© Copyright by A

Dear Reader:

I hope you will enjoy the first installment of the *Dark Ones* saga on the following pages. You will soon see that much more is yet to come.

Every story has many points of view, many different interpretations and versions of the truth. So what about the perspective from the Pure Ones' POV? If you're curious, check out the story that started it all, *Pure Healing*.

Email me at megami771@yahoo.com to find out more. And follow me on https://www.facebook.com/AjaJamesAuthor and https://aja-james.blog/. I will have free chapters and other goodies on Book #3 *Dark Desires*.

I love hearing from you!

Enjoy!

Aja James

Prologue

Vampire.

That is what I and my Kind are called.

Bloodsucker. Demon. Devil's Spawn. Fiend. Incubus. *Monster.*

I cannot say whether I am or am not these things.

I suppose it depends on one's point of view.

To the humans whose blood, and sometimes souls, I take for survival, I suppose I might appear somewhat... *dangerous*. But it is all a matter of perspective.

So allow me to give you mine.

I was born. I was not made.

Nor am I a Pure One who chose the so-called Darkness over an excruciating death when they surrendered their love to the wrong person.

I am simply, and always have been, as I am.

There have been times, oh so many times in the millennia that I have lived, that I resented, raged, railed against my existence.

To the Goddess. To the Heavens. To the Universe at large.

But it wasn't always that way.

I was born into privilege and luxury. Royalty, even.

There was a time, all those thousands of years ago, when vampires ruled the earth. Pure Ones were inferior chattel and humans were our livestock.

And then the Great War reversed the balance of power.

History, as they say, is written by the victors.

And now I and my Kind are hunted like vermin by the very creatures who used to kneel at our feet. There are also human factions who know of us (or at least think they know) and target us for extermination, torture, experimentation, even just for the sport of it. What was once the most powerful civilization the world has ever seen is now in crumbled ruins, its noble citizens degenerating over time into renegades, thieves, lawless parasites.

Few of us True Bloods remain.

Most have either perished in the Great War or in the Purge of the aftermath. Over time, Pure Ones who have lost their faith joined our ranks.

And in this new era, vampires can also be made.

It is this last type of predator that we should all guard ourselves against, for they have no compunction, no morals.

Only thirst.

Never-ending, unquenchable thirst for the blood and souls of others.

But this is no longer my concern—this galactic battle between Good and Evil. I ceased to care which was good and which, evil, the day that *he* betrayed me. I only live for my daughter and son.

My beloved Dark Ones...

"Thou shalt be a benevolent ruler of the human race. Thou shalt not forget thy place, nor that of thy weaker subjects. Except through the Blood Contract, with Consent, or through the Deliverance of Justice, the taking of human blood and souls is forbidden."
—Excerpt from the Dark Laws, verse ten of the Ecliptic Scrolls

Chapter One
Present day. New York, NY.

"Mr. D'Angelo, you may come in now," the nurse said as she exited the hospice room, pushing a rolling laundry basket of used bed linen and towels.

Gabriel quietly thanked the nurse, his shaggy dark hair shielding his expression, his head and eyes slightly lowered, further hiding his face.

Though he knew that he was being rude, he was unable to reciprocate her small smile of encouragement he caught through the filter of his lashes. Instead, he acknowledged her sympathy with a barely perceptible nod and shuffled into the dimly-lit sterilized room after she passed by, closing the door behind him.

As if the click of the shutting door sent a buzz of electricity through his body, turning him on, Gabriel abruptly raised his head and greeted the woman in the mechanical twin bed with a beaming smile.

"Hey beautiful," he said as he moved closer to sit in the deep-seated armchair by her side. "You're looking better today."

"Hey yourself, handsome," the woman bantered back, her eyes sparkling with happiness at the sight of him. Though her voice was barely a whisper, her tone vibrated with good humor.

As if she weren't dying of cancer.

Gabriel determinedly tucked away the dark thought in a remote corner of his mind. He pulled out a folded piece of paper from the inner pocket of his jacket and revealed colorful scribbles before her eyes.

"A gift from Benji," he explained, helping her to raise her head a little bit from the stack of pillows, his warm palm cradling the back of her head with care.

Had her skull always been so small, so fragile? Like egg shells.

The images and colors blurred together in front of her eyes, no longer able to see with clarity, only recognizing light and shadows.

Nevertheless, she proudly proclaimed, "Another masterpiece. Our little man is an artistic genius. I always knew he would take after you."

"It's heaven," Gabriel interpreted the drawing for her so she could picture it in her still vivid imagination.

"There's a red brick house with a chimney and smoke coming out of it in puffs as big as clouds. A snowman with the scarf you gave me wrapped snugly around his neck. You're kneeling down in front pinning the carrot nose on his face. I'm standing on your right side not offering much help. Benji's on your left holding three sticks of marshmallows. He told me to tell you that this is the house he built for you in heaven."

Having painstakingly related the message from their five-year-old son, Gabriel exhaled deeply, silently, as if releasing a great burden that had been suffocating his lungs. He hoped she didn't notice how his hands shook, how his voice grew deeper with barely contained anguish.

"He built me a house," she mused, using what little strength she had to lift her hand an inch to smooth her thumb over a corner of the drawing. "How did I get so lucky? To be sandwiched between the two most wonderful men in the world? Benji has indeed depicted the heaven within my heart."

She turned slightly toward him, he helped her the rest of the way until she could look upon him fully.

After a long silence, he teased, "Do I have mustard on my face? I ate a Crif Dog on my way here."

Self-consciously, he swiped at his lips and chin, trying to avoid her penetrating gaze.

"Don't hide," she said softly. "Let me look at you. One of my biggest regrets is that I haven't gotten a real good look at you in all the years we've known each other. And now my eyesight is misbehaving and I have to concentrate extra hard to see and memorize everything I've…"

"Don't," he interrupted when he saw the sheen of tears in her eyes.

He didn't want to hear about her regrets. He didn't want her to blame herself for a past that could not be changed.

But she took a deep breath and stubbornly pushed on.

"Everything I've stupidly taken for granted for so long."

She wiggled a finger and he was instantly there, holding her hand in both of his, ever in tune with her needs.

But alas, she had never tended to *his* needs, never considered *his* feelings and desires.

Until it was too late.

Selfishness was yet another regret in the long list of sins for which she wished she had the time to atone.

"Have I ever told you that you are the most beautiful man I have ever known?" she told him with a slight curl at the corners of her lips.

When she'd been well, this would have been her most charming, most saucy, most flirtatious come-hither smile. Now it was a mere shadow of a thought of a smile.

"You don't have to say that," he returned, shaking his head a little with disbelief.

He didn't know how much more of her revelations he could take. It was all he could do to hold back the grief, to pull a mask of hope and cheerfulness over his countenance when, inside, he was frozen with despair.

"There are many things I must say before I go," she insisted, her voice surprisingly firm despite the raspy belabored edge. "You must hear them."

When he started to shake his head again, she said, "No. Please let me say them. There isn't much time."

"You're tired," he said, switching topics desperately. "It's time to rest."

She whimpered in distress when he tried to pull away, a tear leaking out of the corner of her eye.

"Don't go. I can't... sleep in peace if I don't tell you." Desperately, she clung to his hand with her last bit of strength, her breathing becoming more ragged from the exertion.

"I'm here," he assured her, relenting to her request, infusing warmth into her icy-cold hand by enfolding it completely within both of his. "I won't leave you."

She took a shuddering breath, and her eyes shut immediately, as if she were preserving her energy to speak and keeping them open would have cost too much.

"I love you," she stated clearly, her voice full and resounding in the silent room. In that moment while she spoke, even the persistent whirring from the radiator by the window could no longer be heard.

Time stood still.

Gabriel squeezed his eyes shut as well, clenching his jaw through a wave of pain that rose like acid in his throat.

"I'm sorry I never told you," she continued, "I'm sorry for many things. Countless things. Sorry for being blind and foolish. For my misguided stubbornness. For making you carry my burdens. For being so selfish. For hurting you unforgivably…"

"Stop," he beseeched her, giving her hand a gentle squeeze, as much pressure as he dared exert on her brittle bones.

"No," she answered strongly and took a deep breath for fortification. "Indulge my selfishness one last time."

With visible effort, she peeled open her eyes, as if raising the heavy lids required strength equal to raising a castle drawbridge. Her pale blue eyes glittering with unshed tears—from anger, frustration or remorse, he could not tell—she pierced straight into his soul with their laser lights.

"I want Benji to have a mother."

Gabriel sucked in a gulp of air and would have interrupted her if not for the quick, resolute shake of her head.

"It is my last request," she told him firmly. "I have all the necessary paperwork prepared."

Gabriel sat straight suddenly as if lightning lit his veins afire.

"Her name is Nana Chastain."

He'd heard of her, but he had never met her.

In the years since the "incident," his wife had sometimes spoken of this Nana with great affection and respect. But Gabriel knew nothing of his wife's friend and confidante, didn't even know how they met, or anything about who she was. Other than his wife's words, there was never even a trace of physical evidence proving that Ms. Chastain's existence wasn't simply imaginary.

As Gabriel's ears rang with inner alarm, his wife went on, "I want you and Nana to raise Benji together. I know Benji will love her madly if he doesn't already."

What? When had their son met this mysterious woman?

"Do it for Benji," his wife implored, "Do it for me."

She didn't add—*do it for yourself.*

Maybe those closest to death had the most insight to life.

Somehow she knew that Nana Chastain was exactly what Gabriel needed to rejoin the living. All the time, energy and emotion he'd wasted on her over the years had worn him down just as surely as disease had worn her down. If not for Benji, she thought he would have gladly, disastrously, chosen to join her in the afterlife.

"Have I a choice?" her husband whispered, his voice shaking, his head bent, eyes squeezed tightly shut.

He already knew the answer. She had made her decision, and she was Benji's mother.

She sighed, hearing the reluctant acceptance in his words, and the strength all at once seemed to seep out of her, her eyes closing again on their own volition, her hand going limp in his grasp.

"You'll like her," she promised, her voice so soft he could barely hear her over the radiator.

Time marched onward.

*** *** *** ***

Inanna watched the couple through the thin wall of the hospice, seeing clearly every hair, every eye-lash.

For the most part, her unique ability could be likened to infrared vision, but it was much more powerful than that: she could see through walls as if they were entirely transparent, and she could zoom distant objects into focus to the finest detail.

His chin-length hair hid most of his expression, but Inanna understood the exchange between husband and wife as if she'd heard every word. She knew what was being discussed; Olivia had told her late last night after Gabriel had taken Benji home.

Benji. Benjamin.

Inanna's new son.

Human son.

How did a four-thousand year-old vampire get into this predicament?

Because she was greedy, that's how. She'd fallen in love with the little boy and his bouncy, blond curls at first sight. And first sight was before he had any hair, right after he was delivered, in fact, at New York-Presbyterian Morgan Stanley-Komansky Children's Hospital.

But who was she kidding, Inanna silently chided herself. She wasn't just in love with the boy.

She was head over heels *in lust* with the husband.

Gabriel D'Angelo.

Inanna turned away from the hospice room and walked briskly outside toward her sun-proofed gun-metal Lamborghini Aventador. Folding her long limbs into the vehicle, she fired up the ignition and raced out of the hospice parking lot, into the pitch-black night.

She would grant husband and wife one last night together before collecting on Olivia's Blood-Contract.

And fulfilling her own.

*** *** *** ***

"You're late."

Maximus cut in front of Inanna as she rounded the corner, moving swiftly toward the Atrium where their Queen was holding court, having issued summons earlier during the night. Simca loped along beside him as always, not an inch away from his legs, moving gracefully as if panther and man were one.

Inanna didn't bother excusing her tardiness. Bringing up the Blood-Contract and her decision to delay yet another night would just open the floor for more questions.

She didn't like questions.

"I notice you're in a rush yourself," she tossed at his broad back, practically blocking all the light in the narrow corridor as he led the way in front of her. "Know what this is about?"

"Negative," he responded in clipped tones, ever a male of few words.

Though Inanna was by no means height challenged, Maximus was quite a bit taller, his legs longer and more powerful, and she had to double her pace to keep up with him. If she had to break into a sprint, it would be too humiliating.

She misjudged the distance between their bodies, though, and almost tripped into his back in her zealous attempt to keep pace.

But before she could take a tumble, a steel-like rope whipped across her shins, causing her to stagger backwards.

"Ow! Can you tell your cat to tone down the annoying protectiveness? She whipped me on purpose," Inanna complained to her Commander, resisting the urge to rub her shins where the panther's tail had slapped her hard.

But before Maximus could chide the feline, Simca was rubbing her long sleek body against his leg, rumbling an apologetic purr, and he heaved a short sigh.

"It wasn't on purpose."

My ass, Inanna thought, spearing a hot glare at the panther's treacherous tail, now undulating carelessly from side to side as if taunting her.

Filing into the brightly-lit Atrium after the Commander of the Chosen and his pet feline, the heavy double doors closing soundlessly behind them, Inanna realized immediately that her Queen was in a dark mood indeed.

Jade Cicada, Queen of the New England vampires, lounged casually in her Chinese-style throne, her voluptuous torso contorting like a coiled cobra.

But Inanna knew that the languid posture belied the fury and seriousness blazing in the Queen's dark eyes. A quick scan around the chamber out of the corner of her eye showed that Jade had already dismissed her harem; only the Chosen and one other were allowed attendance.

Seth Tremaine, the Pure Ones' Consul.

Last autumn, Seth had sought the vampire queen's aid in the Pure Ones' battle with a new nemesis who was forcibly turning warrior-class Pure Ones into an army of vampire assassins. Jade had not shared details, had merely issued an order for the Chosen to lend their strength in one critical battle. Nor did she enlighten her personal guard further after the fact.

Inanna knew that the demon foe was still at large, though it appeared that his army was all but wiped out, at least the one in Boston that they knew about. And Seth Tremaine was apparently at the Cove to stay for the time being. For how long and for what purpose, Inanna and her comrades had yet to glean.

Inanna, for one, did not feel the need to know. Her queen was ever mysterious and private, but Inanna trusted her completely to make the best decisions for the Hive.

"There is nothing more revolting than grown vampires toying with their food and making a bloody mess," the vampire Queen began without preamble, her low, husky voice echoing clearly in the spacious grand hall.

"And nothing more annoying than Rogues who flaunt the breaking of our laws before my face."

The Queen uncurled slightly from her seat and straightened her back, the better to shoot daggers at each and every one of her personal guards from her elevated height on the throne.

"Maximus, report," she ordered.

"The daily human body-count as a result of vampire kills has risen sharply," the Commander promptly related.

"Over ninety-percent of the deaths are non-contractual; the humans did not Consent. In addition, many victims were found not only drained of blood and soul, but their bodies have been torn asunder and left in pieces in the aftermath of a vampire feeding frenzy."

The Chosen shared ominous scowls upon hearing this particular abomination.

"Several of these crime scenes are located in the center of the city and have been blocked off by NYPD. The police's official statement is that this could be the work of gang violence, symbolic of retribution for blood feuds, and the press is having a field day."

Maximus nodded to Anastasia, the Queen's head of security, to continue where he left off.

"Our investigation led us to the source of these killings," Anastasia said, looking into the eyes of each of the Chosen in turn.

"Illegal fight clubs. Organized by humans, bankrolled and attended by vampires who revel in this particularly bloody spectator sport."

"We have not been able to uncover the identities of the Rogues, nor have we been successful in catching them in the act. Fight locations change every time. This secret network of humans and vampires has yet been impossible to infiltrate. All we know is that this is impeccably organized and the members, human and vampire alike, are deeply embedded in New York society. We suspect they even have all of the human law enforcement branches on their payroll."

"You might as well describe how it works," the Queen said with disdain, shuddering delicately as if the sordidness of the crimes made her skin crawl.

"The rules are simple," Ana continued, "there are no rules. Merely to fight until one opponent can no longer fight. Spectators bet on the match and choose the weapons for the fighters. They range from bare knuckles to maces, swords, lead pipes, you name it."

"Some contestants are club regulars and spectator favorites. They usually get the most advantageous weapons. The winner takes a share of the proceeds from the match. More importantly, he gets to go home. Occasionally, death results from the ruthless beating, but more often the loser gets dragged to the 'Cage,' hidden away from the spectators where depraved Rogues drain his blood and steal his soul, and in the feeding frenzy, tear him limb from limb."

She looked to Maximus to continue.

"What's alarming is that these underground fight clubs are multiplying rapidly across the U.S., with the New England territories as the epicenter, and spreading around the world if our sources are right," Maximus said, the black slashes of his brows drawing together in a ferocious scowl. "We've gathered sightings in Moscow, London, Tokyo, Rio De Janeiro."

"The bloodlust and psychotic frenzy are escalating among Rogues," he continued in a low growl. "They have no respect for the Dark Laws and risk exposing our Kind to humans at large. Humans who have aided us in the past are steadily backing out of the partnership. Others who know of us are forming vigilante groups that hunt our Kind to torture and kill in repayment for these senseless murders. If we don't stop this vicious cycle, we will soon have a full-scale war on our hands."

"Enough said," the Queen announced, her face an iron mask of ruthless resolve. "We must stop the Rogues' rampage before the mobs grow more powerful. Maximus, take Ryu to search out the fight club networks and vampire sponsors. Anastasia, take Devlin to notify and partner with our allies, heighten security for our civilians."

With those few words, the Chosen warriors knew precisely what their Queen required of them.

As they bowed formally and turned to leave the Atrium, the Pure One's Consul, all but forgotten in the shadows of the throne, asked quietly, "May I be of service?"

Jade Cicada tilted her head toward the Consul, curled her lips in a darkly ironic smile and said, "And what *service* would that be, Pure One?"

Seth ignored her sardonic tone and answered in all seriousness, "Your warriors are severely limited during the daytime, when these Rogues have the advantage in their human partners. Allow me to consult with the Dozen; the Elite may be able to reach where you cannot. We have a common enemy in these Hordes."

The Queen considered his offer with a slight narrowing of her cat-like eyes.

But before she could reply, Simone interjected, "We cannot trust the Pure One, my Queen. It is too dangerous."

Jade kept her gaze trained on the Consul and ignored the Keeper's warning.

"Inanna," she said, without turning to face the female to whom she spoke, "see what the Consul has to offer. You have my full permission to drain him if he betrays us."

Keeping her gaze glued to his, she smiled more broadly and added, "but leave the last drop for me."

*** *** *** ***

Gabriel collected a sleeping Benji from his next door neighbor and landlady, Mrs. Sergeyev, in apartment 5B when he returned from the hospice.

The elderly woman gave him a brief hug and a wet kiss on the cheek upon seeing him on her threshold, an almost excessive amount of emotion for the reticent Russian. She murmured some comforting words in her native tongue, the smoky bass of her voice blanketing Gabriel with empathy even though he did not understand what she said.

Cradling his son against his chest, Gabriel entered his own studio apartment and locked the door behind him. The cacophony outside his window in Brighton Beach, Brooklyn, was mere background noise by now, and Benji didn't so much as stir in his arms. Gabriel laid the boy in the full-size bed they shared since Olivia became hospitalized and tucked the covers securely around him.

Alone in the dark with his even darker thoughts, Gabriel sat next to Benji with his elbows on his knees, his head in his hands.

He would lose her soon, he knew.

The doctors said it was only a matter of time, varying between a handful of hours to as long as weeks. But there would be no miracle. She would not survive the winter. And in what days she had left, there would be little peace. She would ever shift between physical pain and mental delirium, often both. She would continue to deteriorate until only a dried husk remained.

Gabriel knew that this was the end. He knew, yet he couldn't bring himself to accept the fact. It wasn't in his DNA to give up.

The various doctors and specialists had all said the same: it was a hopeless cause. No surgery, no chemotherapy, no drugs or alternative medicine would be able to make his wife well again.

They'd discovered the second cancer too late. Her rapid decline from a stabilizing cancer patient to a veritable ghost took less than two months.

And in that time, Gabriel had sold his grandparents' house in upstate New York, traded in the classic and impeccably maintained Ford Mustang for a cheap box with wheels, put on E-Bay and Craig's List all of his own worldly possessions, quit his slave-labor job at one of New York's premier architecture firms, got a couple of flexible-hours part-time jobs in the City instead, and moved his family to this rent-controlled five-hundred-square-foot studio in the Russian District.

    It wasn't enough.

    Between Benji's preschool fees and Olivia's medical bills, his bank account was rapidly running dry. Last he checked there was less than two hundred dollars left.

    Gabriel raised his head and pulled out a business card from the inner pocket of his shirt.

    He knew what he had to do.

    This was not how his *shifu* intended him to employ his training, but he had no other choice.

    Quickly, he changed into a black hoodie and loose black joggers. He stopped by Mrs. Sergeyev's apartment to have her keep an eye on Benji and swiftly departed the apartment, taking off at a brisk jog toward the nearby metro station.

    It took almost an hour to arrive at his designated stop. Then, he walked another mile to an abandoned warehouse by the Bay. The night was pitch black save for a pasty moon low-hung in the sky. If not for a few flashes of dim light from the warehouse's broken windows, Gabriel would have thought the Russian mobster who'd tipped him off had lied.

    Now, he cautiously moved toward the dilapidated building, stepping around refuse and broken glass along the way. As he entered, muffled echoes from deep within clanged against the rusted rafters. He followed the distant noise and arrived at an iron door locked from the inside.

    There was no going back.

Taking a deep breath, Gabriel raised his fist and rapped three times on the door.

A narrow bar slid open to reveal two bloodshot eyes that peered suspiciously back at him.

"Get lost," the man on the other side growled in a rough, accented voice.

Gabriel stared back unrelentingly. "I came to fight."

The beady eyes looked him up and down. Gabriel could almost see the accompanying sneer.

"You ain't got what it takes, *eblan*."

"But I bleed just like any other *dumbass*," Gabriel returned. "It doesn't cost you anything to let me in."

A few moments of pause. Then—"Suit yourself. You lookin' for suicide, it's a guaranteed but nasty way to go."

As the man drew out the *sss* in *nasty* like a viper's hiss, he exposed three gold capped teeth in a monstrous grin.

The door opened with a groan after a complex series of levers and locks unwinding, and Gabriel narrowly slipped inside past the tattooed hulk guarding the entrance. Without a word, the Russian led him down a dark corridor to another iron door that opened to a steep flight of stairs, taking them into the hellish belly beneath the warehouse.

Gabriel was suddenly assaulted by the uproar of shouting men, their fists full of bet slips, of cackling women who lost their inhibitions through sustained inebriation, of bottles broken, flesh pummeled, bones cracked, blood splattered.

Welcome to the fight club.

"Thou shalt not covet thy human subjects, nor the Pure Ones who are thy slaves. Subjects must be held at an objective distance, ruled by a fair hand. Slaves must be leashed with tight control, mastered by a strong will."
—Excerpt from the Dark Laws, verse twenty-one of the Ecliptic Scrolls

Chapter Two

It was five o'clock when Inanna slipped back inside the hospice.

She had over an hour of night left, plenty of time to collect on the Blood-Contract and make her way back to the Cove before the early rays of winter sun started to weave their drowsy spell around her.

A little known fact was that Inanna felt less of the sun's adverse effects than other vampires.

Only the Queen was aware of the truth.

To maintain appearances, however, she stuck to the usual vampire routine.

Checking briefly the guest log on the empty reception desk, she saw that Gabriel had signed out before midnight, having stayed much later than his usual visit. Perhaps he sensed somehow that this would be the last hours he would spend with his wife.

When he saw her next, she would no longer be among the living.

Inanna walked soundlessly through the corridors to arrive at Olivia's room. She entered as if one with the darkness, a mere shadow flickering against the wall, and locked the door behind her.

Olivia was in the throes of what seemed to be a nightmare.

She was making pained whimpers, gasping for breath, while tossing and turning on her narrow bed, her hands curled into claws as she fervently scratched the skin around her IV and throat.

A cool breeze drifted through the open windows, carrying the soothing scent of jasmine from the trees that surrounded the hospice, but the writhing patient seemed immune to its therapeutic effects.

Inanna had seen this sight thousands of times.

Hundreds of thousands.

It was the last feverish battle of the dying.

The drugs were losing their effects; the patient's body was rebelling against her. She was flailing against the onset of death.

Inanna knew what she needed.

"I am here, Olivia," the Chosen said, drawing near to sit beside the mechanical bed, taking one of the patient's hands and squeezing lightly to calm the frenzied shaking.

"Do not fret. I am here."

Olivia turned toward the sound of her voice and opened her chapped lips, but only incoherent grunts and mumbles tumbled from them.

As if frustrated with her inability to speak clearly, she began to shake her head from side to side, hot tears slipping from the corners of her eyes.

"Shall I ease your pain a bit?" Inanna asked, not really expecting an answer.

She drew one boney wrist closer and quickly sank her canines into the barely-there vein.

With the first slow draw of blood, the venom from her fangs trickling into the patient's bloodstream like the most powerful sedative, Olivia stopped thrashing immediately and began to breathe more evenly, more deeply.

Stopping after a few small sips so that Olivia was calm and lucid enough to open her eyes, temporarily clear of pain and drugs, Inanna licked the wound closed and regarded the human woman with patience and understanding.

"Thank you," Olivia began weakly, "thank you for giving me one more night with him."

"He needed to hear your heart," Inanna answered. "You have waited much too long to tell him."

"I was a fool and a coward," the patient agreed. "Even at the end I do not think he believed me."

Inanna felt a long-stored anger unfurling in her stomach, stretching its way toward her throat, burning the tip of her tongue with a caustic reply.

Perhaps Olivia sensed it, for she admitted, "I know it's all my fault. I have no one to blame but myself. He has given me, in so many ways, for so many years, a love I don't deserve while I only hurt him with my stupid, thoughtless mistakes."

The patient's eyes took on a faraway sheen as she inhaled deeply the soft flowery fragrance wafting from the open windows and murmured, "Our old neighborhood was lined with jasmine trees. He used to follow me around when we were teenagers, you know. At first I thought it was because we walked the same way to school since we lived across the street from each other, and then I thought this shaggy-headed new kid was stalking me."

She gave a small chuckle. "I was pretty full of myself back then. Being the head cheerleader and prom queen tended to inflate a High School girl's ego."

"But later I realized he was protecting me, since I often went home well past dark. Isn't that strange?" she asked the question, but Inanna did not think she expected an answer.

"He has been protecting me ever since the beginning. But hard as he tried, he couldn't save me from myself. All the terrible mistakes I made."

Inanna kept silent, lowering her gaze.

Yes, she knew everything about those mistakes. She knew the couple's entire tragic story. It didn't have to be this way, she often thought.

It seemed so blatantly *simple* for Olivia to make the right choices, more pointedly, to choose her husband.

Gabriel.

To choose her son, Benjamin.

But the woman seemed wired for self-destruction. Her choices in life not only hurt everyone who loved her, but ultimately, herself.

What a waste!

She felt a slight tug on the hand that still held Olivia's wrist and looked directly into the patient's eyes.

"You will take good care of them, won't you?" Olivia beseeched her with tear-filled eyes. "Please make them happy. I can't bear that my mistakes might outlive me."

Inanna had to swallow twice before she found her voice, made it neutral, soothing. "I always keep my promises. Gabriel and Benjamin will lack for nothing."

Olivia nodded, trusting the vampire completely.

The vampire who had been her secret friend for as many years as she'd been married. Perhaps because Olivia had a rather fanciful nature, perhaps she simply did not care, but she had known from the beginning of their unlikely acquaintance that Inanna was not of her world.

Not human.

They'd met while Olivia was hospitalized after the "incident." She'd shared a room with a patient dying of leukemia because the hospital wards had been over-occupied during the holiday season due to traffic and other accidents. She'd witnessed how this honey-blonde goddess-like creature had all but floated into the room, bent solicitously over the dying patient and whispered words of reassurance, promising to end his pain.

The man had neither family nor friends. He could no longer afford hospital bills and was essentially at the mercy of city charity. He might have been able to linger on for another month or two, but he was in a tremendous amount of pain. Olivia had heard his fervent prayers the night she'd been brought into the ward.

He'd prayed for death.

And death had come for him in the form of an angel.

Olivia had heard some of their hushed words. The woman would stay for hours talking soothingly to the dying man. She'd hold his hand and smile at him with understanding and care.

On the second night that Olivia was there, the night before her release from the hospital, she'd heard them speak of the Contract.

"I told him about you," Olivia said now to her Angel of Death. "As much as I knew about you."

She paused and then said, "Except that you're not quite human."

A small smile curved Inanna's voluptuous mouth.

"What a euphemistic way to put it," she murmured.

Olivia shrugged almost imperceptibly.

"It doesn't matter to me what you are. You've been a better friend to me than anyone else in my life. Except for Gabriel."

She took a deep, steadying breath.

"Do you suppose he'll be angry with me?"

"He has that right as the man who loves you," the Chosen answered. "But what you do with your life is your choice."

"That's not what you said when we first met," Olivia reminded her.

"It was not merely your life at stake at the time," Inanna replied evenly.

"You were right about that," the patient agreed. "Benji was by far the best decision I've ever made."

Abruptly, she turned away, facing the ceiling instead of her visitor.

The trembling in her body began again as she flashed hot and cold. The venom was starting to wear off.

"You'll make sure he doesn't suspect the arrangement?" Olivia asked for what was probably the hundredth time, her voice starting to fade.

"He will not suspect."

"He hates to be manipulated. He has so much pride."

Inanna didn't answer.

Yes, she knew. Gabriel's code of honor reminded Inanna of the most ancient Dark Ones.

Steadfast. Fiercely protective. Self-sacrificing. Nurturing.

Intensely loving.

"Will you be good to him?" Olivia asked.

Inanna cocked her head a bit. Didn't she already ask this? Nevertheless she answered, "He will lack for nothing."

"That's not what I meant." Olivia sighed and closed her eyes.

Her shaking had intensified. She was idly scratching herself again.

"I want you to be kind to him. I don't want him to be lonely. I want you to lo—"

She broke off as her panting got stronger, as she struggled to draw enough oxygen into her failing lungs, arching off the bed in a twist of pain.

"It is time," Inanna said quietly, knowing that the patient no longer heard her.

With a gust of wind, the windows slammed shut, the lights in the hospice room blacked out. In the heavy darkness there was a flash of white fangs.

And then—silence.

*** *** *** ***

Gabriel slid into the studio soundlessly just as the first rays of dawn filtered through the crack in the window drapes.

Benji slept peacefully in the bed, his breathing even and deep, a small warm mound under the covers topped by unruly pale blond curls.

Gabriel paused over his son's innocent form and gently smoothed a thumb down one plump cheek.

Though he was solidly into his boyhood, Benji retained the cherubic sweetness of his toddler days. Perhaps it was the riotous blond curls. Perhaps the rosy cheeks and mouth. Just looking upon his little angel made Gabriel smile, though it was followed almost immediately by a grimace as his split lip split even deeper.

He straightened and, in one smooth motion, pulled the bloodied hoodie over his head, shucking his torn joggers a second later, and made his way, naked, to the tiny bathroom with an even tinier shower stall.

At least the water pressure in the apartment was blessedly strong.

As the blast of hot water drenched him from head to toe, Gabriel closed his eyes and raised his face into the cleansing deluge.

After two gruesome hours in Hell's belly, and six matches later, he was ten grand richer. Enough to pay off three months of over-due rent, which Mrs. Sergeyev had been kind enough to forgive thus far without interest or eviction, plus one month advance, as well as Olivia's hospice bills. He even had a nice little cushion left over for food and emergencies.

And all it took was three bruised ribs, bloody knuckles, a few nasty scratches, a split lip and let's not forget—beating six men into unconscious putty with his bare hands and feet.

His *shifu* would be appalled.

Gabriel clenched his jaw.

He did what he had to do. He would do everything in his power to protect those he loved. As long as he could live with his conscience afterwards.

He'd made sure those men were merely unconscious, a few broken bones and concussions, perhaps, but no debilitating injuries for the long term. They would recover quickly enough to fight another day.

In truth, it didn't have to take as long as it did to dispatch his opponents. A few well-placed jabs and kicks would have knocked them out faster. But he needed to play to the spectators. He had to look like he was struggling, on the verge of losing for a while so that the bets were stacked against him, so that his winnings in the end would be that much greater.

Dragging a fight out to look like he was weaker, taking hits without taking proportional damage, was a tricky tightrope Gabriel had to balance upon. He wondered whether he should have allowed a black eye or two and a bloodied nose to appeal more to the audience's bloodlust. But he had to weigh that against the blood and swollen flesh disorienting his vision, which would have made the fights more dangerous, less predictable.

He couldn't afford to lose his matches.

Absent-mindedly, Gabriel ran the bar of Dial soap over his bruised skin and aching muscles, diligently ignoring his cock stand as he quickly scrubbed the coarse hair around and the heavy sacs beneath. He must be still too pumped full of adrenaline from the fights, he reasoned, his body was simply reacting to the testosterone overload.

Never mind that it had been a long, *long* time since he'd had an erection this hard, this insistent.

Maybe never.

Twenty-six year-old male virgins in today's society were as rare as dragons. Probably even more mythical.

Married virgins were likely nonexistent.

Gabriel didn't choose this path intentionally; it simply was.

His boyhood upbringing by the Shaolin monks on Song Mountain in Henan Province, China, after his missionary parents had died in the Great Earthquake, taught him abstinence, self-control and discipline. Since his grandparents found him and brought him back to the States to live with them, he'd only ever felt a deep connection to one girl.

Olivia.

And despite that she never truly reciprocated his feelings, not even in the end, he'd been intensely faithful. He'd never so much as sought release by his own hand since Olivia's illness. There was something inherently wrong with him seeking his own pleasure while his wife was wasting away in pain.

It was as if the carnal side of his nature had never truly awakened.

Now he looked upon the jutting staff as if it were separate from his body, something of an oddity, something he didn't know quite what to do with.

Of its own volition, one large, long-fingered hand smoothed down his pecs to his tight abdomen, stopping near his navel, where the head of his engorged member bobbed insistently. He stared at it for long moments before carefully, loosely cradling the steely length within his wide palm.

He gasped at the startling sensation, and his penis jumped in reaction. Mind blank of coherent thoughts, eyes closed against the shower that had long since turned cold, Gabriel wrapped his hand tighter around the hot, velvety column, testing himself with a gentle squeeze.

And groaned deeply in response, the shocks of pleasure shooting through his body like lightning rods, making him physically stagger off balance.

Leaning his back against the stall wall, his long, muscular legs braced apart, slightly bent at the knees, he pushed himself further with a few tentative fist pumps.

But it was too much.

He felt too much.

His chest heaving with shortened breath, his jaw clenched tightly against the animalistic sounds that threatened to escape, his penis throbbing, his testicles hurting, Gabriel stood helpless as his long-revered control began to unwind like the fibers of a rope stretched too taut.

Until finally it snapped.

On a sharp intake of breath, Gabriel's eyes flew open. Someone was watching him.

*** *** *** ***

Inanna stared back at the intensely beautiful warrior through the thin wall that separated them.

How did he know she was there? Could he see her as well?

But that was impossible for the human. Wasn't it?

And yet Inanna could see him as clearly as if no sheet rock and wood beams separated them, as if she were right in front of him, a mere four feet away.

As if she were in that shower stall with him, her blood heated to steaming by his passionate display.

She had not intended to come here after her visit to the hospice. She felt wrong about seeing Gabriel and Benji after collecting on her Blood-Contract with Olivia. But it was as if her body had a will of its own, even as her conscience rebelled.

She *needed* to see them.

She told herself it was only briefly, just a few moments to ensure that they were well and safe.

But then he'd stripped bare right before her, exposing the long, sinuous, leanly muscular body she'd battled her own powers not to look upon up to this point.

She couldn't have moved from her spot in the hallway outside his apartment if her life depended upon it. She could only look back, powerless, mesmerized, and so turned on her fangs elongated involuntarily in her mouth, even as molten lava pooled between her thighs.

Dark Goddess, she beseeched in her own mind, *let him finish it. I need to see him come.*

Inanna did not think she exaggerated. Right then, she needed to see Gabriel climax as much as she required breathing.

Absently, she wet her lips, barely noticing the salty tang of her own blood as the tips of her fangs broke through her bottom lip.

Do it, she chanted in her mind, *finish it*.

He seemed to hear her request, for he braced his long legs slightly farther apart, as if to steady himself.

His hand grasped his penis tighter, moving up the rod to hide the plump head within his fist, while the other hand idly cupped his sacs, the thumb kneading in a circular motion.

All the while, he stared intensely back at her.

She could see clearly how his pupils dilated behind the curtain of wet, spiky lashes. She could see his nostrils flaring as his breath came quicker. The edges of his teeth as his mouth opened slightly. The rise and fall of his muscular chest. The contraction of his steely abdominals.

Involuntarily, Inanna leaned forward against the wall that separated them, flattening her palms against it at shoulder level.

Goddess, how she wanted to touch him!

And then he began to move the hand that grasped his penis slowly up and down the long, thick column, squeezing harder at the base and at the head.

Inanna broke her eyes from his as his lids swooped down to half-mast, as the sensations seemed to overcome him.

Her gaze unerringly riveted on his groin and zoomed in precisely until his male member enclosed in that large, long-fingered hand was immediately before her covetous eyes. So close, she could see the painfully swollen glans, the milky fluid that seeped out of its weeping eye, each and every ridge along the blood filled column, the tantalizing veins that stood out against the satiny skin, begging for her attention.

Her fangs ached so badly they quivered in her mouth, enflaming her gums.

Finish it!

His hand began to pump in earnest at her silent command.

Up and down. Up and down. Faster. Stronger. Harder.

The rhythm of his fist around his penis mimicked the pulse of the muscles of her core clenching.

She envied his hand. She wanted desperately to be that fist around him. Instead, her womb felt achingly hollow, her vagina weeping for that hot, hard, velvety organ to fill her.

Inanna moaned soundlessly in distress, dangerously close to the edge of her passion.

But Gabriel was right there with her.

He clenched his teeth together as his testicles drew tight to his body. The plump head throbbed and quivered. Inanna's mouth opened involuntarily. And—

He came on a bone-deep groan in a powerful surge, his hips bucking, his muscles locking, his throat exposed as his head fell back against the wall.

Seemingly endless waves of semen erupted from his tortured sex, flowing like cream down to the root.

Inanna's core contracted sharply in response, and she lost her breath on an almost painful, empty orgasm. It was pleasure, yet it was also agony without his flesh and seed and blood to fill her.

When she regained her composure after long moments, she looked into the eyes of the male who so effortlessly ignited her, as no male in all the millennia of her existence had ever done before.

Again, as if drawn by an invisible force, he was staring heatedly back at her.

But as the fog of passion lifted, his eyes held torment and confusion.

He looked lost.

Haunted.

As if *she* were the one who'd torn from him something he had not been prepared to surrender.

Inanna could look no longer.

She pivoted on her heels and dashed out of the narrow corridor, down two flights of stairs and out into the bitingly cold winter dawn.

Instead of going directly to her Lamborghini parked in a nearby covered garage, she headed down familiar alleys on foot, her body moving by rote, even as her mind had frozen in a confounded haze.

She knew that her continued absence at the Cove would raise no alarm. Jade was familiar with her habit of staying out well past dawn and did not worry. Other members of the Chosen did not ask questions, perhaps more concerned with keeping their own secrets.

Her feet stopped in front of a small jewel of a shop, nestled between two larger brick townhouses deep in the Eastern European hoods of Brooklyn.

It was painted in bright, cheerful colors, trimmed with twinkling white lights, and reminded Inanna of the gingerbread house in the children's fairytale "Hansel and Gretel."

She'd come across it only a few weeks ago on one of her long nightly strolls. It had been built on the shell of what used to be a locksmith-cum-handyman store.

Over a worn green canopy in cursive block letters, the shop heralded "Dark Dreams."

"Come inside before you catch a chill, my dear," an old, ruddy-faced, well-rounded woman greeted her at the door with warm familiarity. The tantalizing scent of freshly baked goods drifted out to enfold her in its sweet mist.

"Come, come," the old lady said as she shooed Inanna unceremoniously into the shop. "I was expecting you this early morning."

She gently pushed Inanna through the shop toward a private corner. There were no windows for prying eyes to peer inside, and it was softly lit with an array of one-of-a-kind antique lamps from around the world.

"Sit, sit," the woman urged in her liltingly accented voice, its foreign origins difficult to trace. It somehow reminded Inanna of a heterogeneous mix of Middle Eastern, Greek and the deep American South, of all places.

While the Chosen sat obediently in a small, ornate, velvet-backed chair, Mama Bear (as Inanna affectionately thought of her) bustled about, ducking behind a curtain of beads into the back room and returning with a teapot, taking out two intricate china cups and saucers from a glass cabinet, plopping bulbs of dried flowers into each cup and pouring hot water over them.

"Sugar is in the bowl," she said to Inanna, gesturing to the crystal lidded bowl shaped like the genie's lamp in the Arabian Nights in the middle of the sturdy tea table carved from an ancient Cyprus cedar root.

"Help yourself. I'll be right back with the croissants. You arrived just in time to sample my first batch."

Humming as she went, the old lady disappeared once again behind the curtain of beads, leaving Inanna alone with her thoughts.

She came here when she needed comfort and guidance, Inanna realized with a flash of self-knowledge. Or simply when she needed someone who listened, who nodded with understanding even if she did not, in fact, understand. Jade was the only other person Inanna felt comfortable confiding in, though she did so very rarely.

The other Chosen were different. They used to be either Pure Ones or human. They were not like Inanna.

They were vampires made.

Inanna often felt like an outsider looking in.

Alone and unique in her existence.

True, she once had a father and a mother. But they had long since been lost to her. As far as she knew, her father had perished toward the end of the Great War, though in her heart of hearts she refused to believe it, and her mother...

Inanna wanted to believe that her mother was still in this world. She didn't remember the female at all, having been separated from her since birth. But her father had always assured her that her mother was alive. He'd seemed unwilling to believe otherwise.

And so Inanna nursed the corner of her heart that still pulsed with hope. Even after four millennia of searching, she had not given up.

Surely one day... someday... she would find them both.

"Here we are," Mama Bear said as she laid down a tray of freshly baked croissants on the table.

She took the seat across from Inanna and folded her hands under her chin, elbows on the table.

"Now tell me what's troubling you, my dear. You look like you've seen a ghost."

Not a ghost at all, Inane thought wryly, *but a flesh and bone full-blooded male.*

Out loud, she said, "I saw something I want, but it is not something I should have."

"Ah," the old woman murmured, the one word resonating with immeasurable ancient wisdom to Inanna's ears.

She nodded with understanding. "I know how that feels. Now tell me, is this guilty feeling you have akin to a child consuming too many sweets before supper or..."

She pushed a croissant toward Inanna and gestured for her to take a bite.

As the Chosen did so, her eyes drooping with pleasure as she savored the hot, buttery treat, the old woman continued, "Or is it akin to stealing a lover from another woman?"

Suddenly, Inanna was overcome by a coughing fit, choking on the flaky layers of her croissant.

The old woman patted her back, unconcerned, and offered her a drink of tea.

"There, there," she soothed, "it can't be as bad as all that."

She waited until Inanna regained her composure and sat back, regarding the seemingly younger woman with empathy and affection.

"You know, my sweet girl, there is no such thing as stealing another's lover," she stated softly with a knowing smile. "Love cannot be stolen. It can only be given. And it always takes two to make it happen."

"If you see something you covet," she paused to spear Inanna with her sharp intuition, "then take it."

"But—"

The old woman interrupted Inanna's protest with a wave of her hand.

"Oh, I'm not suggesting you break any laws."

And then she said almost inaudibly under her breath, "Unless they are meant to be broken."

More loudly, she said, "I am merely saying life is too short to deny your deepest desires."

She cocked her head at Inanna. "And for those who live unfulfilled, life can be much too long. If I had a thousand years, five thousand years even, I would exchange it all to have my heart's desire for just one more day."

She paused momentarily as if lost in thought, but then looked wistfully back at Inanna.

"Wouldn't you?"

"The superiority of our Race is witnessed by our immortality, sustained by restraint and wisdom. The frailty of the human race is witnessed by their fleeting existence, sustained by their penchant for violence and self-destruction and the inability to learn from mistakes."
—*Excerpt from the Ecliptic Scrolls*

Chapter Three
Six years ago, Christmas Eve.

The young woman about five months pregnant was likely still in college, if she was pursuing higher education.

Her pale blonde hair was pulled back by a butterfly clip from her face, revealing an ethereal beauty that suffered only marginally from her concentrated frown as she peered down at her slightly rounded belly in the half-reclined mechanical hospital bed. From her unhappy, ferocious expression, one would have thought she was going to give birth to a two-headed monster.

Whatever the reason, one thing was clear: she did not want this baby growing inside of her.

This was the third day that the young woman shared the same room with Inanna's Blood Contract, a middle-aged homeless man dying of cancer.

It did not escape Inanna's notice that the girl watched her closely every time she came to visit, and leaned so far over her bed she almost fell off several times to hear the exchange between Inanna and the dying man. Inanna hoped it was simply curiosity, but something told her the young woman saw too much, heard too much, and wanted that which she should not.

This would be the last night Inanna visited the man in the curtain-separated twin bed a few feet away from the girl's. Before dawn, she would return to collect on the Blood Contract. Having soothed the cancer patient into a dreamless slumber, Inanna pulled the curtain closed between the two patient beds and tried to take her leave before the young woman expressed her dark desires.

"Are you an angel?" the girl asked just as Inanna passed by the foot of her bed to the door.

She could have ignored the question, could have pretended she didn't hear and rudely leave without bothering to acknowledge the girl's presence. But Inanna's feet would not obey her.

As if pulled by an invisible string, she turned toward the girl and met her light blue eyes for the first time.

"I am no angel," Inanna responded softly but clearly, "you will do well to remember that."

"But you have come to grant his wishes, isn't that right?" the girl persisted, her large eyes getting even larger as she stared intensely at the Chosen, as if trying to solve an unsolvable puzzle.

"I heard him ask you for relief and I heard you promise he would have it."

"Forget what you think you heard, little girl. It does not concern you." Inanna knew that she should leave.

Now.

Her instincts told her that if she stayed, the decision would irrevocably impact the whole of her existence.

And yet she stood her ground. Somehow, she knew that this barely-legal young woman was a guidepost in her destiny.

"Could you do the same for me?" the girl asked in a gasping whisper, her cheeks suddenly flooding with color at her own audacity.

Inanna felt as if the longer she gazed into the woman's eyes, the deeper she was plunging into a bottomless pool. Resolutely, she tried to pull herself out of it.

"You do not know what you ask," the Chosen said. "Someone such as you have all of life to look forward to. What could you possibly need relief from."

It was not a question, but the girl answered it anyway, an edge of desperation in her voice that increased until she was all but shrieking.

"I don't want to live! I have no family, no friends! And this-this-*thing* inside me will keep growing and growing and I'm getting so ugly and fat and *he* doesn't want me! He only likes skinny girls who can party and have a good time and I'm fat and ugly and he dumped me! And he's disgusted that I got this way, that I wasn't careful enough and he blames me for it! He doesn't believe that it's his! I don't want it! If I can't have him I don't want to live!"

Youthful hysteria aside, there was a raw hopelessness and despair in the young woman's countenance that made Inanna consider her more carefully.

Something about the girl was not quite right.

She was obviously frightened and despondent, but there was also a pervasive cloak of depression about her, a darkness in her heart that the brightness of her beauty could not eclipse.

After millennia of witnessing the various emotions, desires and regrets of the dying, Inanna recognized a Lost Soul when she saw one.

Against her better judgment, Inanna closed the distance between herself and the nearly frantic girl, her chest heaving with the exertion of her outburst, hot tears running down her cheeks. Inanna pulled up a chair to the girl's bed and enfolded her cold, damp hands within her own warm grasp.

It was then that she noticed the gauze bandages around the girl's wrists.

So it was not a whim, then, this desire to quit the living.

Even though she was rescued and brought to a hospital, even though a new life was growing inside of her, the girl was still looking for a way out.

Inanna did not know her troubles and was therefore not equipped to judge, but on a basic level, she could not wrap her mind around the antipathy that the girl held toward her unborn child, especially at this late stage. For a four thousand-year-old vampire who may never have children, Inanna could not help but rebel inwardly at the girl's selfishness and callousness. Nevertheless, she kept her expression neutral and her tone soothing.

"Surely there is someone," Inanna said with encouragement.

She looked around the room briefly and noticed the vase of fresh flowers on the nightstand. Searching through her peripheral memory, she realized that, everyday, the vase was replenished with diligent care.

"Who gave you those flowers? They must not be easy to acquire this time of year."

The girl's breathing calmed somewhat at this reminder, her expression softening with wistfulness.

"I guess I have one friend," she whispered in a barely audible voice. "I don't deserve him though."

"Lucky for you that he seems to disagree," Inanna said. "He obviously still thinks you're beautiful and lovable if he brings you these gifts of affection everyday."

The girl sniffed as she considered Inanna's words. Her face scrunched into a small, mystified frown as she said, "I don't know why he's always so nice to me. He's been that way since we were in High School. It's not like I encourage him or anything."

"Maybe he just likes you because you're likable," Inanna offered. "Maybe if you ask him, he will give you the help and support you need."

The young woman looked down at her belly and said, "He already offered to help. He said he'd marry me and take care of me and the baby as if it were his. He said it would be the best gift anyone ever gave him if I agreed. It's his birthday today, you see. He's the one who found me in my bathtub that day…"

The girl's expression darkened again in memory.

Abruptly she shook her head as if to clear it and lifted her eyes to Inanna. "But why would he do that? Offer to take care of me and the-the- baby?"

At the last word, the girl's voice was barely a whisper, as if giving name to the entity within her would make it too real.

More loudly, she said, "I don't even like him like that. What could he possibly get out of it?"

"Sometimes people help others simply because they want to, because they care," Inanna responded. "Sometimes they aren't asking for anything in exchange. They simply want to give."

"Like I said, I don't deserve him." The girl's lower lip started quivering again. "I think I'll make him miserable. I'll treat him something terrible and he'll end up leaving me too, just like everyone else. I *know* it."

Inanna tightened her clasp of the girl's shaking hands, trying to infuse heat into her cold palms. Suddenly, she was overwhelmed by sympathy and understanding toward the girl, despite her initial resentment and disappointment.

She had felt alone too. Strange and alone. Living in limbo.

If not for her father, and… there was something else. Some*one* else.

But the moment her mind caught onto this thought, the inkling vanished as if it never was.

Inanna blinked to orient herself again.

If not for her father's courageous, unconditional, healing love, she could not have overcome the doubts and fears that plagued her, could not have found the strength to make her own way in life.

Even if the girl was a Lost Soul, she did not deserve to be abandoned.

At that moment, Inanna made a choice.

"You are not alone," Inanna said, resolute and strong. "You will never be alone. I, for one, would be delighted to be your friend. And now you have at least two people you can count on in this world."

The girl peered at her disbelievingly and a little shyly. "Really? You want to be my friend? But you don't know me at all? And I'm so-so-"

Inanna shot her a look that effectively silenced whatever disparaging thing she was going to say about herself.

"I'd like to get to know you," the Chosen said, her sincerity beyond doubt. She let go of one of the girl's hands and held onto the right hand, giving it a firm pump.

"Hello, my name is Nana Chastain. It's nice to meet you."

For the first time, a faint smile hovered on the edges of the girl's chapped pink lips. "Hello," she replied, "my name is Olivia."

An hour later, leaving her new friend in better spirits and more optimistic about the life she carried within her, Inanna rode the elevator down to ground floor.

She'd stayed in the hospital longer than she intended, but it was time well spent if she could convince the girl to hold onto hope and give herself and her baby a fighting chance.

She would return early the next morning before dawn to collect on the other patient's Blood Contract on Christmas Day.

As Inanna walked toward the reception area on her way to the exit, her attention was arrested by a tall, leanly built young man leaning over the check-in counter with a bouquet of fresh flowers. Involuntarily, her footsteps slowed as she drew closer.

"It will just be ten more minutes or so," the receptionist said to the young man. "We need to move Ms. Brown to another room."

"Nothing wrong, I hope?" the man said with immediate concern, his low, husky voice pricking Inanna's awareness like a thousand needles.

"Not at all," the receptionist smiled back reassuringly. "It's just that the other patient sharing her room requested to be alone tonight. And as it's Christmas Eve, we try to grant as many requests as we can within reason. And Mr. Stevens hadn't made any requests up 'til now."

The young man nodded, his broad shoulders relaxing slightly with visible relief. He signed in, picked up the flowers and a hefty satchel of papers from the reception desk, too busy tucking it under his arm, and didn't look where he was going.

Abruptly, he crashed into someone else, crushing the flowers between them and dropping the satchel to the floor, papers flying out everywhere.

Out of pure reflex, he wrapped his arms around the unlucky obstacle that got in his way and tried to prevent the both of them from falling. But downward momentum got the better of him and he could only twist his body at the last moment so that he landed on the hard ground first, his body breaking the impact of the other person's descent.

"Are you okay?" he asked when he was able to take a small breath. "Are you hurt?"

Inanna could not believe that she'd made such a clumsy ass of herself. After four millennia of honed senses and combat training, she hadn't fallen on her face since she was a toddler. What was she thinking to be so ridiculously distracted?

Her body all but vibrated with pleasure as the young man's hands smoothed their way down her back, petting her in a comforting motion.

What was it he asked? Oh yeah, he was checking if she was hurt.

With a muted groan, not of pain but of mortification, Inanna stretched to a sitting position with her arms bracing her weight, her hands flat on the ground, and looked down.

All coherent thought evaporated as she stared into the face of her gallant rescuer.

It was the face of an angel.

A beautiful, passionate, warrior angel.

And so fresh and innocent with youth it almost hurt to look upon him.

At that moment, Inanna Fell.

For the first time in her long, lonely existence, she longed for something, *someone*, she should not have.

Craved him at her very core.

Deep, chocolate brown eyes gazed back at her, first with concern, and then with confusion, as if he too became suddenly aware of the inexplicable tension humming between them.

Before he could speak again, she disengaged from him, and without a word or a look back, Inanna left temptation behind.

*** *** *** ***

Present day.

Gabriel sat woodenly on one side of a twelve-foot mahogany desk.

The funeral home's sales representative droned on about the various types of cremation and burial services they offered, along with a wide range of price tags, sprinkled in with false sympathies and condolences.

For the past four hours since receiving the call from the hospice's attending physician, sleep had morphed into nightmare, and nightmare had become reality.

Pain, anger, disbelief, numbness, shock... a thousand different emotions churned through Gabriel's chest cavity until gnawing emptiness loomed where functioning organs used to reside.

In those four hours, he'd calmly gathered Benji out of bed, brought Olivia's best dress, fresh underclothes and shoes, drove to the hospice within the speed limit and without the impediment of morning work traffic; met with the physician on call to listen to the details of Olivia's last moments, though he heard not a single word; changed Olivia out of her hospice gown and into her "Sunday Best" with the help of the nurse; struggled with putting on her left shoe because rigor mortis had made her swollen foot too stiff to fit inside, almost broke down in a fit of rage and tears because of it, but managed to pull himself together to prevent a full-blown spectacle; held Benji while he cried and said goodbye to his mother, Gabriel's own eyes remarkably dry; ordered Olivia's belongings into bags and suitcases, and waited for the funeral home to pick up the body and take it to temporary storage.

They'd even had time to pick up a McDonald's breakfast along the way, and Benji was now slurping his chocolate milk and munching on hash browns in the funeral home's reception area, away from the "serious business" on which the adults conferred at this never-ending mahogany desk.

"Cremation," Gabriel said, the surprising sound of his interruption like a shotgun blast in the freezing conference room.

Startled to a stop mid-speech, the sales rep opened and closed his mouth before recovering his train of thoughts. "Of course. We offer three different levels of cremation—"

"And yet the result is still ashes," Gabriel interrupted again.

As the rep struggled anew for another sales angle, he quickly and decisively declared, "Level one cremation. No urn. Just give me the bag. When can I expect to retrieve it?"

"Well..." the sales rep blinked like an owl behind his Ray-Ban glasses and darted his eyes from side to side, no doubt scrambling for persuasive tactics to get a higher price out of the grieving widower.

"Make it before closing today," Gabriel stated, "charge me the fees for express service."

Without waiting for a response, he stood and walked out of the too-frigid room, signaling a definitive end to the meeting.

Down one corridor to the surprisingly sunny and cheerful reception area, Gabriel found his son finishing the last of his milk, sitting atop one of the cushioned chairs, his small legs swinging carelessly a couple of feet above the floor.

"Let's get out of here," Gabriel said with a determined smile, "let's go somewhere fun today, anywhere you want. How about it?"

He scooped his son into his arms, disposed of the McDonald's breakfast bag, and exited the funeral home as fast as he could without looking as if he were running away.

"Can we come back later to see Mo-I mean- Olivia?" Benji asked, already forgetting that the goodbyes a few hours ago were, in fact, permanent.

The slip was not something Benji made often.

From the time he could speak, Olivia had insisted that her son call her by name, not Mommy, not Mother, not Mama, not Mom.

Not any moniker, in fact, that reflected their relationship.

Only since she found out about the cancer had Olivia encouraged Benji to call her Mommy, but the habit had already been formed and was difficult for the boy to break. He continued to call her Olivia despite her best efforts to persuade him otherwise.

That he involuntarily began by calling her Mom showed Gabriel just how upset Benji still was.

Swallowing the lump in his throat, Gabriel infused his voice with patience and tried to sound carefree.

"We can't see Olivia any more, remember? She's going to be invisible from now on. But she'll still see us even though we can't see her. So you better be good."

Benji nodded in all seriousness and wrapped his arms tighter around his father's neck, burying his face in the warm, comfortingly smelling nook between his father's chin and his shoulder. For a few moments, the boy was silent, as if contemplating the truth of what Gabriel had imparted to him.

And then he said in a small, shy voice, "Can we go see Nana?"

Gabriel almost stumbled a step as a surge of fury charged through him.

Why did Olivia do this?

Make him share custody with a woman he'd never even met! Barely ever heard of until this point!

He always knew that Olivia had lived a separate life from him in the first few years that they'd been married.

They were like friendly roommates who shared the responsibility of taking care of an infant they both loved dearly. He'd never questioned her comings and goings during that time.

He knew she had lovers and considered him as more of a close relative than a red-blooded man with feelings, desires and needs, and he'd never pressed her in any way to see him differently. He'd wanted her to rebuild her self-confidence and feel secure in his devotion without condition.

For a while, she seemed to get better, seemed to be happier. But she never truly *saw* him until the very end.

Though she'd been discreet about her extramarital affairs and never flaunted them in his face, she hadn't tried to hide her relationships either. At least she'd refrained from bringing men home with her. To Benji, Olivia and Daddy loved each other, were friendly and affectionate, and they both adored their son.

Gabriel was quite certain that Olivia had never introduced Benji to any of her lovers, least of all the boy's real father.

But apparently, she'd brought this Nana Chastain home or had brought Benji out to meet with the woman. And amazingly, both mother and son had managed to keep Gabriel in the dark all this time.

His prolonged silence was making Benji squirm with nervousness, as if the boy felt his father's inner turmoil.

Gabriel lowered Benji to his feet as they reached the car and helped him into his booster seat in the back.

Trying to keep his tone light, Gabriel said, "So you really like this Nana, huh? I'd like to meet her too."

Benji raised his eyes to look inquiringly into his father's face as he got buckled in.

When he could detect no trace of unhappy emotions, he shared exuberantly, "Nana is Olivia's Angel. Mine too. And yours too, Daddy."

"Really?" Gabriel asked encouragingly, "how can you tell?"

Benji impatiently waited for Gabriel to get into the driver's seat before answering, visibly excited by the topic of conversation, as if he couldn't hold in the juiciest secret in the world any more.

"She's really *really* pretty," the boy gushed with enthusiasm, "she looks like an Elf princess from *Lord of the Rings*! Olivia is a human princess, but Nana is a *fairy* princess. She's *magical*." The last he said in a hushed whisper, full of awe and reverence.

Then he added, "Olivia said Angels are shy. She said if I told anyone, Nana would disappear."

Ah, Gabriel thought. So that's how Olivia managed to keep the secret between the two of them.

"So where does this Angel live?" Gabriel asked in the same light tone, though his hands tightened involuntarily on the steering wheel as he started the engine.

He could see Benji's shrug in the rear-view mirror. "I dunno," the boy answered. "We always met her in the Park. Olivia would pick me up from school sometimes and take me there."

"Central Park it is, then."

Gabriel pulled his tin can of a sedan out of the funeral home's parking lot and headed in that direction. He was determined to meet this Nana face to face before the day ended.

Heaven help her if she denied him.

*** *** *** ***

Sergei Antonov regarded the sleek, expensively-clad woman sitting across from him in the deep-seated, mohair sofa with undisguised lust, muted respect and just a hint of buried fear.

Never let them see you sweat, as the Americans were fond of saying.

As the Russian mob boss with dominion over Greater New York City, the trickle of fear inching like a meandering leech down Sergei's spine was a first-of-its-kind sensation. Since escaping from persecution in Russia to the U.S. by stowing away on a human trafficking boat at the age of ten and working his way through any means fair or foul up the mafia ranks, he'd cultivated a healthy respect for pain and death along the way, but had never feared them.

What was sitting not four feet in front of him, however, promised fates far worse than death in her pitch-black eyes if he did not tread carefully.

"I expect you are satisfied with our rapidly expanding network of clubs," Sergei started with somewhat feigned self-confidence.

Never let them see you sweat, he repeated in his head.

"Three well-established hubs in the City, two starting in Jersey and D.C., and let's not forget the growth internationally."

"You expect wrong," the woman answered softly, in a husky feminine voice, the kind that purred, evoking images of twisting bodies in the throes of orgasm.

The edge of malice underlying her tone did not escape Sergei, however.

"In our agreement, I provide the funds," she continued, "you provide your reach and influence, and together, we grow our little enterprise from one seed to a hundred, a thousand trees that flow rich with the blood of men."

Strange, how she could sound so poetic while talking about death and destruction, Sergei reflected.

"And yet," she said, pausing briefly to pick a nonexistent spec of lint off her Valentino overcoat, "there are only a handful of clubs thus far in half as many cities. Hardly the explosive growth you promised me."

This discussion was not going well, of that Sergei was clear.

He knew by pure instinct that this was not the time to negotiate. It was not about asking for more funds, for she seemed to have an infinite supply. It was not about asking for more time, for her patience was obviously wearing thin. If he did not come up with a creative solution to accelerate the expansion of the fight clubs, she would simply choose a different partner—after disposing of her current one.

Sergei was nothing if not creative.

"I have a plan," he shared with a spark of conspiracy in his eyes as he leaned forward, elbows on knees, to fully capture her gaze. "Right now, the growth of the clubs is generated purely by word of mouth, exclusive and shrouded in secrecy. If we want to truly accelerate the expansion, we must make it viral."

She tilted her head slightly at an angle and considered his words. "Interesting. Go on."

"The Internet reaches where our vast, yet limited networks cannot," Sergei continued, his confidence bolstering, "and with the right technology platform, the best coders, we can create a virtual fight club that spans the world instantaneously. As the addiction and frenzy spreads, real fight clubs will spawn themselves everywhere at once. We just need to lay down the ground rules and keep close tabs on where and how they get established so we can maintain control and help remove barriers if need be."

The woman's gaze glowed with both appreciation and unholy excitement at Sergei's plan.

"We will need to market the fights properly, won't we," she suggested, quickly latching onto the idea. "Make sure we have the best fighters and the most gruesome displays, the bloodier the better."

"Leave that to me," Sergei responded, nodding in agreement. "It just so happens that a prized specimen joined our club last night. Unknown yet whether he's a repeat or a one-off. But we shall be *persuasive*. He will make a reappearance very soon."

Faintly, the woman stretched her lips into a smile of anticipation, revealing just the tips of her brilliant white upper teeth, including two razor sharp canines.

"You have video footage, I assume."

Sergei stood smoothly, surreptitiously letting out a long-held breath as he did so. Looked like he passed this round. His partnership status was still secure.

"Right this way," he said, holding out an arm to usher the woman forward, as she stood gracefully as well, though Sergei was careful not to touch her person. "I believe you will be duly impressed with the ferocity of this particular fighter."

She craned her smooth pale neck toward him as she walked past and speared him with her black eyes over the rim of her designer sunglasses, which she had retrieved from her Prada handbag to perch on her perfect nose.

"Haven't you learned by now how to manage expectations? Be careful that you don't promise too much."

"Then I shall let the lady judge for herself," Sergei said smoothly, his self-possession in tact. He knew enough to discern when she was teasing and when she was truly displeased.

Right now, she was in a good mood.

The video was sure to put her in an even better one.

"On occasion, despite the rules that bind us, destiny reveals an alternate path. Only the courageous, the faithful and the stalwart succeed in walking this path to the end, wherever it may lead."
   —Excerpt from the Lost Chapters of the Ecliptic Scrolls.

Chapter Four

The sun was already starting to set over Central Park, and there had been no sign of the mysterious Nana Chastain all day.

In a corner of Gabriel's mind, he knew that expecting her to show up just because he wished it was foolish. And yet, he expected her appearance nevertheless and even felt justified in his building resentment when, hour after hour, she remained unseen.

Gabriel had spent the past several hours entertaining Benji with the bounties of the Park and its surrounding winter festivities.

Delighted with this unprecedented length of devoted attention from his father in a very long time, Benji had smiled, chatted, and laughed with a carefree joy that contrasted sharply with the cold ball of sadness and loss growing within Gabriel, the emotions seeping into his body with the icy chill of winter.

Now he sat alone on a bench surrounding the Wollman Rink, keeping an eye on Benji as the boy tried to stay upright on his rented ice skates, while Gabriel's own thoughts, long suppressed, flooded his mind with brutal clarity.

For almost two years, he'd known that Olivia's battle with cancer would end sooner rather than later. That she'd held on for so long was a rare surprise to her doctors.

They'd pretended that life was normal for as long as they could despite the drugs and radiation, the increasingly frequent visits to the hospital. Olivia had wanted it that way. She'd even quit her job as a portrait photographer at a well-established studio in Manhattan and went independent when she'd found out about the illness. She'd wanted to stay home and spend more time with Benji.

Ironically, it was as if the illness had awakened her from a sluggish slumber and infused her with new vitality. She'd stopped meeting her lovers.

Stopped seeing *him*.

Olivia became a stay-at-home wife who greeted Gabriel when he finally trudged home from work, often past ten at night, her welcoming smile brilliantly on display despite the mess she'd made of the kitchen trying to save yet another failed recipe in her brave but doomed efforts to cook.

Gabriel couldn't wrap his head around it, but the truth was: finding out she had only a short time to live had made Olivia happier.

What took them all by surprise was the appearance of the second cancer that accelerated her decline dramatically. But even then, she was unworried about the prospect, though she sometimes seemed harried as if she were making plans but didn't know if she could see them through.

And if what the attending physician said was right, Olivia had passed without pain, with nary a worry to line her face. In fact, as Gabriel recalled—the shock of her death easing enough to allow memories to surface—Olivia had died with a smile on her face.

She'd looked incredibly relieved, finally at peace with herself and the world.

It had hurt to look at her. To know that death had given her the comfort he never could.

"Daddy, Daddy!"

Vaguely, Gabriel heard the distant echo of Benji's shouts from the ice rink. He looked up to see his son waving his arms in wild excitement, his cheeks glowing red from the exercise as well as a grin of sheer, undiluted joy.

It was then that Gabriel noticed the tall blonde woman standing behind Benji, her hands on the boy's shoulders as if to help him stay vertical on the slippery ice. But even from the distance, Gabriel could see that she held Benji also with familiarity and affection.

Dark blue eyes steadily held his gaze as she inclined her head briefly in greeting.

Before he knew what he'd done, Gabriel had already bounded from his seat and closed half the distance between the bench and the ice rink, maintaining the woman's gaze without even a blink of distraction.

Some unreasonable part of him feared that if he took his eyes off her even for a second, she'd simply disappear.

A few long strides later, Gabriel was not three feet from the woman holding his son, her gloved hands tightening ever so slightly on the boy's shoulders as if he were her shield.

"Hello Gabriel," she said, her warm, rich voice low and familiar.

It sent shivers of awareness throughout Gabriel's body.

Why did he feel he'd heard her voice before?

Staring intensely at the woman's face, he barely prevented himself from staggering off balance when the recognition hit.

He'd seen this face before.

Where or when he could not recall, but he *knew* he'd met her before. Hers was not a countenance one could ever forget.

Benji swiveled his head back and forth between the towering adults and tried to understand why they weren't ecstatic to see each other.

Here were two of his favorite people in the world, meeting for the first time. Weren't they supposed to smile and hug and chat happily while swinging Benji between them? Olivia had said Nana would be his new mother and Daddy's new "partner." Didn't that mean Daddy would treat Nana just like he treated Olivia?

Crossing his fingers, Benji waited for the adults' next move.

Finally, Gabriel seemed to snap out of his personal fog, but as he parted his lips to speak, his cellphone buzzed in the back pocket of his jeans. It took several vibrations before Gabriel turned with a soft "excuse me" and answered the phone.

It was the funeral home. The ashes were ready for pickup, but they would close in thirty minutes, so he'd better hurry. Gabriel made his mono-syllable replies in clipped tones, rushing the conversation to an end.

But when he turned back around, the mysterious Nana Chastain was nowhere to be seen.

*** *** *** ***

Running away was a cowardly thing to do, and not an action Inanna took lightly, if ever she did before.

But she simply wasn't ready for the encounter.

It had to happen sometime, of course.

Sometime soon.

She shared custody of Benji with him, for Goddess' sake. The sooner she established an amicable relationship between them the better.

Safely behind the darkened windows of her Aventador, Inanna leaned her arms forward on the steering wheel and knocked her forehead none too gently against it in self-disgust.

The problem was that she didn't want to be amicable. She wasn't even sure she wanted a *relationship*. She just wanted the man himself.

Over her, under her, all around her.

Inside of her.

She wanted his body, his sex, his blood, his seed. All the carnal, sexual, lustful things her long-ago childhood tutors had tried to discipline her against.

For the most part, she'd been an angel in this regard. She'd never suffered from urges she couldn't control, was always a master of her own emotions and actions. Sexual intercourse was not something she took lightly, and over all the millennia of her solitary existence, there had only been a few partners and only for short durations.

For all her self-discipline, she might have been mistaken for a Pure One.

But she was Vampire. Her nature now boldly and undisputedly asserted itself. It made her long for that which she should not. Made her fangs elongate with thirst and need. Made her body hum with the recognition of its mate.

Determined to get herself under control, Inanna raced away from Central Park, putting as much physical distance as she could between herself and her dark longing.

Upon arrival at the Cove, Inanna was all about business.

She rode the hidden lift from the sixty-sixth floor of the Chrysler Building to the no-public-access level two floors above. Everything above the sixty-sixth floor was sealed off to the general populace. Most people thought there was only an abandoned tower above the last floor; they would never have guessed that the five stories above were actually the converted three-level headquarters of the New England vampire hive.

Inanna got out on the floor where the Chosen resided when they chose to stay at the Cove rather than their own lodgings and where their "business" meetings were usually held, unless the Queen decided to hold court at the Penthouse Atrium.

"You're late," Maximus grunted as Inanna rounded the last corridor to one of the main conference rooms where the leader of the Chosen, with his ever-present pet panther Simca, herself and Ryu, the Queen's personal Assassin, were to meet.

Inanna let her eyelids droop to half mast, giving Maximus a lazy look. "That seems to be a favorite phrase of yours," she greeted in return.

"Don't wind him up," Ryu said with a sideways smile from where he lounged bonelessly on one of the luxurious leather chairs, looking like Simca's feline twin.

Inanna almost grunted at the warning. More than anyone else in the Chosen, Ryu Takamura took great pleasure and pride in winding their Commander up whenever possible. The only other person who could compete was Devlin.

"What is your report?" Maximus demanded immediately, just as Inanna's butt hit her seat, which she wisely chose to be across the large conference table from the pesky and possessive panther.

Thankfully, her leader was looking at the Ninja, not her.

"There was another fight club arranged last night, down by the waterfront. One of our remaining human partners was able to infiltrate into the crowd," Ryu began.

"It takes fifty grand just to be considered for entry into the club as an observer, and most of the time, the stakes are much steeper. Only the highest rollers are admitted, and there's a background check more hair-raising and thorough than the CIA uses."

"What did the human observe?" Inanna asked. Finally, they were making some progress.

Ryu lifted his shoulders in a nonchalant shrug that belied the intensity of his gaze. "The usual. Blood, gore, death, money. The stakes are getting more expensive with each fight club event. Whoever the organizers of this network are, they must be amassing a staggering fortune."

"But there was one noticeable newcomer to the club," Ryu imparted as he leaned more alertly forward on his elbows. "A *real* fighter, if our source is correct, unlike the usual crazies out for violence and adrenaline highs. Trained in mixed martial arts from what I've gathered. It was his first appearance at a club. We don't know yet if he'll be a repeat. He made quite an impression on the spectators though."

"Which means the organizers will most likely want him to be a repeat," Maximus mused. "If we can get to him before they do, we may have a deeper in to the club."

"*If* we can convince him to work with us," Inanna added, "that's a big if. Humans are not exactly willing to be open minded about blood-suckers these days. Many of them only pretend collaboration to get close enough to strike where we are vulnerable. We have to decide how much we reveal to him."

"If we don't involve him in entirety, we might as well not involve him at all," Ryu said. "He'd be no more help to us than the other humans we still count as friends."

"Agreed," Maximus joined in. "Let's do our own surveillance and find out as much as we can about this fighter before we engage him."

He turned to Inanna. "You have the deepest human cover, Angel, you would arouse the least suspicion."

Angel.

Inanna's moniker within the Chosen. The full title was more to the point: Angel of Death. It was her responsibility and her chosen cross to bear.

To her Commander she said, "I'm on it. Ryu, let's download all the details."

*** *** *** ***

Leaning over the railings of the esplanade in Battery Park City, lower Manhattan, Gabriel watched the last of Olivia's ashes flutter with the icy night breeze into the Hudson River below.

She'd wanted to be set free.

Sometimes in her dreams or nightmares, he could not tell, she would murmur and plead: "I want to be free."

Free from what, Gabriel never figured out.

Until now.

He'd often blamed himself for not being enough for her. She'd often shown her resentment toward him for taking care of her. He'd feared that she'd wanted to be free of him, free of the marriage, free to do whatever she pleased with whoever she wanted. And so he'd turned a blind eye, giving her all the freedom and space she needed. But still, it was not enough.

She'd wanted to be free of life.

Gabriel used to think she did the things she did to purposely hurt him, but now he realized she was merely hurting herself, hating herself. It went beyond depression; she was truly *hopeless*.

Lost.

A time bomb waiting to detonate.

Looking back with twenty-twenty hindsight, Gabriel admitted to himself that perhaps he'd always known the source of Olivia's struggles. Known that he couldn't save her. No one could. But he was a stubborn fool. Likely masochistic as well. He couldn't countenance giving up.

It wasn't in him to bow in defeat.

The monks on Song Mountain had taught him that all life was precious, every life worth fighting for, worth saving. If you were born a king, a peasant, an ant, a tree, it didn't matter. It was all part of your journey, and there were valuable lessons to be learned along the way. Seeking death before the designated time was a coward's way out.

At least Olivia's soul would not be burdened by that mistake, Gabriel thought with some consolation. She had fought the good fight in the end, taking the grueling cancer treatments in stride. Perhaps her smile at the last was because of that—she hadn't given up.

And maybe, just maybe, Gabriel had given her some of the strength to conquer her demons.

"I thought I'd find you here."

Gabriel straightened from the railing and pivoted abruptly to face the owner of that haunting, familiar voice.

Nana Chastain. Olivia's Angel.

The shock of seeing her not two feet away, right now, this moment, knocked the very breath from his body. He could only stare wordlessly at the woman who was both terrifying stranger and soul-deep intimate.

The familiarity her words implied completely escaped him.

She turned half away from him toward the river, gazing out into the dark night and choppy waves.

"I should have come forth sooner," she said, "I apologize for the abruptness of my appearance. You must have been...taken aback by the terms of Olivia's will."

When he made no response, Inanna turned to face him fully and could barely keep her response in check as his body heat and subtle, clean scent, even from two feet away, pulled her toward him like the most powerful magnet.

Still he did not speak. His dark eyes speared into her with such intensity she had to fight herself to not step back.

Inanna wondered what he saw. How much he was able to discern just by looking at her.

Could he see what she was beneath the polished façade? Could he glean the predator and warrior within? Was he in tune to her barely contained desires for him? How her body temperature rose just by being in his presence?

Whatever he saw, he could not make sense of, for he asked in his low, husky voice, "Who are you?"

What Gabriel really wanted to ask was: *Who are you really? Why do I feel this way around you? I barely know you and yet I feel naked, vulnerable and lost before you. What power do you have over me? Over my family?*

Inanna responded to the face value of his words.

"I am Nana Chastain. I have been Olivia's friend for many years, and it's remiss of me not to have introduced myself to you sooner. I apologize for that."

Every word she uttered was like a brick she laid on a fortress wall between them, shielding him from the real woman on the other side.

"I own a conglomerate that dabbles mostly in foreign real estate," she continued, and Gabriel felt that the more she told him, the less he knew about her. "Perhaps you have heard of it—Chastain Development & Company International."

Yes, he'd heard of it. It was the parent company of the prestigious architectural firm he used to work at, the one Olivia had recommended him to look into, saying she had a friend on the inside who could put in a good word for him.

Just how much was this woman involved in his life? In his family?

Gabriel remained silent, his thoughts a frenzy of dots swirling to be connected, his emotions a jumble of fleeting memories and feelings he tried desperately to piece back together.

Thinking back, he realized Olivia had mentioned Nana Chastain more frequently than he first recalled. Perhaps all the times she'd said she was going to stay with a friend for the night, it was actually Nana she meant, not another lover as Gabriel had assumed.

"I suppose Olivia told you of the arrangement," she went on, when he did nothing to fill the pregnant pause. "It is primarily a matter of legality. I am open to discuss however you wish to collaborate on Benji's upbringing. Please don't worry that I will forcibly inject myself between you and your son."

Her words were meant to be reassuring, Gabriel comprehended, but instinctively he knew that his life would never be the same again.

"That is the extent of your arrangement?" Gabriel knew she was hiding something. In his gut he *knew* there was more she wasn't telling him.

Her long, dark lashes fluttered down briefly, shielding piercing blue orbs from view. When she revealed her eyes to him again, they glinted with unfathomable emotions. "The rest of the arrangement is you."

Gabriel's heartbeat picked up pace.

"Olivia gave me Benji… and you, Gabriel."

*** *** *** ***

Jade Cicada gently glided her fingertips along the sheer silk drapes that served as the only barrier between her bedchamber and the luxurious hot pool that was her private sanctuary at the end of each night, before she succumbed to the first rays of dawn.

No one, not her harem of young, gorgeous, succulent vampires and venom-drugged humans, nor her devoted Sentries, ever entered this private bath hall except to clean and prepare it for her use.

Until recently.

Through the translucent multi-colored curtain, the shades of the sky as dusk approached, Jade imagined, she could see distinctly the enticing dark masculine shape of her Blood-Slave, lounging seemingly relaxed against the edge of the pool. His chest and abdomen rose above the waterline, the smooth olive skin shadowed with the hills and valleys of his leanly defined muscles. Below the waterline, she could only make out shadows.

Mysterious, tantalizing, provocative shadows.

She deftly parted the silk as she approached him.

He turned the strong column of his neck gracefully toward her, acknowledging her presence, even though he did not raise his eyes to meet hers.

Undoubtedly he'd known she was there behind the curtains watching him, taking his measure with hungry eyes and aching fangs. But he never betrayed any nervousness or unease. Except for the first time they met, Jade had never seen the Pure Ones' Consul so much as startle.

He was calm and tranquility personified. Dignity and equanimity in the flesh.

How she craved to unbalance him.

"Any progress?" she asked as she stepped closer to the pool, as if they were continuing a steady stream of conversation.

He did not bother to clarify. Reading her thoughts unerringly, he answered in the same nonchalant tone to match hers, "A sub-group of the Dozen is on their way here. They will make contact with Maximus tomorrow, I expect."

She effortlessly peeled away her long black, semi-translucent sheath and waded naked into the heated pool from the side directly opposite him.

"Hmm. Leaving the Shield dangerously unprotected, don't you think?" she mused with a sardonic smile. "Dark Goddess forbid your enemies learn of this weakness."

He finally raised his eyes to hers, and there was an infinitesimal moment of distraction betrayed by an involuntary flutter of his lashes when he realized how close to him she was, mere inches away now.

But his voice remained smooth and firm as he said, "The base is secure. The need for our attention is much greater here."

"Indeed?" she murmured silkily, her startling dark blue eyes becoming hooded with arousal as she closed the last distance between them until her peaked breasts lightly touched his muscled chest, and her lower body languidly enfolded his, her long legs wrapping gently around his hips.

"I certainly need your undivided attention, Pure One."

Helplessly, a slight shudder racked his torso as her skin molded to his, the water only magnifying the erotic friction.

Per their agreement, however, she did not take him inside her body, though he could not have been more ready for her to do so, his staff pulsing with need. Instead, she opened her core against his swollen cock beneath the water and lapped against the root of him in small, undulating circles, driving him to the brink of sanity.

Clenching his jaw, he forced himself not to react outwardly to her teasing onslaught. Unfortunately, his raging erection he could do nothing about.

So much for his well-earned moniker, "the Monk."

Since he first laid eyes on Jade Cicada, Seth's body had no longer been his own.

"Surely you've had enough attention for one day," he responded in a low, steady voice, no inflection whatsoever to betray the spike of pain within his chest as he thought of the harem she'd dismissed a mere half hour ago.

It was the same every night before she took to her bed before dawn. Half a dozen well-oiled, deliciously-scented nude males would parade into her bed-chamber, where they entertained her sometimes for hours with their sculpted, lithe young bodies and fed her their hot, sweet blood.

And she made him watch her take her satisfaction every time.

It was their bargain: his punishment for withholding sexual intercourse, though she'd never spelled it out as such.

It was understood that a Blood-Slave gave both blood and body to his/her master. In Seth's case, he'd negotiated a compromise that only surrendered his blood. She could try to seduce him, and surprisingly she hadn't made much of an effort in the past few months.

That her glorious, naked body was currently wound around him like a second layer of skin was mere child's play where the Queen of the Vampires was concerned. He knew from witnessing her orgies that she could do far worse. But try as she might, she could never take him without his consent. That was their bargain.

Seth cursed his own arrogance. He'd sorely overestimated his self-control and completely underestimated the vampire Queen's powers of persuasion.

"Mmm," she purred as she nuzzled his throat, breathing in his subtly musky scent, mixed with the refreshing fragrance of the bath. "Not enough of the attention I desire most," she said as she kissed a wet path along his jaw.

He could feel her smile though he could not see it. He knew it was a full, teasing tilt of her lips.

This was all a game to her.

That he burned feverishly with unfulfilled arousal and deep, dark need—it only amused her more.

Without warning, she undulated her hips slightly and her nether lips closed around the head of his penis in a luxurious kiss before settling back against the root of him.

Seth gritted his teeth to prevent a hiss from escaping as his scrotum tightened painfully and his cock jerked and shuddered. Though his arms ached to wrap her in their steely embrace, he resolutely kept his limbs relaxed against the wall of the bath. Beneath the water, however, his fists tightened until his knuckles turned white.

Against his throat, he felt her smile spread wider.

"Just say the word, Pure One," she taunted him with her rich, womanly voice, "you'd enjoy our Contract so much more if you just let yourself go."

"Dying an excruciating death over the course of thirty days is not what I call enjoyable," he replied in an even tone.

Her soft laughter rumbled from the tips of her toes to the top of her head, finally to flutter out between her rosy lips like tinkling dragon flies' wings. Seth could not help but appreciate her ability to laugh with her entire body. It was as if her whole being vibrated with good humor.

It also did not escape his notice that *he* was the object of her amusement.

"Come now," she said when the laughter subsided like effervescent champagne bubbles, "surely you don't pretend that I'm ignorant of the *real* meaning behind the Cardinal Rule." She lifted her head and faced him directly, her arms wrapped loosely around his neck.

A small smile still in place, she lowered her lids and looked at him coyly from beneath her lashes.

"You do not waste away in thirty days unless you give yourself in love to your partner, body, blood and soul. Mere sexual congress for the fun of it means nothing. You could fuck me all day and all night anywhere, any way, and you'd be immune to the fearsome Decline." She paused for effect as her careless words made him shiver hot and cold.

"Unless, of course, you have *feelings* for me." Her smile was spreading again as she licked from the base of his throat to the tip of his chin. "Surely, you, of all males, would not make that mistake."

Seth had no response, no ready quip to banter back. Words eluded him in this moment of truth. Whatever it was between them, it was not a game to Seth. And though he struggled not to feel, his emotions grew stronger and more complex with each passing day.

To block out further conversation, *dangerous* conversation, he tilted the pulsing vein in his throat against her lips. His hands reached for her hips beneath the water and he brought her core tightly against his, grinding his cock in a voluptuous twist from root to tip through her swollen nether lips, hitting her clitoris in one long, mind-numbing glide.

She moaned deeply and clutched his shoulders, her nails digging into his skin. Almost immediately her elongated fangs sank into his vein, and she took a deep, drugging pull.

And then, finally, there were no more words.

"She who loves a Dark Mate shall be rewarded with peace, passion and prosperity. She who covets a Pure One shall be delivered pain, destruction, and death. She who desires a human shall be forced to witness the wrath and endless despair of mortality."
—Excerpt from the Dark Laws, verse sixteen of the Ecliptic Scrolls

Chapter Five

Sophia spun on her heels a full three-sixty degrees in the middle of Times Square, right outside the subway exit on Forty-Second Street.

Every time she came to the Big Apple she was awed and thrilled anew by the towering skyscrapers, bustling streets and cacophony of sounds. She would never *live* in New York City, it was too intimidating, too loud, too in-your-face. Too overwhelming.

But she loved to visit.

This time, she was here for a whole month, using a special exchange program between Harvard and Columbia University as cover. She even got to stay on campus. Well, in a five-million dollar four-bedroom apartment in Morningside Heights reserved for dignitaries, tycoons and movie stars.

But still, she was *on campus*!

Unfortunately, she didn't get to choose her roommates. Though they looked young enough to be graduate students in their early twenties, and they always would, the younger of her two guardians was almost two thousand years old if you counted all his incarnations together.

Fortunately, Sophia liked these two particular body guards. Aella was her best friend and Cloud... well, Cloud was the source of her best friend's greatest frustration, if things continued the way they were. Sophia had never seen the Amazon goddess confounded and thwarted by any male, and now that she finally met her match, it was rather fun being an interested, third-party observer.

"Tell me again why we had to take the subway when there are plenty of taxis and limos at our disposal? Or even Uber for Goddess' sake," Aella griped as she wound her wooly red scarf more securely around her throat.

Aside from that one concession to the winter cold, she was all sleek black leather and golden blonde hair that cascaded in waves to her lower back. Even the unshockable citizens of New York City stared in awe at her perfect beauty as they passed by.

"We're on a mission, remember?" Sophia answered with a smile, knowing her friend's complaints had less to do with the subway and more to do with the male at her side. "Two missions, actually."

Sophia rubbed her ungloved hands together and breathed heat into them to warm them up. "We need to help the Vampire Queen and also try to recruit more Pure Ones while we're here. Where better for me to find Pure souls than the crowded subway?"

Sophia, while human, did possess the Gift of being able to detect Pure souls. After the Shield was attacked this past Fall, they desperately needed to rebuild their numbers, especially to recruit more warrior-class Pure Ones. With the enemy still at large, they had to move fast.

"And the same reason applies for our promenade through Times Square now?" Aella asked, a small smile on her lips. Apparently, her good humor had returned as the threesome began strolling down Seventh Avenue.

Sophia shrugged, putting an extra bounce in her footsteps. "Sure. We can chalk it up to the mission, but really I just wanted to breathe the city in."

"You want to inhale the pollution, car exhaust and trash fumes?" Aella needled.

Sophia gave her a sideways look. "Nothing you can say can dampen my mood. Why don't you wrap your arms around Cloud's like you want to instead of whining for attention?"

Aella darted a hasty glance at the male walking on the other side of Sophia. Seeing that he was busy surveying the area and people around them, not paying attention to their bantering, the Amazon breathed a sigh of relief.

Just in case, she pinched Sophia on the upper arm hard enough that the young Pure Queen felt it through her goose down coat and layers of clothing.

"Ow!" Sophia rubbed her sore spot and glared at her vindictive friend.

"Everything all right?" Cloud asked, half with concern, half indulgence.

He was used to Aella and Sophia's harmless bickering by now. They reminded him of the two Stooges sometimes with their teasing and antics. He hoped that didn't mean he was supposed to be the third.

Still eyeing Aella suspiciously, Sophia leaned closer into Cloud's side and wrapped both her arms around the warrior's left. Cloud took her sudden show of affection in stride like an older brother who was used to spoiling his baby sister, and Sophia sent Aella a triumphant look.

Green-eyed with envy, Aella gave herself a mental shake and focused on the task at hand.

To Cloud, she asked, "Seth said to meet the Commander of the Chosen this evening after sundown, correct?"

Keeping his gaze sharpened on their surroundings, the Valiant answered, "Yes. At Penn Station, in front of the main departures board."

"Will he be alone?"

"Seth did not say, but I assume he may bring one or two of the Chosen to even the odds."

While the New England vampires and the Pure Ones had an informal truce of sorts, neither side moved without precaution.

Trust was earned, never assumed.

"Word has it that Maximus Justus Copernicus is one of the most fearsome warriors in the entire vampire race, not only because of his experience and skill, but his ability to anticipate his opponents' moves two or three steps in advance," Aella reported with grudging admiration.

"You've been doing homework," Cloud acknowledged, glancing at her briefly before focusing on surveillance again.

"Naturally," Aella said, no boastful inflection in her tone.

It was her job, after all, as the Pure Ones' Strategist to scope out options and take careful measure of their friends and foes.

"I've made a study of the members of the Chosen over the past few months. Their fighting prowess during that critical battle was most impressive. We could not have overcome the odds without their assistance."

"*Oooh*," Sophia chimed in, "you must have all the juicy gossip on the vampire Queen's personal guard. Do tell."

When Aella "made a study" of something or someone, she left no stone unturned.

Aella did her elegant non-rolling-eye expression, giving her young charge a look of condescension. "Beg pardon, I do not gossip. My research is nothing short of art."

Sophia did roll her eyes at that, perhaps too immature for a woman who was now old enough to vote, but she couldn't help herself when Aella was around to goad her.

"Share in your knowledge, oh wise one," she intoned, "What did you find out about the Chosen?"

Needing no further prompting, all seriousness once more, Aella reported to both Sophia and Cloud, "As you know, Maximus is the Chosen's Commander. Besides leading these elite warriors, he trains new recruits and enforces the law among the vampire kind within the New England territory. He is seldom without his panther Simca, who is also an immortal, like your stallion."

Cloud nodded in understanding. Simca, like his steed, White Dragon, was both eternal companion as well as formidable weapon, an extension of the warrior himself.

"His second in command is Anastasia, call sign Phoenix," Aella continued. "Her ability is telekinesis. And then there's Ryu Takamura, the Assassin."

At this, a small frown knit Aella's dark blonde brows together. "His abilities I am still researching. Most likely there is more than one. He is perhaps the most dangerous of them all, a deadly Ninja in his human life."

"I recall three blondes at the battle," Cloud asserted. "A male and two females."

Indeed, the three fair-haired warriors had stood out in the dark catacombs of their nemesis' lair like fallen angels in the pit of Hell.

Aella nodded. "The male is Devlin Sinclair, call sign Hunter. As his moniker describes, he's responsible for hunting vampire Rogues. Maximus, Anastasia and he often work together. I'm not sure that he has a special ability besides those that are trained and honed through experience. Few vampires, in fact, possess special gifts."

Only those who were once Pure Ones retained their Gift when they became vampire. That, and True Bloods. But the latter were all but extinct after the Purge of the Great War.

"One of the females had the uncanny ability to know exactly where enemy vampires were coming out of the tunnels," Cloud recalled. "I observed her catching most of them by surprise with moves that anticipated their entry into battle."

"Ah yes," Aella agreed, inwardly impressed by the warrior's attention to detail. "That would be Nana Chastain, call sign Angel. She has the ability to see through solid barriers as well as hone in on objects far away, rather like an infrared telescope, but far more powerful. I have not been able to trace her origins, but word has it she's the eldest vampire of Jade Cicada's inner circle, older even than the Queen herself."

This was a noteworthy anomaly, which the threesome tucked away for future reference. Typically, hives were ruled by the eldest vampire, for they were usually also the most powerful.

"And last, we have Simone Lafayette, the Keeper. She oversees the queen's affairs, serves as her advisor and assists Maximus in his duties. Perhaps her most important role is being the guardian of the Ecliptic Scrolls."

"Like the Zodiac Scrolls?" Sophia inquired.

Aella gave one nod in the affirmative. "I don't know the details, Eveline is sure to know more, but I believe the Ecliptic Scrolls were written during the time that preceded the Great War. Some say they predate the Zodiac Scrolls, but no one can confirm since there are few recorded survivors, vampires and Pure Ones alike, from that age."

As they digested that, Cloud switched back to the topic at hand. "And the Queen, Jade Cicada, what is her power?"

Aella gave him a sideways glance and hesitated. She paused long enough that Cloud looked over Sophia's head directly at her, piercing her with his unusual laser-blue eyes.

Aella looked away abruptly and answered, "She can take energy from others, even absorb their powers if they have any, for a short period of time. This she does through the taking of their blood, their souls if she's so inclined, or her most preferred method… through sex."

Aella surreptitiously darted a look at Cloud. Seeing no visible reaction, she went on, "They say the vampire Queen is nigh irresistible sexually to males and females alike if she turns on her seductive powers. She is reputed to be one of the Great Beauties of all time."

They had turned at some point during their leisurely stroll and were now in front of Rockefeller Center, overlooking the skating rink on the Lower Plaza.

Trying to distract her friend from over-speculating about the vampire Queen and her seductive prowess, Sophia said loudly in a cheerful voice, "I'm hungry. Let's get some lunch and digest afterwards with a little shopping. We don't have to meet Maximus and company until sundown, right? We'll have plenty of time to strategize later."

"And by the way," she added in a lower voice, "I'm pretty sure I detected two Pure souls nearby, within a fifty-foot radius. Maybe one or both of them could be a new recruit."

*** *** *** ***

"Daddy, look! I can go backwards!"

Gabriel skated forward while Benji painstakingly shuffled backwards on his skates, but Gabriel made sure he was always within arm's length of his son in case the boy took a tumble. He clapped his hands in encouragement and couldn't help smiling at Benji's effervescent joy.

Just one more day, Gabriel told himself. One more day of pure enjoyment and distraction from the stark reality that his five year-old son no longer had a mother, that Gabriel no longer had a wife, and that his recent "earnings" were rapidly dwindling. He'd misestimated the amount of hospice bills and cost of cremation services.

Apparently, without health insurance, the average American tax payer couldn't afford basic services other countries provided free of charge.

Gabriel needed money fast, or Benji would have to start missing school. He could probably stall another couple of weeks with the month's advance he was going to give to Mrs. Sergeyev, but he'd have to find a stable, sufficient nine-to-five job very soon. The most obvious avenue would be to go back to work for an architectural firm, but the pay was abysmal and the hours were long. He couldn't afford to work seventy to eighty hours a week as a single father with a five year-old.

Gabriel took out a business card from his jacket pocket.

On the front it said "Chastain Development & Company International" with contact information and office address. On the back, written in elegant cursive was the number to the Columbia Graduate School of Architecture Assistant Dean's mobile.

"Give him a call," Nana had said last night by the river. "I hear he is looking for some gifted teaching assistants, and the positions pay very well, including a benefits package that is available to all university employees."

He had not extended his hand to receive her generous offer, still reeling from the suddenness of their encounter and how her very presence seemed to turn his world upside down, his emotions inside out. She'd taken his hand and tucked the card within his grasp, the skin-on-skin contact firing up all his nerves like a jolt of electricity.

The rest of their conversation, or rather, her one-sided monologue, was a distant blur.

He barely recalled anything she said. He'd been too busy feeling confused and overwhelmed by the voluptuous emotions she evoked by her mere nearness, spikes of sensations he'd never felt before, yet somehow seemed eerily familiar.

Even now, all he could remember was the subtle fragrance of her hair in the night breeze, the haunting blue of her cat-like eyes, the blood-red of her full lips and the achingly familiar sound of her voice.

It's like he *knew* her. Body and soul.

But he couldn't for the life of him figure out when they might have met before. The knowledge of her seemed to be imprinted in his DNA, irrefutable and everlasting.

Benji had grabbed hold of his hand and started pulling him toward a long, snaking line of skaters, joined by their hands, in the middle of a group game.

Gabriel followed listlessly, still caught up in his inner turmoil. He'd chosen the Rockefeller rink for a reason—he did not want to chance a second encounter with Nana Chastain at the Park so soon after their first (and second) fateful meeting.

He didn't know what to think, how to feel; he didn't understand why she had such power over him.

It was as if he was finally awakened after centuries, millennia, of oblivion.

Suddenly, Gabriel tensed and looked up.

At his twelve o'clock, less than ten feet away stood two Eastern European-looking men staring pointedly back at him. They stood out like hulking ogres amidst children and families with their bulky build and towering height, even without wearing ice skates.

One of them jerked his chin toward his left, keeping his eyes trained on Gabriel. The other one subtly pointed toward Benjamin and stretched his thin lips into a threatening smile.

Gabriel got the message. Go with them or expect trouble.

He murmured a few words to Benji, and the boy nodded, grasping a little girl's hand instead of his father's, keeping the skating ring intact, and shuffled away happily. Gabriel waited for the skaters to pass and slowly made his way toward the two men.

"Can I help you?" he asked when he was immediately before the strangers.

The more expressive of the two smiled widely, revealing two gold capped front teeth. "The question is, how can we help you," he said with a strong Russian burr.

"I don't see how," Gabriel responded, refusing to play their game.

"Come now," Mr. Smiley said, "you don't consider our letting you walk away with ten grand in one night being helpful?"

Gabriel kept his expression neutral, betraying none of the alarm he felt tingling down his spine. "I won that money. You *let* me have nothing."

Mr. Smiley and his companion shared a dark look, after which Mr. Smiley responded, "We did not expect you to be so ungrateful, D'Angelo. After all, it is by our rules, with our permission, that you managed to score your wins."

"I paid the club's cut," Gabriel said, knowing that this conversation was going downhill fast, and he had no leverage with the mafia.

"Well, there is that," Mr. Smiley conceded. "And for your cooperation, we'd like to offer you an even bigger event. How would you like to quintuple your winnings in one night?"

"I'm not interested," Gabriel replied without hesitation. It was a one time deal. He had known the risks he was taking, and he did not intend to tempt fate again.

Mr. Smiley heaved a put-upon sigh, dipped his chin down, and stared at Gabriel through sunken eye sockets from beneath bushy eyebrows.

"Did I ask if you were interested?" he said in a low, menacing voice, his tone no longer flippant. "Did I say you had a choice?"

A muscle ticked in Gabriel's clenched jaw.

He did not foresee this. He would never have taken the risk if he'd known this was where it would lead. What did the mafia want with him? Why had they even bothered to find out his real name? The fight clubs were supposed to be anonymous. But he didn't have time to sort it out.

"And if I don't play your game?" he asked, knowing he would not like the answer.

Mr. Smiley straightened to his full height and stretched his lips into the simile of a smile again. "Then we might have to invite your lovely boy Benjamin to play instead. We know where you live, we know where he goes to school, we could—"

"Enough," Gabriel cut in, "name the time and place and I'll be there. If you go anywhere near my son, I will hunt you down and destroy you even if I have to do it from hell."

Something in Gabriel's steadfast stare, in the conviction of his voice, made the two men pause. Somehow they knew that this warrior did not make idle threats.

Shrugging off the moment's hesitation, Mr. Smiley said, "You'll be hearing from us soon."

And in another second, the two men had disappeared into the crowds surrounding the rink.

*** *** *** ***

Inanna watched the exchange on the skating rink from the observation deck one level above. She'd zoomed in on the conversation as soon as it started, reading the speakers' lips.

She understood perfectly.

Gabriel. Fight Club. Benji. Danger.

Whether it was out of concern, obsession, or helpless attraction, she did not care: she was thankful to her instincts for pulling her out of bed in the middle of the afternoon to tail Gabriel and Benji to the Rockefeller Center.

Though she was not as susceptible to the sun's effects as others of her Kind, she still felt the pull of slumber strongly despite being bundled in black from head to toe, with nearly opaque sunglasses shielding her eyes. She came wide awake, however, as soon as Gabriel approached the two Russians.

She should have been surprised that Gabriel was involved with the fight clubs, but she was not surprised that he was a fighter. Since the first moment she laid eyes on him, she'd sensed the warrior within. The way he moved, the way he perceived his surroundings, everything about him declared that there was much more than met the eye.

Inanna berated herself for not grasping his financial straits fully. She should have prevented him from going to such extremes, but there was no turning back.

She had to help him.

Even at the risk of exposing her identity to the vampire Hordes. She had the deepest human cover, true, but if the fight clubs' vampire sponsors ranked among the society's elite, and it was almost certain that they did, Inanna would not be able to maintain her cover for long. The Chosen were well known among their Kind.

But she could not risk exposure right away. That might bring Gabriel more trouble than help. She had to somehow track him, infiltrate the club and ensure his protection from afar.

Inanna turned and started walking south, toward Penn Station, where Maximus and she were set to meet the representatives from the Dozen in one hour.

Perhaps the Pure Ones could assist in the infiltration. They were not well known in the City, after all. She'd be taking a chance in trusting them, but she had no choice.

She would risk all to ensure Gabriel and Benji's safety.

*** *** *** ***

Directly beneath the main departures board at Penn Station, three Pure Ones tried to blend in with the crowd and not attract too much attention.

It was an effort in futility.

Victoria's-Secret-super-model-Sports-Illustrated-Cover-Girl looks and stature aside, Aella's waterfall of golden blonde hair was like a lighthouse beacon for ships stranded at sea. The throngs of travelers parted and swelled around her like schools of curious fish, awed and helplessly pulled to a mythical mermaid in their midst.

The golden goddess's male companion was equally magnificent, his edgy, austere, Asian-style attire making him seem as if he'd just stepped off the set of a new *Matrix* sequel. If the masses paused to consider the other-worldliness of the pair, they might begin to raise some questions.

But the piercing aquamarine gaze of the male left their observers in a state of calmness and acceptance, as if it was an everyday occurrence to witness such striking, almost inhuman beauty.

Next to Aella and Cloud, Sophia felt disconcertingly like an ugly duckling (who was unfortunately *not* a long lost cygnet in disguise) stuck between two outrageously gorgeous swans.

Though she'd officially been the Pure Ones' Queen for eleven years, she was still an awkward eighteen-year-old trying to make sense of the world around her. Thankfully, she did not have long to dwell on her insecurities and feelings of inadequacy, for their sometime vampire allies had arrived.

Without making contact or breaking stride, the leader of the Chosen made a subtle gesture to a nearby stairwell and led the way there with his partner. The three Pure Ones followed closely behind.

Through a "Staff Only" door they went, up a couple of flights of stairs, through another corridor and private door, finally to arrive in what looked to be an operations room. Once they were all inside, the Chosen's Commander and his partner turned to the three Pure Ones and bowed formally in greeting.

Sophia and her Elite warriors bowed back and introductions were made. The Commander got straight to business.

"How much do you know about the fight clubs?" he asked without further preliminaries.

"Everything you have shared with Seth we know," Aella answered, "as well as what we have learned from our own research into the matter."

The female vampire named Nana Chastain tilted her head a bit in consideration. "What have you learned?"

Aella and Cloud shared a silent look before Aella addressed her question. "That the vampire sponsors behind all this reach into the Elites of your society, including perhaps one or more of Queen Jade's inner circle."

That the two vampires did not react by unsheathing their weapons in rage at what could be considered a condemning accusation meant that they had already come to the same conclusion.

Maximus confirmed by responding, "This is why we need your help. No one, including the Chosen and the Queen herself, should be above suspicion. If indeed one or more of the inner circle is the traitor, we cannot trust the investigation to our own, and we cannot send the Chosen to infiltrate the clubs as each of us are well known within our society."

"In addition," Inanna put in, "you are not restricted to the night as we are. It is a handicap we cannot afford to have in this mission."

Aella nodded. "Agreed. We have already contacted our human networks in the area to begin gathering intel."

"Let's work together on the human side of the equation," Inanna offered. "I have deep networks you can leverage as well."

They discussed detailed logistics of the partnership, immediate actions, roles and responsibilities. Inanna shared the information she'd recently acquired about a fighter named Gabriel, and Aella agreed to pull on one of the Chevaliers to infiltrate the club once they learned of the time and location of the next event. Aella and Cloud going in directly would be too risky, for strong vampires could sense Pure Ones, especially those with a Gift, by their aura. They would smell a trap a mile away.

Finally, Maximus asked aloud what Sophia had been thinking all this while, "Why do you trust us, Pure Ones? Why do you help us?"

Cloud, who had been mostly silent up to this point, responded quietly, "We do not trust you. Nor would we expect you to trust us. As you said, no one is above suspicion. We have a common enemy and a shared goal: maintain order in the human world as well as the secrecy of our Race."

The two Chosen warriors nodded their alignment.

Thus they went their separate ways, the Chosen disappearing almost immediately into the crowded terminals, while Sophia and company exited on Thirty-Fourth Street.

As they headed North, Sophia turned back and scanned the crowds that had already enveloped the vampires and a slight frown creased her brow.

"What is it?" Cloud asked, noticing her hesitation.

Sophia worried her bottom lip with her teeth and turned back around. "It's so strange, but for a second I thought I sensed a Pure soul in the Angel."

Aella glanced at the young Queen briefly but kept silent while filing away this tidbit.

Sophia shook her head in confusion. "I must be wrong. My Gift still eludes me sometimes. It's like trying to catch smoke tendrils—it just slips through my fingers. Of course she couldn't have a Pure soul. She's a vampire after all. If she once was a Pure One who turned to the Dark side, she would have sacrificed her Pure soul. It's either one or the other, isn't it?"

Both Pure warriors knew that the question was rhetorical, but both instinctively also knew that the answer wasn't that simple.

*** *** *** ***

Having left a happily exhausted Benji with Mrs. Sergeyev, Gabriel made his way to the fight club's new location, sent to him by a shred of note slipped under his studio door, a few minutes before midnight.

Hands in his hoodie pockets, pace brisk, expression grim, he didn't bother to side-step puddles that had collected in the numerous ruts in the cracked pavement of the junk yard as he headed toward a windowless warehouse that seemed abandoned.

But knowing what lay within, he could hear, just barely, muffled shouts and echoing clangs. This time, when he stepped up to the heavy iron door, the guard immediately let him in without a word or question.

As he followed the hulk through a trap door in the floorboards down a short flight of stairs and through a dark, wet, putrid sewer tunnel, Gabriel filed away the twists and turns they took in his head. By his calculation based on the study of the city maps he made earlier this evening, the way he entered was not the only way out. He had two other exits should he need them, one that took him close to the river and another, longer route, that took him through a manhole in the center of Chinatown.

He could not afford to lose tonight, but would they really let him walk away if he won? He doubted it.

He'd already made preparations with Mrs. Sergeyev for Benji. She was to contact Nana Chastain as soon as he left the studio. Ms. Chastain had assured him that though the card she gave him was her business contact, she could always be reached at that number and address. If he didn't return before dawn, he'd left instructions for her to take Benji and keep him safe.

Gabriel knew that he would not return by the designated hour.

Doing so would put his son in danger, and he'd already made that mistake once. Whether the mafia let him live to fight another day or whether he escaped the club, he could not reunite with Benji in the near future. They would try to use his son as leverage to make him do their bidding. He had to protect Benji at all cost. He was trusting Nana Chastain to keep Benji safe.

Strangely, though he barely knew her, he was certain that she'd move heaven and earth for his boy.

"You're up next," the hulking guard said as they reached the makeshift locker rooms behind the fight club arena. "Lose the clothes and put that on."

Gabriel glanced at the loose black trousers with a drawstring waistband draped haphazardly on a beat`up bench.

"And those," the guard indicated with a jerk of his chin at a set of hand wraps, a bucket of thick glue and a large lidded vase beside it on another bench.

"Five minutes," the hulk warned as he trudged to a corner and folded his thick hairy arms over his barrel-like chest, watching Gabriel's every move with hostile wariness.

Gabriel lifted the lid of the vase and peered in.

Crushed glass. The spectator's choice of weapon for the fight this night.

"Dark Ones hold themselves superior to all other beings. True Bloods, the noblest of us all, are born to rule the land. Their blood contains the history of our race, the wisdom of the ages, the ingredients of our Destiny. As such, the purity of Dark Blood must be preserved at all cost."
—*Excerpt from the Ecliptic Scrolls.*

Chapter Six

"Right! Right! Eye socket! Eye socket!"

"Get'im! Get in there!"

"Oh my god! Is that blood that just shot in my mouth?"

"Pin him down! Come on! Arrggghhh!"

Five rounds of brutal dog fight later, Gabriel had completely tuned out the shouting, cursing, hysterical laughter and jeering.

He wasn't going to last many more rounds.

These fighters were nothing like the ones he confronted before: they knew what they were doing and they fought to kill. Two broken ribs, a blown-out ear drum and countless bleeding gashes from the swipes of his opponents' glass-shards-wrapped-fists later, he could feel his strength rapidly seeping out with copious amounts of his sweat, blood and spit.

His left arm was starting to get numb, having taken one too many twists and punches. Vision was impaired by a haze of red in his right eye, and he knew that before long, the lid would completely swell shut. It was time to get out of this hell hole.

Landing a forceful and precise roundhouse kick to his opponent's jugular, he didn't wait for the knockout to be pronounced before banging on the steel barb-wired door to be released.

The hulk leered menacingly back at him from the other side. "You'll get out of here when I say you can. Get back in there and fight."

Gabriel's upper lip peeled back in a ferocious snarl, but before he could bang the gate again, his new opponent's fist swiped three knuckles-worth of six inch gashes diagonally across his back, leaving a bloody, fiery trail of agony.

Gabriel pivoted with a spinning back kick and landed on all fours from the cracking impact. As he caught his breath, he forcibly blocked out the searing pain from his new wounds and refocused on his opponent.

From his first match, he hadn't bothered to play to the crowd like before. His sole purpose was to buy enough time to ensure Benji's safety. The thugs who threatened him earlier at the ice rink had been tailing and watching his every move. Their job was to make sure he showed for tonight's fight. If he resisted, they would have dragged him here, likely using Benji as incentive for his cooperation.

Gabriel methodically closed in on his giant of an opponent who was at least a foot taller at over seven and a half feet and built like a mountain. Using his peripheral vision he took in the ten-foot barbed-wire fence that enclosed from four sides about three hundred square feet of floor area. There was one entrance and exit through the locked steel door the hulk was guarding.

Except for the open ceiling.

Gabriel knew this was his best chance.

The giant was a human battering ram but a slow-moving one. Gabriel crouched low and suddenly sprinted straight on for the fighter who also hunched his shoulders in anticipation. At the last possible second, Gabriel leapt sideways, hitting the wall closest to the giant with one foot, then the other. Using his body's velocity and torque, he pushed off the wall and landed one foot across the right eye of the giant, followed close by the other foot which stomped out the vein in the giant's temple.

As his opponent teetered sideways like a tree about to be felled, Gabriel kicked out one more time to the back of his head and gained enough momentum to leap another three feet in the air, elongating his body to reach as far as he could. Having gained the top of the wall, he flipped backwards off of it into the roaring crowds on the other side.

Gabriel zeroed in on the exit to the West and easily shoved his way through the stunned audience who posed no real barrier, some even cheering him on, others shouting for him to get back in the fight. Several yards away, the hulk and a half dozen guards rallied to action, but made slow progress as the frenzied crowds swarmed around them.

With barely a pause, Gabriel kicked down the flimsy wood door that barred the exit and increased his speed as he entered the sewer tunnels, lit dimly by a few scattered safety lamps secured to the walls and low ceiling.

At his current speed, he could reach the manhole exit to Chinatown within three minutes.

The chaos behind him grew more distant as he sprinted through the winding tunnel. Even if his pursuers managed to catch up with him, they would only be able to come at him one or two at a time in the narrow passage, lending him enough advantage to take them out despite his injuries. Once he reached the manhole and escaped into Chinatown, he could easily lose them in the meandering alleyways. Another few strides and he would be there.

And then everything plunged into pitch blackness.

Gabriel stopped immediately to take stock. Slowing his breathing and calming his thundering heart to listen, he could hear only the slow drip of water from a short distance away. He must be close to the manhole.

"Leaving so soon?" a faint echoing whisper sifted through the dank air of the tunnel, so faint he would have thought he imagined it but for the dark feminine laughter that followed.

Hackles raised, muscles tensed, Gabriel stood silent, barely breathing, awaiting for the unseen opponent's next move.

Suddenly, something slashed across his right thigh, and almost instantly he went down on one knee, his entire leg losing feeling. A beat later he was down on both knees, his head lolling back as if too heavy for his neck.

Before he toppled completely to the dirt ground, however, an unseen force wrapped around his jugular and pulled him bodily up against the tunnel wall until his feet barely touched the ground.

As he struggled to breathe around the vise of a fist, a face pressed close to his in the darkness.

"Mmm. You smell *so* good," his captor hissed in his ear, and he felt a wet tongue lick a long path up the side of his face, taking in the trail of blood that was seeping from his eye wound.

"I have watched you fight," the demon continued to rasp, now nuzzling the crook of his neck and collarbone.

"Magnificent," it said on a drawn out hiss, mingled with delighted laughter.

The hand that was not holding him suspended roved down his chest and stomach to his groin and wrapped around him greedily, squeezing and kneading.

"You make it so *hard* to choose," his tormentor continued, now licking around his mouth, making Gabriel want to gag, but concentrating on drawing breath was all he could do.

"On the one hand I want to save you for another fight. You are such a sight to behold. Such power, such precision, such deadly skill."

The wandering hand now moved back up his bare torso, dragging sharp nails across his skin, leaving long bloody scratches in their wake.

"On the other hand, watching you arouses me to a feverish pitch, makes me want to devour you whole, preferably after a good long *fuck*."

Revulsion jerked through Gabriel's body like an electric shock though he remained damnably paralyzed from head to toe.

Who was she?

If indeed it was a she.

His opponent was definitely shorter than him and slighter of build from what he could make out in the darkness. Yet she held him with one arm fully stretched taut, dangling two hundred pounds of flesh and bone from her fist as if he were as harmless and light as a kitten. Though the lack of oxygen must have impaired his judgement, he knew the situation to be impossible.

No human woman could be so strong.

"Alas," she sighed long and forlornly, "I have neither the patience nor the desire to resist such a tantalizing morsel such as you. A quick meal it would have to be."

She struck hard and fast before her words fully registered, sinking two sharp daggers into his neck.

No... not daggers. Her *teeth*?

Now immobilized not only by whatever drug she'd used on him, Gabriel was frozen by disbelief. And yet...

Suck, suck, suck. Swallow. Suck, suck, suck. Swallow.

There was no denying it. Even as he felt the blood drain rapidly from the vein she had punctured, a trickle leaking down his neck and onto his chest, he realized she was taking it all within herself.

She was drinking his blood!

But then there was no time to think.

He could barely even feel as a bone-deep exhaustion took over and he lost his last tenuous hold on consciousness.

Through the throbbing pain of his wounds, the agony of the creature's feeding at his throat, Gabriel entered a dark tumultuous world of hallucinations and dreams, so vivid they seemed like long buried memories released from an ancient prison.

*** *** *** ***

Third millennium BC. Silver Mountains Colony, hinterlands of the Akkadian Empire.

Alad caught the huddled figure sitting atop her habitual stone bench out of the corner of his eye as he effortlessly parried with his mock battle opponent using a short sword.

"Spying on you again, is she?" Sargon, his partner for the workout, said with a half grin. "I wouldn't mind having a beautiful girl worship me like she does you, my friend."

Alad did not respond to the teasing with words, instead catching his opponent by surprise with a low sweep at the shins, followed by an elbow jab to the sternum, effectively knocking him to the dirt ground with a heavy thud.

"Perhaps if you concentrate more on your training, you will gain more favorable notice," Alad said without change in expression, offering to help his partner up with extended arm.

Getting to his feet with a groan, Sargon shook his head. "I will never gain favorable notice being paired with you. Between that face of yours and your skill as a warrior, no Pure female between the ages of ten and ten thousand would look in my direction."

Ignoring the remark, Alad replaced his sword back on the weapon rack and shot the parting words at Sargon, "Watch your legs. Don't always rely on attack. You must have an effective defense also."

Sargon waved away the advice as he walked off the training grounds toward the bath hall a short distance beyond. Verily, there was no Pure warrior who could equal Alad, with but one exception perhaps. Sargon could continue honing his skills for another thousand years and not be his comrade's match on the battlefield.

Alad quickly wiped off his torso and pulled on his tunic before reaching the girl on the stone bench in a few long strides.

Her soulful blue eyes tracked his approach with admiration and affection. And something else Alad could not define.

"Libbu," Alad greeted her gently, "is something amiss?"

Inanna gladdened slightly at his endearment for her as she always did.

Ever since she could remember, her father's right-hand, the fiercest of all Pure warriors, Alad Da-an-nim, had called her his "heart." He had always been there, as constant as her papa, and though she had lived only thirteen summers and he had lived many more, she didn't think anyone could love him as deeply and as fiercely in a thousand years as she did in her short time in this world.

She gave him a brief smile, a sad shadow of her usual effervescent grin whenever she beheld him, and replied, "I just wanted to see you. One day, I will convince father to let me train to be a warrior too and I will be able to fight by your side."

It was something she always said, since she was old enough to know the business end of a sword. It was something he indulgently accepted as the whim of a child, but which she held as a solemn vow, first as a determined, stubborn girl, now as a young woman sure of her mind and heart.

Alad peered closely at his young charge. Something was definitely amiss. Her usual sunny, joyful self was encased in a grim countenance that bordered on ashen, and a slight form that hunched over as if in pain. Spikes of awareness and worry pricked along Alad's spine.

Verily, she looked quite unwell.

Inanna slipped down from her bench and began walking away from the training grounds, knowing Alad would keep pace with her. As she was her father's daughter, he always made sure she had adequate protection, and when available, he always escorted her himself. She wondered whether he spent time with her because of duty or desire.

Recently, this question had been weighing increasingly on her heart.

"You must tell me if aught bothers you," her bodyguard persisted. *"Let us return to the fort so the healer can attend you."*

Inanna shook her head. "You worry needlessly. I am only experiencing the onset of my woman's time."

That silenced her escort effectively, as she intended. Out of the corner of her eye, she could see a slight flush creep up the back of his neck.

She delighted in taking every opportunity to remind him that she was growing up. Even before her woman's cycle unceremoniously announced its arrival, she felt her heart changing, her thoughts expanding, especially where her father's Second-in-Command was concerned. She might be innocent and she might be a newling, *but she had an old soul. And her soul had recognized his from the very beginning.*

Mine, *the word whispered through her consciousness like a spell or a wish from the deepest recesses of her heart.*

She strode determinedly over a hill and down a winding path and up some steep mountain terrain toward the grove of tamarisk trees that bloomed on a secluded cliff overlooking the fort and surrounding villages below.

Normally, this trek would hardly wind her, though it was a good distance away and the climb required some nimble maneuvering. But this time Inanna fought to keep her shortness of breath to herself, hidden from the sharp detection of her companion.

She did not want more questions from him.

Her body in the past few weeks had become a mystery even to herself. It came suddenly upon her—this change. *She felt weary and sleepy during the day and alive with excitement in the darkness of night. No matter how she tried, she could not fall asleep after the sun had set, staying awake full of nervous energy, writhing in her bed until the sun rose again.*

She started sneaking out of her room at night. Sometimes so full of life, she ran through the valley and surrounding forests at the base of the mountain for hours on end, until the sun's first rays imbued her young, lithe body with exhaustion, calming her overactive senses, slowing her erratic heartbeat.

And then there were the other changes.

The constant thirst that parched her throat.

Unable to be quenched no matter how much fluids she took in. The aching upper gums that throbbed in her mouth, the pain especially acute during the nights. The feverish heat that blistered her skin, making her scratch bloody streaks down her arms and legs. The bottomless hunger that gnawed in her stomach, and yet whatever she ate could not satisfy the beast, only making her nauseous at best, vomit everything back up at worst.

She could feel her thinning figure when she dressed each day. Her father was away on a scouting expedition and so was not here to witness her rapidly changing form and looks, but he would return within a day, two at most, and she loathed to worry him when he already had so much on his shoulders to bear.

Finally reaching the tamarisk grove, she sat beneath the largest one, leaning her back against the knotted trunk and closed her eyes. She was so weary she could barely keep upright. And yet, Alad's presence gave her added energy, and she felt something more than her usual joyous excitement whenever he was near.

She felt a fissure of something darker. Something dangerous and greedy.

"You are not taking care of yourself," Alad chided gently, sitting down beside her, spreading his long, long legs wide and bent at the knees, one hand casually draped there, the other brushing a wisp of hair from her face.

Inanna hissed involuntarily at the delicious contact, and he jerked his hand back as if scalded. She breathed in and out deeply for several moments, willing the dangerous desire within her to subside.

What was wrong with her?

"You are one to talk," she returned with a bit of her old sass. "When you are not riding into battles, you are endlessly training in mock battles. Have you even healed from the wounds you sustained a fortnight ago? And if you train, you should at least teach me how to fight so I can do my part in the war."

Alad could only shake his head. Stubbornness mixed with a blade-sharp intellect, wrapped in a maturity that belied her years, his charge had at times bemused him, befuddled him, and more recently, beguiled him.

"Your part is to help keep the fort safe and liven the villagers' spirits as only your smile can do," he told her teasingly but firmly.

She plucked at a blade of grass at her feet as her expression turned mulish. "And how can I defend the ones I cherish if I don't even know how to defend myself?" she argued. "Other Pure females train to be warriors, it is not so uncommon—so why not I?"

"You know why," Alad said quietly, though he knew her question sought no answer.

She knew the reason as well as he did. She was simply bucking at the constraints of her role, now and in the future.

Inanna was the prophesized daughter of the leader of the Pure Ones in the Great Rebellion, at least that was what the Scribe and Seer said.

She was supposed to hold the key to their collective destiny.

Already, under her father's leadership, the once Blood Slaves of the Vampire race had broken free of their shackles. Still many Pure Ones remained in captivity, some even by choice. Facing a new life without the old rules to bind them, without a well-traversed history to guide them, many Pure Ones felt like dandelion puffs in the wind, uncertain where the fates would take them, dizzy with the endless possibilities of the consequences from the choices they would have to make.

Inanna did not know why she had to be the Light-Bringer.

She was struggling hard enough as it was just to grow into womanhood with some semblance of grace and dignity and not be a burden to her awe-inspiring papa. She wished fervently and often that the keepers of the Pure Ones' past and future had gotten it all wrong.

"Still does not mean I cannot fight," Inanna said obstinately.

Alad considered this point in all seriousness. The Great War had already demanded countless casualties on both sides. Pure Ones had the disadvantage, for their roles had always been subservient, even the guards and warriors who safeguarded the Dark Ones during the daytime when they were most vulnerable.

They were not born aggressors; they defended, sheltered, protected.

Those who were once human might have had a different, more violent history, but Alad could not empathize. He was born to two Mated Pure Ones, peace-loving civilian farmers who lived simple lives. Until their village was burned to the ground and all the inhabitants within.

When vampire soldiers had come to pillage and set an example for the Pure Ones' rebel forces, no one had been able to stop them. No one knew the first thing about fighting back.

Alad had been ten at the time. And he had fought like a wild animal blinded by bloodlust. Somehow he had survived and escaped, and the Pure Ones' leader had found him, starving and on the brink of death. The General took him in, fed him, sheltered him and trained him to be one of the Elite warriors of the race.

He stole a glance at the child-woman beside him.

She was right. He would never forgive himself if harm befell her because of his neglect.

"I will teach you to fight," Alad said finally. "But we will take it slow. You must train your body on flexibility, speed and endurance first. We can make a plan tomorrow at sunrise. Let us return now lest we miss the evening meal."

She shrieked with excitement and hugged him tightly, albeit fleetingly.

But as she started to rise, a subtle breeze shifted the air around them and carried his unique scent to her nostrils, made muskier by his recent exercise.

A bone-jangling shudder racked through her body, and a sharp pain stabbed in her belly, doubling her over.

Immediately, Alad was before her, taking her by the shoulders, his gaze stricken with worry, roaming rapidly over her face, her body.

"What is it, Libbu*?" he asked urgently, willing her to meet his eyes and tell him. "You are unwell. We must get you back to the fort."*

When he tried to take her in his arms, she resisted, pushing with surprising strength at his arms, his chest.

"You. Get away! You are making me..." Inanna gasped as her face contorted in agony and she tried to crawl away but could barely move for the pain. To her shame, she let out a whimper and felt tears leaking out of her eyes.

Alad could no longer bear it.

To see her in pain was a thousand times worse than any torture he could ever imagine.

When he took her in his arms again she did not protest, perhaps she lacked the strength. Instead, she curled into a tight ball, her knees drawn to her chest, and her arms wound tight like tentacles around his neck, her fingers nervously pulling at the hair at his nape.

"Inanna," he said, trying to make her concentrate on him rather than her painful struggle.

Rarely did he use her name. Somehow it was too intimate. It was a woman's name; it hardly fit the girl he cared for from a wee babe.

"Inanna," he said again, turning his face to hers, starting to rise with her secure in his arms. "Hold on—"

Before he could finish the command, she abruptly pushed him back down, so strong and sudden that he landed hard on his back with her straddling his lap.

For only a split moment he gazed into her dark blue stormy eyes and saw the raw hunger in them. Then she bared her teeth, two sharp canines elongated from swollen gums—

And struck.

"Immortality is bequeathed only by the grace of our Dark Goddess. She who seeks to unbalance the cycle of life and death by giving Dark Blood to humans shall reap the sorrow she sows. Without the Goddess's spark the creatures shall be mindless monsters, bent on violence and blood, and the creator shall lose her grasp on sanity with each Turn. Such will be her punishment."
  —*Excerpt from the Dark Laws, verse nineteen of the Ecliptic Scrolls*

Chapter Seven

Benji was fast asleep as he was delivered gingerly into Inanna's arms when she came to retrieve him from Mrs. Sergeyev's apartment after midnight.

Laying her precious bundle on the passenger seat of her Lamborghini, she drove smoothly into the City toward Morningside Heights.

The Pure Ones had readily agreed to watch over Benji when she called in a favor she hadn't earned. He would be safest in their care for the time being; even the Russian mafia couldn't possibly uncover the connection.

Meanwhile, she had business to attend to.

Despite the risk of blowing her cover, she had to go to Gabriel.

When Mrs. Sergeyev called her, she could hardly countenance the immediacy of the situation. Another fight night so soon! She was not prepared. With advance planning, she could have taken the time to train Gabriel, explain at least the basics of what they were up against. She could have pulled on her human partners to infiltrate the club and come to his aide if necessary. She could have researched the location, the setup, the potential fighters he might be pitted against.

But she had no time. No warning. And she had no choice.

No matter the cost, she was going to get him out of that Hell pit alive and whole.

She left her ride a few blocks away from the location Aella had given her and sprinted silently the rest of the way, a fleeting shadow in the darkness. She visually scanned the area as she ran, zeroing in through concrete walls and steel doors as if they didn't exist, quickly isolating the fight pit, whose audience and participants had become embroiled in a free-for-all of mayhem and destruction.

He was not there.

She leapt with long, powerful bounds on top of a rusted crane and surveyed the surrounding area. The pit branched out into a couple of tunnels leading West and South. There was movement in the West path, close to a manhole in the middle of Chinatown. Her eyes grew sharper as she telescoped her vision from still a distance away.

Gabriel.

Held by a Vampire.

Dying.

Inanna's body leapt back into motion like a missile even as her heart fought to keep beating. *No no no no no!* She was not too late!

As she reached the manhole, she unleashed her chained whip, the three-pronged hook at the end latching onto the heavy metal of the cover. With a flick of her wrist, she removed the barrier, sending it crashing with a clang against a nearby wall.

The street was deserted but for a homeless man huddling against the building. He started at the loud noise and looked about, but Inanna had already disappeared into the tunnel below.

A hiss of pure venom greeted her as the vampire realized her approach. Inanna let fly her whip again but the vampire was quick, dodging the hook at the last possible second and spinning away from her prey.

The vampire was fast, Inanna registered barely, and well-trained. No ordinary civilian could have evaded her whip.

The vampire did not give her time to contemplate further, nor did she wait for Inanna's next move, instead disappearing into the darkness of the tunnel, leaving a faint echo of laughter in her wake.

With the immediate threat gone, Inanna fully focused on the man lying limply against the tunnel wall, blood still seeping from the gaping wound at his throat. The vampire had torn through his flesh in her feeding frenzy.

Inanna did not hesitate a moment more to check his vitals, instead lifting him bodily in her arms and leaping in one long bound out of the tunnel through the manhole. She had no time to lose.

Every moment could be his last.

She sped down a darkened alley and rammed her shoulder through the nearest door at the end, and staggered into a pawn shop closed for the night. Quickly she scanned their surroundings and ascertained that it was secure. She took them into a large closet-cum-warehouse in the back and settled with Gabriel against the wall, holding his head with one hand, clutching his hand with the other.

Only now did she feel his pulse and check his heartbeat. Too slow. His breath was fading.

No no no no no! Inwardly she screamed over and over. She could not lose him. Not now, not ever!

What could she do? What should she do? Think, Inanna, *think*!

The ugly wound at his throat was still leaking blood, though the flow was much slower now, reduced to a trickle. Involuntarily, she bent forward and licked at the twin punctures and the torn tissues around them, trying to help them close.

As the first salty-sweet tang of his blood hit her tongue, Inanna reared back with shock.

The first thought she had was: *she'd tasted him before*.

She could not recall the time or place, but she knew deep inside that she'd had him before. She *knew*.

The second thought she had was: *Mine.*

And then she felt it.

The slight shudder that passed through his body. The almost inaudible sigh as his last breath left his chest and the hand she held grew instantly colder.

Inanna's own breath froze along with her thundering heart. Everything came into focus in these few moments, before his soul permanently left his body.

She knew what she had to do.

*** *** *** ***

The vampire returned to her lair before the first rays of dawn, shutting her chamber door with a soft click and divesting her body of the constraining leathers.

So close.

She'd been so close to taking the delectable human fighter's soul as well as his addictive blood.

Hissing her impatience, the vampire walked nude to stand before a full-length mirror.

A beautiful female stared with blood-red eyes back at her, all but glowing with strength and vitality, the recent feeding adding a sheen of radiance to her skin, a rosy blush to her cheeks.

Oh his blood had been so strong, she thought with renewed desire, not at all the weak watered down version that flowed in most humans. Only *its* blood could surpass the power that sang through her body as she consumed each drop.

How was it even possible that a human could possess such ambrosia in his fragile veins? His soul, she knew, would have been magnificent as well, and if she'd had the time to properly enjoy her delicious reward, she would not feel the thwarted dissatisfaction that even now tasted of acid in the back of her throat despite the fullness of her body.

And his body, oh his body.

She reached down to touch her hairless core and watched her eyes close half way in the mirror with barely leashed lust.

She envisioned his long, lithe leanness, the way he moved like a lethal warrior from ancient times, his fighting maneuvers as beautiful and graceful as they were precise and deadly, his angular, fallen-angel's face with its full, wide mouth...

Aaaahhhh, the vampire moaned as her come seeped down her thighs, wetting her fingers.

She brought her hand to her face and licked the fluids meticulously, holding her own gaze in the mirror.

If only it was his seed on her fingers, flooding her mouth, dancing on her tongue. If she had thought more clearly, she would have brought him to her lair, perhaps kept him alive for a while to enjoy properly.

Maybe even indefinitely.

But alas, her bloodlust had overcome her reason and she was too hasty with him. Even so, the vampire thought as she turned away from the mirror and wrapped a satin robe around her body, it was not entirely her fault she'd wasted this rare opportunity on a mere feeding frenzy.

It was Inanna's fault.

How did she discover the location so quickly? The vampire had made certain her human sources were silenced already. *It* would not be pleased with this setback, for it seemed the Chosen had more resources that they estimated.

The vampire scoffed, her upper lip curling in a sneer.

One of these days, she would deal with the Angel of Death. It was all part of their plans.

She just had to be patient.

*** *** *** ***

Something sweet and thick trickled in a steady drip into Gabriel's mouth, the aroma awakening his senses, the taste blossoming on his tongue.

Vaguely, he registered the tingling that was beginning in his extremities, like thousands of needles prickling his burned-out nerve endings.

Was he sleeping? Was he awake? An ever-present exhaustion weighed down his limbs, paralyzing his body, numbing his mind.

He was so tired. Surely he could rest a while longer...

Third millennium BC. Silver Mountains Colony, hinterlands of the Akkadian Empire.

A long, languid sigh flowed sweetly from Inanna's lips. Such a wondrous feeling that surrounded her, glowing within her. She'd never felt better in her life.

Loathe to bring her cozy nap to an end, she slowly raised her eyelids, still heavy with drowsy contentment. She was so warm and comfortable, as if cocooned in sunshine and clouds. She felt as if she were floating in a dream.

Perhaps this was the promised Sanctuary of the Goddess, where Pure Ones' souls returned after a long, fulfilling journey.

Through the curtain of her lashes she saw something that reminded her of a lush plum, though not so dark in color, and the seam that divided the halves of the plum was horizontal, not vertical. She blinked rapidly and tried again.

Her vision suddenly grew sharper so that she could see fine lines radiating from the dark seam. Her eyes rolled slightly to the left, then to the right. The long dark line was bracketed by deep indentations on either side. Her vision suddenly became even more acute so that she saw what appeared to be giant individual hairs spouting from crater-like pockets all around the indentations.

What in the Goddess's name—?

She sat up abruptly and knocked her forehead into something sharp and hard.

"Ow!" Inanna and the object she bumped into voiced at the same time.

With a small shriek she leapt to her feet, swiveling her head from side to side, taking in her surroundings. It took a few moments for her eyes to adjust, the images she took in gigantic and up-close one moment, tiny and faraway the next.

She tried again, concentrating hard.

The tamarisk grove. The mountain cliff. Alad reclining with his back against the knotted trunk. The villages and fort below the...

Alad!

She turned back to the Pure male in question.

Alad was breathing deeply and slowly, as if he had just run a long distance and it took great effort just to draw air. His eyes were half-closed, his body relaxed.

"Glad to see you are well again," he murmured in his deep, husky voice though it was barely a rasp at the moment.

Inanna desperately tried to think, to remember.

She had gone to watch Alad train as per usual this afternoon. She had been feeling wretched yet full of nervous energy, and being near him had only made it worse. They had walked together to their habitual spot. She recalled inhaling something intoxicating and enlivening, and then she was overset by one of her nightly fits, though much, much worse. After that she...

Inanna gasped as her gaze focused on his throat.

Though she wanted to deny what she saw, her enhanced vision took in the two perfect puncture marks in the vein that throbbed visibly in his neck. Like a bird of prey, her irises dilated as she tracked the single drop of blood that seeped from the wound like a tear.

Mine.

The word echoed in her consciousness with ferocity, covetousness and savagery. Her fangs began to descend from her upper gums as she once again felt the fiery thirst.

"Take more of me if you wish," Alad's quiet voice broke into her mindless bloodlust. "You have been starving after all."

As the words registered, Inanna let out a tortured whimper and took a step backwards, then another. The meaning of what he said became all too clear and she crashed to her knees on a keening wail.

What had she done! Oh, what had she done?!

He moved to get up and reached for her but lacked the strength to stand. He kept his arm extended, his hand outstretched and beckoned her, "Come here, Libbu. *Stop your thoughts. We will work through this together."*

"Come," he motioned with his hand, his deep voice reverberating inside her head, as if his voice came from within her, and she was drawn by an irresistible force to obey his command.

Uncertain and ashamed at what she'd done, at what she was, Inanna slowly approached her victim, the male she loved most in this world, even more than her papa.

When she was within reach, he gently caught her upper arm in his weak grasp and pulled her into his lap. Loosely he held her against his chest, resting his chin on the top of her head.

For a time, she stayed silent and still within his warmth, soaking in his soothing scent through every pore. Finally she swallowed on a gulp, choking on her words through free-flowing tears.

"I am so, so sorry," she stuttered, "I do not know what happened. I-I-" she bit her lip to stop her shameful blubbering. "I am a monster," she whispered, "I deserve to be punished."

"Do not worry, Libbu. You are still you," his voice rumbled low and calming against her hair. "There will be no punishment. One cannot help one's nature."

She risked a glance upwards into his face, and saw that his eyes were closed, as if he could barely stay awake.

"I do not want to be a-a- vampire," Inanna could scarcely even utter the word. Doing so made it all too real.

She felt his brief smile rather than witnessed it. "And yet it appears that you are a Dark One nevertheless. We do not get to choose who we are, but we do determine what we do."

"But I do not want to take innocents' blood and souls!"

Inanna began to feel frantic and trapped again. It was a prison from which she could not escape, for the prison walls were her own skin and flesh.

"I do not want to hurt others! And yet I hurt you terribly," she ended forlornly, her voice breaking and full of regret and self-hatred.

He wrapped his arms around her more tightly and took a deep breath.

"You did not hurt me. Verily, I feel full of health and vitality, if a bit sleepy. I felt no pain when you... fed."

In truth, the process was startlingly pleasurable, and he almost embarrassed himself with sexual arousal.

But not quite.

Instead, his blood hummed and heated languidly, his muscles relaxed even as his skin became ultra-sensitized, his manhood thickened but did not harden. He was suspended on the verge of release, but mercifully he did not, although he doubted he would have had any say in the matter.

While she drank from him, he seemed to have lost all control, his body a pliant and willing slave to her needs.

Was this what it was like to be a Blood Slave?

Alad never knew. He had been born free and fought to remain so. Was he a slave if he consented? Although he'd made neither gesture nor word, his heart had opened to her gladly, somehow knowing he had what she required to become well again.

"How will I face Papa when he returns," the precious bundle in his lap murmured with apprehension, and he felt another wellspring of tears on the horizon.

"I suspect he knows," Alad said with half a smile. "He is your father after all."

"But he never said anything!" Inanna suddenly found her fire, "why did he not warn me! I thought... I thought I was Pure like everyone else."

More softly she said, so that he had to lean in to hear her, "I thought I would grow up, fall in love and find my destined Mate like the stories he used to tell me."

Alad considered how to respond.

"As I understand it, Dark Ones grow up and fall in love too. I believe their other half is called Blooded Mate. I am not certain how it works, but the Scribe told me once that in their Scrolls, something like the ones we have, there is mention of ancient lineages from the bond of Blooded Mates."

"But I want—" abruptly Inanna bit back her words even as they began to tumble out.

"What is it you want?" Alad pressed patiently when her silence stretched on.

For a long time, she kept her thoughts secret, and they relaxed together against the tree, watching the evening breeze stir the leaves and fragile blooms.

"I want you.*"*

The words were so soft, they seemed like the wind's whisper in the air. But Alad heard them in his heart, in his very soul.

He smiled and laid his cheek against her fine, golden crown.

"Then you shall have me," he promised her. Teasingly, he tugged a lock of her hair. "But you have to grow up first, Libbu. *You must stay strong and vital."*

"You will wait for me then?" she asked him innocently, full of effervescent joy once more. "You will not have any other female?"

He doubted she fully comprehended her request, but he answered her solemnly nevertheless.

"Aye. I will have no other female. When you are a woman and if you still want me, I shall be yours without contest."

As I already am.

*** *** *** ***

"I'm pretty sure I'm right this time."

Sophia leaned in more closely as she stared unblinkingly into a face that was growing out of the cherub stage but with cheeks still rounded and eyes still wide with angelic innocence.

Said eyes stared right back at her, also unblinkingly, framed by long, lush lashes that made Sophia a bit envious, truth be told.

She nodded in conviction. "He has a Pure soul, I can see his aura glowing bright white."

Benji sat on a bar stool in the kitchen of a very large room, maybe more than three times the size of his home with Daddy. There were floor-to-ceiling windows along an entire wall. Below, he could see a small park and garden. On the horizon, the sun was beginning to peak through wisps of clouds.

The strange place and his unfamiliar surroundings did not hold his attention, however. He was more interested in the three beautiful elves who stood around him, all staring at him with concern and concentration.

They had to be elves, like the ones in *Lord of the Rings*. He and Daddy had watched the movie more times than Benji could count. And he could count pretty high.

He was smart. In fact, he was even starting to read the children's illustrated version of the books without Daddy's help. In the books and in the movies, the elves had similar features to the strangers before him—except for the pointy ears.

They were all three tall and slim, like Daddy. And they looked *eth-real*. Benji was proud of himself for remembering that word. Really hard to say, especially when he tried to say it repeatedly to memorize it better. He looked it up in his pocket-sized Merriam-Webster Dictionary. It meant "a: of or relating to the regions beyond the earth. b: celestial, heavenly. c: unworldly, spiritual."

Of course, he then had to look up a bunch of the other words in the definition itself, but he got the gist.

Two of them even had long hair almost down to their waists, just like the elves. The shortest one with shoulder-length brown hair was more normal-looking, but still really pretty in Benji's estimation. She was the closest, so he reached out and poked a finger into her cheek.

"Are you an elf?"

She reared back as if shocked that he could speak. Come on, he was five-and-three-quarters, well, two-thirds, but who was counting.

"I'm hungry," he said next when no response was forthcoming from the group around him, followed quickly by, "where's Daddy?"

The golden one spoke up, smiling at Benji in a worried way, as if she feared he might cry or something. Geez, adults could be so unnecessarily nervous.

"Your father will be back soon. Your friend Nana left you in our care while she went to get him."

Benji nodded at that, and when he didn't burst into tears, the blonde elf seemed to relax. "I'm Aella, by the way," she stuck out a hand as she said, "nice to meet you."

Benji took the hand in his warm little grasp and squeezed firmly like Daddy taught him. "I'm Benjamin, but you can call me Benji."

She then included her companions in the introduction, "This is Cloud," she gestured to the tall male elf with long, pulled-back black hair and laser blue eyes. He nodded and Benji gave a little wave back.

"And this is Sophia," Aella said as she put a hand on the young woman's shoulder.

"Hiya," Sophia grinned her greeting. "So you're hungry are you?" She checked what looked to be a bracelet on her wrist. "It's six o'clock. Guess an early breakfast will do everybody good. What do you feel like having? Waffles? Eggs and bacon? Cereal?"

"Waffles please," Benji replied, getting more comfortable with the elves. If they were Nana's friends, they were his friends too.

As Sophia began preparing the necessary ingredients and Aella took out the waffle iron, they bickered good-naturedly back and forth about Sophia's cooking skills or lack thereof. Cloud watched the exchange with Benji and the males shared a silent, meaningful look.

Women, the look said. They perfectly understood one another.

Benji liked his new friends. Elves were his favorites in the *Lord of the Rings*. They even spoke their own magical language.

Benji wondered what Sophia meant when she said he had a Pure soul.

*** *** *** ***

In the dark, windowless storeroom, there was no sign of daylight, but Inanna sensed that the sun was rising slowly but surely this cold, winter morning.

She wrapped her arms more tightly around Gabriel as she cradled his head in her lap. The last few hours had been exhausting and agonizing for both of them.

As his body contorted, shook and shuddered through the Change, it was like dying a thousand deaths. For her, watching him endure the seemingly never ending torture, the process was only slightly more bearable.

Her only consolation was that he had not been conscious through the ordeal. His body had been on auto-pilot.

Finally, he had stilled, his chest heaving, his skin covered with cold sweat, pulled tight and taut over his bones and flesh, his newly charged veins standing out like tree roots against it.

She smoothed back the sweat-matted hair from his face and saw the flesh starting to knit around his right eye. The swelling was subsiding visibly. It was working—the Dark blood that now flowed through his veins.

His chest rose on a deep pull of oxygen, and he slowly, painstakingly opened his eyes.

As he blinked her into focus, he shook his head free of her loose hold and gingerly raised it from her lap, drawing his body to a sitting position.

His voice barely a rasp, he said, "Where am I?"

"You're safe," Inanna replied, "and so is Benji."

Gabriel somehow knew she spoke the truth and accepted it.

Slowly he raised one hand and examined its back.

The knuckles were raw and red, but none were bleeding, the skin around them intact. He shook his head again to clear it. Flashes of memory came to him, blinking in and out like lightbulbs that needed to be changed.

There was a fight.

No. There were several.

He had sustained heavy injuries.

But he had escaped the pit.

Where did he go?

Someone had caught up with him. Who...

A blinding stab of pain exploded behind his right eye, and he gouged the heel of his hand into his eye socket in an attempt to stop it.

Gasping from the still dizzying pain, he tried to search his mind again, but it was no use. He could not recall anything after escaping into the tunnels.

Strangely, however, he remembered the faint, bittersweet fragrance of tamarisk blossoms. Yet he was certain he had never seen the tree up close and personal, certainly not in New York City. He was somewhat shocked he even knew that there was such a tree by such a name.

Gabriel took several deep breaths and tried to collect his scattered thoughts.

He was currently sitting on the cold floor of a storeroom full of dusty trinkets and tattered wares. Nana Chastain sat patiently beside him, regarding him with concerned, but opaque eyes.

She was hiding something.

Even so, he couldn't help but trust her. At the same time, a wave of resentment and confusion burned through him.

"You brought me here," he said rather than asked, looking back at his hands. The wheels of his mind whirred even more slowly when he gazed upon her.

"Yes," she agreed. And that was all. No further explanation forthcoming.

"How did you know where to find me?" Gabriel questioned, the haze in his brain starting to lift, though barely.

She inhaled deeply and let out the breath slowly. "There is much to tell you," she answered at length, which told him exactly nothing. "Let's get back to Benji first. You must also rest."

"I can't," Gabriel shook his head. "The Russians—"

"Will not discover your location," she finished for him. "I have made certain of it."

He glanced at her sideways, for the first time taking in her attire—skin-tight black leather with hidden compartments for weapons, a shoulder holster that crisscrossed behind her back, the handle of something visible to the side, knee-length combat boots and fingerless gloves on her hands, her golden hair bound in a tight braid lying like a fishtail over one shoulder.

Clearly, she had not been out making social calls when she'd found him. She knew about the Russians, knew about the fight club. What else did she know?

Who the hell was she?

Benji first, Gabriel decided, questions later.

He levered himself up on both arms and tried to get to his feet. His body ached and throbbed everywhere, and it took him an inordinate amount of time to get up, but finally, he stood, weaving only slightly off balance.

Gabriel had to stand still for several moments as the world slowed its spinning around him. He felt lightheaded and nauseous in addition to the ever-present gnawing pain in his muscles, his bones.

"You will need to rest," she repeated, putting one of his arms around her shoulders, supporting some of his weight.

"And to feed."

"A Blooded Mate shall be the only other which she requires to complete and sustain herself. She shall take his blood, his seed and thrive with the nourishment of his body. He shall take her blood, her essence and bask in health and vitality."
—*Excerpt from the Ecliptic Scrolls.*

Chapter Eight

Gabriel lay exhausted and aching but wide awake in the king-size bed he shared with Benji in a luxury apartment unfamiliar to him, inhabited by complete strangers.

Who seemed to be acquaintances of the resourceful Nana Chastain.

Benji was obviously becoming fast friends with the two women, a veritable chatterbox when Gabriel arrived shortly after a breakfast of waffles by the looks of it. His son seemed rather in awe of the lone male in the group, but it was a shy reverence rather than fear.

Gabriel could sense no danger or threat from Ms. Chastain's friends, and it made sense that even the Russian mafia would be hard pressed to find them here.

Gabriel himself would not have ever expected to find them here.

Brief words were exchanged among the group, mere introductions and greetings, and no questions were asked. The younger woman with dark hair gave him a long penetrating look, but that was all.

Gabriel found that strangely unsurprising. Something told him they were inured to seeing half-naked battered and bruised strangers with pint-sized children who randomly made use of their abode.

Ms. Chastain—Nana, though he felt wrong using her name, she didn't seem like a *Nana*—departed on her own after a few words with Benji. Sophia and Aella set up PS4 on the wireless TV and roped his son into an adventure game. Cloud, whom Gabriel recognized as a seasoned fighter just by observing his stance and movements (and Aella as well), showed him to his room which had its own en suite bathroom and gestured wordlessly for him to take a rest in the rumpled bed that was previously occupied by his son.

When Gabriel gave him a loaded look, the warrior said, "There will be time enough for questions later," and quietly closed the door behind him.

As Gabriel contemplated the ornate ceiling above his bed, his stomach roiled with hunger and loudly protested his negligence. But the thought of food made him nauseous, even as his belly clenched on emptiness.

His mind too busily whirring, he got up to take a shower.

Opposite the mirrored wall behind the vanity, he doffed his blood-stained, tattered clothes and inspected his naked body. Dark bruises covered most of it, but no open wounds remained. The gashes he remembered sustaining from glass-wrapped fists were nowhere in sight. Only thin, pale pink lines indicated that he hadn't dreamed it all.

Impossible.

Mentally, he knew this. But he took it in stride as just another bizarre observation in a day that made the Twilight Zone seem staid.

He turned on the hot shower spray and got under it, letting the powerful blast rinse away the grime and blood that stuck to him like a second layer of skin.

As he soaped his face and neck, he paused at the side of his throat. The skin was smooth and unblemished, but the area he touched felt tender.

Gabriel staggered off balance as a wave of nausea overtook him.

Slowly he slid down the glass wall of the shower until he sat on the porcelain floor tiles, hot water continuing to rain down upon him, misting the stall in a dense fog.

Why couldn't he remember?

He closed his eyes and concentrated. A bright flare of pain exploded behind his eyes and against his temples.

Darkness enfolded him.

*** *** *** ***

Third millennium BC. Silver Mountains Colony, hinterlands of the Akkadian Empire.

Inanna blocked the spear jab with her shield, twisted her body to one side, and used the momentum to swing hard and fast with her sword at her opponent's torso.

He leapt back just enough to avoid getting sliced wide open, but remained close and continued to advance upon her, now swiping the long spear at her feet.

She anticipated the move and somersaulted backwards as he continued to attack her lower body with lighting fast jabs. He was too quick despite her nimbleness and caught the heel of her boot with the point of his spear, taking her off balance.

Down she went on her elbows, but only for a moment. It was long enough, however, for him to keep her there with the spear tip at her throat.

Inanna huffed and blew a tuft of hair out of her face, leaning her head back and pulling her long tresses free of their braid. "One of these days, Alad the Great, I shall defeat you. Just you wait."

Her mentor extended a hand and a smile to help her up. "I await that day with breathless anticipation."

Inanna tried getting to her feet, but cried out when she put weight on her ankle.

Alad was immediately crouched before her in worry. "What is it, did you hurt—"

Still clasping his hand, she tugged hard, and as he fell, she rotated them both until he was lying on the dirt ground and she on top of him, straddling his lap.

"Ha!" she crowed with victory, "are you breathless still?"

Alad relaxed and lay prone beneath her, closing his eyes while a smile played on his lips. "You have defeated me, Inanna the Mighty. I beg your mercy."

She leaned forward until her long hair shielded them both behind a cascade of gold. When he felt petal-soft lips meet his, Alad's eyes came wide open.

The touch was so brief it was but a tickle, like the flutter of butterfly wings. Slowly she pulled a little bit back and stared deeply into his eyes.

"You shall have no mercy, etlu *mine," she murmured with a soft smile, "I will have all of you forevermore."*

Alad shivered from head to toe at her husky words, his body growing heavy with need. Uncertainly, he wet his lips, wondering how he should reply.

But she was on her feet in a flash, pulling him up with her. She grinned widely and declared, "I am hungry from defeating the race's most fearsome warrior, starving really. Feed me before I faint."

Before he could react, she dashed away, sprinting like a gazelle toward their mountain cliff beyond the hills.

"Come, oh Slow One," she called from already some distance, "do not keep your mistress waiting!"

Alad shook his head at her playful good mood, dismissing the feelings her casually given words had aroused, and jogged after her.

When he caught up with her, Inanna was already sitting against their chosen tamarisk tree, eyes closed, a mischievous smile twitching on her lips.

Alad sat down next to her, keeping a respectful distance between them.

He gave her his arm and said, "Here, you said you are hungry," and raised his wrist to her lips.

Instead of taking what he offered and sinking her teeth into the strong vein there, Inanna held his hand and entwined their fingers.

She did not want to feed from his wrist this day.

She had not lied when she said she was famished. She truly was. But it was for more than just his blood.

For seven summers she had fed from him on a weekly basis, sometimes more, sometimes less. But only Alad.

Despite her fears that she would transform into a greedy monster like the vampires of lore the Elders told children to scare them into obedience, she never needed anyone else's blood, nor did she desire it. Not even a twinge.

Only her father and Alad knew about her "condition." Everyone else treated her as ever before.

When she had confronted Papa about who she was, and more to the point, who her mother was, he had provided no illumination. He had admitted that her mother was a Dark One, but that was all. No matter how many times she asked, almost every day, multiple times a day, from the time she was a small girl, he never revealed much about her mother.

Inanna knew that her mother had dark hair and dark eyes, that she looked nothing like her, and only seven summers ago did she learn that her mother was a vampire.

That was all.

Having matured into a woman well-tuned to others' emotions, Inanna had long since stopped badgering her father about the woman who birthed her. Every time she questioned him, his face became a mask of pain, so stark and excruciating, her heart broke for him.

Her father had made one thing abundantly clear, however. No matter who she was, what she was, she would always be his daughter, and he would always love her, provide for and protect her.

And so gradually, Inanna sealed away her curiosity. Nothing was worth hurting her beloved papa.

She looked down now at her fingers entwined with Alad's.

Aye, she had fed from his wrist for seven summers. He had made her powerfully strong and kept her secret safe. As her body transformed from that of a girl to a full-blooded woman, her heart also changed.

Not that she no longer loved him, never that. But rather that she no longer held him in awe. She had lost the girlhood infatuation and gained a woman's deep, multifaceted, all-consuming love.

A sensual love. A sexual love.

A ravenous, gnawing desire that only he could fulfill.

She had been patient, oh so patient, waiting every day for him to reciprocate her feelings.

Verily she wore her heart on her sleeve.

But Alad was nothing if not respectful. His touch was always brisk and purposeful on the rare occasions he initiated the contact, his gaze ever focused on her face, though she knew her body had filled out in all the right places to please a man.

It drove her mad.

Clearly, she would have to take matters into her own hands.

She raised his wrist to her lips, still holding his hand, but instead of biting it, she planted a kiss there.

Alad's breath froze in his throat as he watched her intently. She unwound their fingers and held his hand in both of hers, gently rubbing a finger down each of the grooves that lined his palm.

"The Elders tell stories about how these lines reflect our fates," she said as she beheld his palm in fascination.

Alad could barely hear her words, too busy trying to calm his rapidly accelerating heart and ignore the throbbing ache that was spreading through his body, coalescing below his waist.

She turned to face him and trailed one hand gently down his face, his neck, stopping to rest where his heart thumped double-time in his chest.

"I wonder if your fate includes me," she murmured, "for I cannot imagine a future without you in it. You promised to be mine and only mine, remember?"

Alad swallowed and gazed, mesmerized, into her deep blue eyes.

For the life of him he could not speak or move. He feared the things he would say and do, for his tenuous hold on self-control was stretched taut to breaking point.

Aye, *he wanted to tell her,* I am yours whether you accept me or not. My blood, body, heart and soul are yours to do with as you wish. There is nothing I would not give you, nothing I would not do to please you, though this love between us is forbidden by virtue of what we are.

A union between Pure and Dark Ones was strictly prohibited, punishable by death within both race's laws. But even if the law was not exerted, lore had it that a terrible wrath and calamity would befall the offenders regardless. True, Dark Ones, especially those of the upper echelons of society, often kept Pure Ones as Blood Slaves, but the bond was merely physical, not emotional or spiritual.

Alad was well aware that Inanna wanted more than just his blood, his body, just as he knew that whether she wanted them or not, he had already given her his heart, his soul.

They were playing with fire, and the heat was blazing hotter with each passing day. He had tried his utmost to prevent them from getting burned, but more and more, he was tempted to give in to the delicious inferno.

"I want you," she said clearly, firmly, still holding his gaze captive. Deeply, she drew in a breath, inhaling his scent, and nuzzled her face in the crook of his neck. "I shall feed here," she murmured, her warm voice and hot words making his muscles draw tight.

Her fangs sank into the vein at his throat smoothly.

Alad jerked at the indescribable pleasure-pain that consumed him. As she drank from him, gently drawing on his vein, moistly sucking on his skin, the edge of pain dissipated and only a mind-numbing pleasure remained.

So this was what it was to Nourish his mate, Alad thought as his arms came around her and drew her closer until she straddled his thighs, her legs locking around his waist, her core rubbing against his.

Inanna gasped at the tantalizing friction. Maintaining the seal of her mouth on his throat, she ground down on the hardness of his manhood in an ancient rhythm as old as time.

Goddess above she wanted more! She wanted them to be skin to skin, wanted to crawl inside of him, take his body inside of hers, his blood and seed filling her to the brim.

*Mine, a growl vibrated deep in her core.
Forevermore.*

*** *** *** ***

"So you have *turned* a human," the vampire Queen said softly, almost bemusedly, "have you come for your punishment?"

Inanna was allowed a private audience with Jade Cicada in the Queen's personal chambers after she returned to the Cove. Briefly, she'd explained her discovery of the fight club and the vampire assassin she encountered. She then reported her transgression, and now awaited judgement.

"I accept whatever retribution you deem appropriate, my Queen," Inanna answered and went down on one knee, head bowed.

Jade was wearing one of her sheer black dresses that covered her from neck to toes but left very little to the imagination.

Slowly, she uncoiled her body from the massive bed she was lying upon when she bid the Angel entry, but she did not leave the warmth of her silken sheets, only straightening to a sitting position.

She was loathe to leave her comforts, for the male who presently shared her bed still reclined behind her, his naked body radiating a delicious heat, his scent surrounding her.

"Did you *turn* him against his will?" Jade asked her personal guard with mild curiosity.

Inanna shook her head. "He was dying. I… I could not lose him."

Interesting choice of words, the Queen thought to herself. Not "I wanted to save him," or even "I did not want to lose him," but a reply that suggested her Chosen had no choice in the matter of letting this human depart from the living.

Jade strongly suspected this *turning* was more than just a whim of the moment. Inanna did not volunteer more information, and Jade did not ask.

The Queen inhaled deeply on a drowsy sigh. "Then it is perhaps good news for you that I find meting punishment for such transgressions too tedious to contemplate this morning."

She trailed a covetous hand down the torso of the male behind her, dipping beneath the sheet that pooled low around his hips. "I have more important matters to attend to."

Inanna raised her head in question, saw what her Queen was referring to and looked down once more, a blush suffusing her cheeks.

The intimacy the Queen displayed was not something new; Jade Cicada was a deeply sensual creature who literally hummed with sexual energy no matter where she was, and with whom.

And Inanna was certainly no virgin.

But the male in question whose cock was being steadily and lazily stroked beneath the sheets had the expression of someone holding back great pain, torment, and...shame.

"But perhaps I am not doing you a favor," Jade continued, still playing idly with her toy. "The Ancients say that such acts engender their own reward. Perhaps your *reward* will still find you in time."

"I will not run from it," Inanna vowed grimly.

Indeed, when she finished here, she intended to go back to Morningside Heights and answer all of Gabriel's questions, including who and what she was and what she had made him.

"Then so be it," the Queen stated with finality and waved her hand toward the chamber door.

"Alert the others of last night's events," she ordered, turning momentarily serious, "we must snuff out this wildfire before it spreads further."

"Aye, my Queen," Inanna answered, rose to her feet and exited quietly.

Jade turned back to her not-quite-lover, her grasp on his hard, swollen member tightening.

"I do believe this is the first time in the many millennia of her long life that the Angel has ever transgressed," she murmured as if to herself. "I wonder what provoked her to exceed her powerful self-restraint."

The male made no answer, and she did not really expect one. Surely it would be difficult to form a reply when all the blood had gone to one's penis rather than to one's head.

She peered at her gorgeous pet through her lashes.

Hmmm. Perhaps he was miffed at her for torturing him so—his jaw did look as if it might break with the way he was clenching it so tightly.

"It is fascinating what people can be moved to when their emotions are involved, don't you think?" Her question was muffled against his throat as she leaned in to place a voluptuous kiss there.

"I wonder what it would take to move you," she said languorously as she bit into his neck.

Seth Tremaine turned his body to give her better access, hands fisted in the sheets at his sides.

He feared not whether he could be moved, but how irrevocably and with what consequences.

*** *** *** ***

Inanna braced her arms on the stainless steel table where multiple giant digital screens sat, playing various angles and images of last night's fight club.

Her comrade Devlin Sinclair, the Hunter, sat in the leather chair immediately before her, manipulating a virtual keyboard with fingers so fast they were almost impossible to track by sight.

"There," he pointed to a particular image in the middle screen and slow-moed it back three seconds. "Does that look familiar to you?"

It was a shot of one of the tunnels connecting to the pit. A dark shadow of a figure in flowing robes and oversized hood concealing its hair and face moved stealthily through the passage. That was the only image they had found of the vampire Inanna encountered after reviewing various footage of the night's events for several hours. Unfortunately the area below and above ground near the Chinatown manhole where the confrontation occurred had no surveillance.

Or if there was, it had been disarmed.

Inanna stared intently at the screen, but she could not be certain of what she saw. "It has to be her," she finally answered. "There were no other vampires in the vicinity as far as I could detect. But this image doesn't give us much to go on."

Unfortunately, Inanna's ability did not allow her to see through layers in captured images. As such, the identity of the vampire assassin remained a mystery.

"Well," Devlin drawled nonchalantly, "at least we know it's a female. That narrows our target population down by fifty percent, give or take."

Inanna regarded her comrade with two parts chagrin, one part exasperation.

It didn't matter the urgency, magnitude or direness of any situation, she had never seen Devlin lose his cool. His eyelids were ever at half-mast, as if he were perpetually sleepy or bored and couldn't be bothered to exert himself in any shape or form.

She knew it was a guise, for his mind was razor sharp, his gaze brilliantly discerning. But there were times...she wanted to light a fire under his ass.

A faint smile hovered near his lips as if he sensed her frustration. "Think about it. Within our ruling perimeter, there are two thousand three hundred and forty-six vampires. Of those, only one hundred eleven are combat-trained. And of that number, a dozen, maybe fifteen if you really stretch it, are capable of evading your whip. Coincidentally, eight of the fifteen are male, seven are female."

By the time he swiveled around to regard her, Inanna was already smiling back at his cleverness.

"O ho! Serious One," Devlin teased, "we happen to know the names and locations of all seven of the females in question, two of whom are right here at the Cove, three if you count our Queen, lucky you. Though I'm only guessing about Simone's abilities. She's not warrior-class per se, so perhaps we can discount her."

"Unless the vampire is an outsider," Inanna said.

Devlin considered this for half a second, "Possible but not likely. Our border security is pretty damn tight, if I do say so myself," and since Devlin patrolled said borders on a regular basis hunting down rogues and unfriendlies, he should know. "I would have been alerted if a foreigner entered our midst."

That made things simpler, if it were true.

"The Pure Ones corroborated our conjecture that one of the Chosen might be involved," Inanna recalled, a frown furrowing her brow, taking up Devlin's suggestion of starting the investigation close to home.

"Maybe more than one," Devlin returned, his voice soft but tinged with steel. "It could be me, it could be you for all we know."

Inanna speared him with a hard look. "It is not you, Hunter, I'd bet my life on it."

"I wouldn't if I were you," he murmured silkily, then leaned back in his chair and folded his arms behind his head in a devil-may-care pose.

"So what do you intend to do? Confront our two comrade in arms, go to Jade herself, and demand to know which of them gorged on human blood last night?"

Vexation, thy name is Devlin, Inanna thought to herself.

"How is our little human doing by the way? You never said whether he lived or died." Though the question was casually asked, the Hunter's keen eyes glittered knowingly.

Inanna had not wanted to share the events surrounding Gabriel with anyone outside of the Queen herself, but she needed Devlin's tech expertise to do some digging and he needed to know what they were looking for. There had been plenty of screen time of Gabriel in the fight pit, shot from a multitude of different angles, but none after he exited into the West tunnel.

"He is of no consequence," Inanna replied off-handedly, ending their exchange by walking out of the control room.

Devlin stretched like a great big feline in his luxurious leather chair and stared bemusedly at the ceiling fan.

"Maybe not to me," he said quietly, listening to her boot steps echo down the hall, "but that human is of definite significance to you, Angel."

*** *** *** ***

The vampire sleekly made her way through the thick darkness that pervaded the dance club, illuminated only by flashes of laser lights from overhead projectors.

No one inside would have known that it was actually midday outside. They likely didn't know the day of the week, month or year and didn't care for that matter.

A remix version of *Heathens*, by Twenty-One Pilots was thumping through the crowded warehouse, so thick with human cattle, a vampire could lock herself inside and gorge for weeks.

Not this vampire, however. She'd had her fill last night and was still more than satisfied where her bloodthirst was concerned.

Now, as to her other lust... that was lamentably unsatiated still. Which was why she moved purposefully through the human peons, ignoring come-hither looks, boastful words and clumsy grabs.

She knew that she attracted abundant sexual attention, from both men and women, despite the dark and anonymous surroundings. That she dressed in a white bodysuit that looked as if it was painted on her, revealing more of her lean yet voluptuous figure through strategic cutouts than the material concealed, was probably one source of attraction.

But mainly it was her aura. She all but throbbed with danger, hunger and raw sex.

These peasants couldn't begin to meet her needs, however. She had an altogether different craving.

Disappearing through a private, steel-encased door with an intricate locking mechanism that could only be opened from the inside, her irises dilated further to adjust to the complete blackness that enveloped her. The same song kept playing within the chamber, but sound-proofed walls blocked out all other noise from the club.

"Shouldn't you be tucked in bed asleep by now?" whispered a sinful voice in the darkness.

The vampire stopped four feet in front of a raised dais piled with furs and pillows. Even with her keen night vision, she could only make out the outline of something reclining casually on the bedding.

"I've missed you," the vampire said, waiting for the creature to invite her closer.

A humorless chuckle ensued. "Have you." It was not a question, and the tone suggested that the object of her desire could care less.

"I have also brought you tidings," she continued, a shiver of anxiety crawling up her spine at the lukewarm reception. "Last night's performance has gone viral as expected. Over three million hits by now globally."

"Hmm," came the nonchalant reply, a mere vibration of vocal cords. "And how do you intend to repeat the performance without the star attraction?"

The vampire held her breath. How did it know?

Sharp white fangs flashed bright in the semblance of a smile.

"Did you think to conceal your little faux pas from me? I would have thought that one as ancient and as well-trained as you would have just a tad more control than you exhibited with the human." A series of *tsks* followed by a weary sigh traveled to her ears.

The vampire could form no reply.

In truth, she didn't know why the temptation the human fighter presented had been so irresistible. It was definitely not part of the plan to end his life early: he was ridiculously high in demand by spectators, human and vampire alike. They could have used him at least two or three more times before injuries or death in the pit provided a natural end.

But she did not resist his temptation. She could not. Just the thought of him now made her burn, reminding her why she had come here.

"I will think of something," she finally said to the creature taunting her. "I always do. Everything is going according to plan. I am here to collect a small reward for my services."

Silence greeted her. Then, the creature's upper lip curled back in a toothy smile. Or was it a sneer?

"Come and get it then," it beckoned.

Anyone else might have paused at the blood-red eyes that stared at her, speared through her, but the vampire had other priorities.

The unpredictable danger made the sex all the more explosive.

"Choose your Blooded Mate wisely, for the Bond shall be irreversible. Enter into it with clarity of mind, wholeness of heart and acceptance of soul. Dark Ones must remember: your other half could be any and all, but always only One."
—*Excerpt from the Lost Chapters of the Ecliptic Scrolls.*

Chapter Nine

It was night by the time Gabriel ventured from his room, still unsteady on his feet, just as Benji entered it.

He stayed a while longer to tuck his son in and chat a bit, following Benji from one topic randomly to the next in a pattern of logic only understandable to five-year-olds.

As Gabriel finally kissed the top of Benji's head goodnight, his son inquired sleepily, "Are you going to marry Nana, Daddy? Will she be my mother?"

Gabriel closed his eyes and held back a sigh. Had it really been less than forty-eight hours since his world had imploded? And it all centered on one woman—Nana Chastain. So help him, he would get his answers *now*.

To his son, he replied, "We would have to be friends first, Benji. I barely know her."

"But I do," the boy said fervently, "I've known her forever. I like her a lot. You will too."

"We'll see," Gabriel murmured noncommittally, "good night."

"Good night, Daddy. I love you," came the prompt response, the same one every night.

Before he even closed the door, Benji was fast asleep.

Gabriel padded on bare feet, dressed only in borrowed trousers tied loosely at the hips, to the open living and eating area.

All four of his new "friends" sat around the kitchen counter, apparently waiting for him if their identical stares were any indication.

Gabriel raked a hand through his unruly hair, bracing himself for this interview. It looked like he was going to get what he wanted: answers, now.

He grabbed a bar stool on one end of the massive marble island and rested his arms on the counter.

"Tell me," he commanded without preamble, and no one asked him to clarify.

"Would you like the good news or the bad news?" the youngest of the quartet asked and cringed slightly as if she were already sorry for what he was about to hear.

The Amazon called Aella laid a hand on the younger woman's shoulder in a clearly communicated "let me handle this" and said:

"We are at war."

Fantastic start, Gabriel thought but kept his silence.

Whatever crazy speeches got made tonight, he was going to listen to each and every one. Hopefully by the end, the madness would start to make sense.

"There are more races on this earth than the human race," Aella continued, "at least two that we are intimately familiar with, but I would not be surprised if there are others."

Somehow, Gabriel didn't think she meant race as in ethnicity, especially when uttered in the combo phrase "human race."

"There are the Pure Ones, of which Cloud and I are citizens, and there are the Dark Ones, of which Nana belongs."

"And Benji and I would be human," Sophia added, lest Gabriel assumed otherwise. "Sort of."

The last bit was not reassuring. He noticed that they had not categorized him—yet.

"There are many things to explain, which you will learn over time, but suffice it to say for now that the main difference between our Kind and humans is that we live much longer lives if we stay whole and safe."

Aella began to count off her fingers. "Because we heal ten times as fast as humans, we seem never to age. Our senses are much keener, and our souls are much older."

"But once in a while a human is born with a Pure soul when our souls get recycled, because after all, we are not really immortal. It's just when you've lived thousands of years, you might seem that way," Sophia explained helpfully.

Gabriel gave her a pointed look.

She ducked her head. "Well, not me, I've just lived eighteen years thus far and it hasn't been easy, let me tell you."

"I thought you said you were human," Gabriel interjected. His dizziness was worsening by the minute listening to these explanations that explained nothing at all.

"Sophia," Aella said in a chiding tone when the girl opened her mouth to speak again. Promptly she shut it and huffed, folding her arms, a look of defiance on her face, but she stayed silent.

"We are also physically much stronger," Aella went on where she left off as if Sophia never interrupted. "We do all the things humans do—drink, eat, sleep, and so on, but both Pure and Dark Ones have Cardinal rules we must abide by or suffer fatal consequences."

"You have police like ours to uphold the laws?" Gabriel asked, trying to relate what she was saying to something familiar, mundane.

"Yes, but that is a separate issue," came the Amazon's response. "We have warriors who are tasked with catching and bringing to justice those who break our laws. But what I was referring to are the laws of our nature, laws that are biologically programmed into each and every one of us, such that punishment is guaranteed for those who stray."

Before Gabriel could pursue the topic further, Aella redirected to her original statement, "We are at war, our three races. It has not escalated to common knowledge in the public sphere yet, but war is insidiously eating away at the fabric of our civilization like a rampant disease in hidden corners all over the world. The fight club you've been recruited into is the current virus we're tracking. Someone wants to promote violence, chaos and bloodlust in the human world. We know that certain Dark Ones are involved as financial backers, perhaps even the masterminds behind it all. If this continues, it won't be long before the mayhem grows beyond the fight clubs. Already we have seen an escalation in deaths by violence—three times the normal average over the last month."

If the Grim Reaper was an orator, he couldn't produce a better end-of-the-world monologue, Gabriel thought.

"I take it this is the bad news?" he asked. It wasn't like him to dish sarcasm left and right, even in his own thoughts. But what was a man to do when the Apocalypse was apparently upon him?

Aella darted a look at Nana Chastain, who had been silent as a tomb thus far. Cloud not speaking Gabriel could understand; the warrior didn't like to waste his breath, especially since his companion was doing such a bang-up job. But Ms. Chastain had some serious explaining to do.

The woman in question took a deep breath as if to brace herself and looked directly into Gabriel's eyes.

"You are one of us now. You are a Dark One."

Gabriel narrowed his gaze but didn't blink. "Which means exactly what?"

She held his penetrating stare and answered, "Humans have called us many things over the course of time, but perhaps one epithet will resonate the most: vampire."

*** *** *** ***

"No trace of the club remains," Anastasia, the vampire Queen's head of security, reported. "But we have enough footage of the fights and the spectators to begin tracking some leads."

Three of the Chosen, Ana, Maximus and Devlin, had set out to the fight club's location as soon as the sun had set, but the Russian mafia had been busy during the day, removing all evidence of the previous night's events.

The only items they had not destroyed were the infrared cameras hidden and installed in strategic locations by the Pure Ones' human infiltrator. They did not know the identity of the person, both as a means of protection for the human but also because the Pure Ones, wisely, did not fully trust Jade Cicada's intentions.

They did provide the Chosen with access to the video footage, however, which came in handy.

"It is not only the Russian mafia organizing these events, which they have begun to stream live internationally through an encrypted channel," Maximus disclosed. "The Italians, Irish, Chinese, Koreans, inner city gangs—perhaps more that we have not yet discovered—are all getting involved. This racket is throwing off more profit than the drug, arms and sex trade combined. And its attraction and reach are growing exponentially through the Net."

Jade sighed impatiently, her nails clicking in a staccato beat on the armrest of her luxurious throne. "We must cut off the head of the serpent," she said softly, thoughtfully, "but we must find it first."

"We do know that at least one seasoned warrior from our fold is either the mastermind or a conspirator," Devlin spoke up in his careless tone, as if he could just as well have kept this information to himself. "I did some homework during the day and narrowed it down to a few possibilities."

When no more was forthcoming, Simone Lafayette, the Keeper, grew exasperated on behalf of present company. "Well? Who are they?"

Devlin smiled and ignored her question. Holding the vampire Queen's gaze, he said, "With your permission, my Queen, I shall hunt the serpent down, but I do it alone."

Jade considered him for a few heartbeats.

"So be it," she finally declared. As Devlin bowed and left on his mission, Jade turned to the remaining Chosen and delivered rapid-fire orders.

"Ryu, see if you can hack the encryption and block further broadcasts. But first piggyback onto their network to ascertain their next moves."

While the Assassin lacked Devlin's genius with all things technology, he could still take down a CIA firewall with ease.

"Maximus and Anastasia, follow the money trail and seize what accounts you can. If cash doesn't exchange hands, we'll at least take out some of the oxygen fueling the blaze."

When only the Keeper remained, Jade rose from her seat and stepped down to stand before the glass wall behind the throne, overlooking the cityscape below.

New York was so beautiful at night, but with *his* blood, she could also enjoy it during the day, though she did no more than bask in the wintry sunlight for a short while and watch the hustle and bustle of the city awakening.

"My lady, what task do you have for me?" Simone inquired when Jade remained silent for a long time.

Finally, when she thought Jade would not answer, the Queen said, "Find out what you can about Seth Tremaine. His role as the Pure Ones' Consul. His immortal... and his human past."

Readily, Simone accepted her assignment. She was only surprised that the Queen had not asked her sooner. It was an investigation she had started on her own from the moment Tremaine set foot on the premises.

Now she had the full backing of the Cove to complete it.

*** *** *** ***

Gabriel took a deep gulp of January air, then another, and another.

Though he was bare chested and bare footed on the concrete terrace that stretched along the wall of windows in the living area, and the winter wind was whistling in the air, he did not feel the cold.

Was this another trait of his new state of being? Immunity to extreme temperatures? In truth, he felt as hot as a volcano about to erupt despite the sub-zero conditions.

The woman behind him made no sound, but he was as aware of her presence as his own furiously thumping heart.

She had not said a word since she followed him out onto the balcony and the Pure Ones had dispersed inside the apartment, and neither had he. He needed to sort through his chaotic thoughts first.

Strangely, upon discovering that he was no longer part of the human race, his first reaction was acceptance, and even a certain amount of gratitude, for somewhere in the back of his mind he knew that he would have died otherwise.

And he needed to live.

For Benji. He found that he was not ready to leave his son in someone else's care, even though that individual had proven to be a reliable guardian in the past two days, despite the adversity of their current situation.

The second reaction was an uncomfortable realization: he wanted to live for himself.

For the first time in his life, he felt truly awakened, as if he had been in a haze all along, and though his mind was still blanketed by a dense fog, interrupted by alarmingly frequent blackouts, he finally felt as if the wall around his consciousness that he hadn't realized existed was beginning to crumble.

The third recognition was that *she* had triggered it all.

Though it made no sense and he wanted to bang his head on the concrete column next to him in frustration, he knew that Nana Chastain was the one who had breathed life into him—perhaps literally.

He turned now to face the woman who had saved him. Made him.

"You turned me into a... Dark One," he stated, rather than asked.

She gave one slow nod, holding his gaze intently.

"How?"

She inhaled long and deeply and kept her position by the sliding doors, as if she wanted to run from him but knew that she had to stay. She seemed always to run from him.

"When you died, before your soul departed your body, I gave you my blood to keep you there."

Said so matter-of-factly, without any inflection or change of expression. *When you died. I gave you my blood.*

"That's all it takes to make vampires out of humans?" Gabriel wondered why there weren't more bloodsuckers running around.

She shook her head. "A vampire would have to share a part of her soul with the human. In most cases, the human's soul has already departed, because the process of forcing another consciousness into the body is very... arduous. The result of typical *turnings* is that the vampire loses part of herself in the human shell, and the new vampire is not quite whole. Both the creator and the creation could turn to madness if they do not control themselves, if the shared soul is not strong enough."

"In most cases," Gabriel picked up on her phrasing, "but not in mine."

She did not reply for a long time. He did not prod her. If he was truly what they said he was, he could afford to keep waiting.

"Not in your case," she finally agreed and said nothing more.

He continued to stare at her, but she did not seem to have the inclination or will to continue. Her eyes flickered as if she lacked the courage as well.

"And how does it work, exactly, if my body is now crowded with more than just my own soul?" he asked quietly. There was no way he would let her escape from answering.

She swallowed as her eyes lowered momentarily, her long, gold-tipped lashes fluttering as if she were fragile and vulnerable.

Gabriel clenched his jaw as the ridiculous desire to comfort her almost overwhelmed him.

When she looked back into his eyes, he saw a steely determination there, as if she were bracing herself for retribution against a wrong she'd committed but was not sorry for.

"We are Bonded, you and I, until one of us perishes," she stated in a clear, steady voice. "In my Kind, we would be called Blooded Mates. In the human world, I suppose the closest thing would be marriage, except there is no divorce, no going back."

Ironic, that, Gabriel thought. Just a while ago, Benji had wished for their marriage.

"And I had no say in this?" his words were but a whisper, seemingly innocuous yet lethal.

Was it his imagination or did her deep blue eyes fill with unshed tears? Gabriel ground his back molars. There went that stupid instinct to protect her again, even against his own inquisition.

"I am sorry," she said huskily, and he felt her pained contrition as if it were his own. "No, you did not choose this path consciously. You were beyond choice at that point. I am solely accountable for the decision."

Gabriel took a step toward her, so that mere inches separated them.

He braced an arm beside her head, his hand on the sliding doors behind her, and leaned in so that she was barricaded by the lean, muscled wall of his body, his heat surrounding them both, his breath fogging the air between their faces.

"Why me," the question was more of a statement, a low, rumbling rasp that raised the baby fine hairs all over her skin.

Inanna could have prevaricated.

She could have given him half-truths.

I saved you because Benji needs his father. I saved you because you could probably give us information about the fight clubs that would be the key to blowing up the scheme and capturing those responsible.

But the truth was none of those things.

When she Bonded him to her, Mated them to each other, she had been thinking of none of those things.

Only one word blocked out all else in her mind: *Mine*.

"I wanted you," she said at last, holding his mesmerizing gaze. "So I claimed you."

His pupils dilated at her words, fleeting expressions of confusion, fury and lust chasing each other across his face.

She closed the last bit of distance between them until they were flush against one another, chest to chest, thigh to thigh, the chunky heel of her combat boots giving her extra height to almost match his. Her lips were exactly level with his jawline, so she rested them there as her arms came around his back, her hands flattening against his spine, then traveling downwards until they each cupped one of his buttocks and exerted pressure enough to bring his groin into the notch between her legs.

"I want you," she breathed against his throat, the whispered words like a vow that sealed their fates.

All at once Gabriel's control snapped like a live wire twisting loose with electricity. He crushed her with his torso to the glass doors and took her mouth with a savage growl.

There was no preamble, no warning. He thrust his tongue inside her wet warmth and plundered, demanded, punished. He wasn't remotely gentle. This wasn't a kiss by any means. It was an assault, and he intended to make her pay.

Exactly what he wanted from her he didn't know and didn't care. All the pain, chaos and fury inside of him needed an outlet, and she was it.

It didn't matter that he'd never done this before. It didn't register that he was shaking from head to toe with an undefinable emotion as if he was coming apart. His tongue thrust into her again and again, imitating what his hips were doing against her middle. He bit her, licked at her, devoured her, and the more he came at her, the more she took.

Inanna angled her head to better receive his attack, like a fortress lowering its drawbridge to enemy invaders.

What was a woman to do when she loved the enemy?

Ah, but that was the wrong analogy. He was never her enemy. Not even now when she'd pushed him to the point of no return.

It didn't matter that he came to her in anger. It only mattered that he was hers, anger and all.

Finally hers.

She devoured him right back, tangling her tongue with his, sucking at his lips, nipping his lower one until she drew blood, pulling him deeper into her until his hardness pushed mind-numbingly against her pleasure spot. Even through the layers of their clothes, she was on the verge of orgasm from the inexorable pressure.

Abruptly, Gabriel pushed apart from her and staggered back a step until they were no longer touching.

Chest heaving, heart hurting, brain near exploding, he swiped his forearm across his mouth, wiping her away.

Inanna's throat closed up at the gesture.

What did she expect? That he would welcome her with open arms when he learned of their forced union? That he would suddenly return the feelings she had built up and stored over the last six years?

He barely knew her. And if he knew her role as the Angel of Death, her role in his immediate past, he would most likely hold her in loathing and disgust. And now he was tied to her forever.

Until death do us part.

Wordlessly, he stalked past her, careful not to touch her in passing, and went inside the apartment.

That went rather well, Inanna thought as she leaned back against the glass doors that slid closed, her legs having turned to rubber.

And she hadn't even delivered the coup de grace: as Blooded Mates they depended on one another for continued survival.

Blood and sex.

*** *** *** ***

The creature lounged on the monstrous, luxurious bed in its silent, sound-proofed chamber, pitch black save for a dish of small flickering candles on its bedside table.

Alone again.

The eerie glow illuminated a chess board with a game in progress propped on top of a square pillow on the bed. The creature examined each individual piece with meticulous care, almost lovingly, picking them up, polishing them, replacing them back on the board in their exact places.

Satisfied, the creature lay back among the satin sheets, its head supported by goose down pillows, and looked up into the giant mirror that formed the bed's canopy.

An impossibly beautiful man-woman looked back.

Long, dark hair spread beneath and around it on crimson bedding. Translucent pale skin, smoother than ivory. An oval face with a sharp, angular jaw. Full red lips moist with wine and... other things. Sleek arching brows over almond-shaped, thickly lashed eyes.

The eyes, though, were the ugliest part of it, in its own opinion at least. Bottomless voids of nothingness.

Was it true that eyes were the windows to the soul? If so, the creature wondered whether its soul was as black as the pupils that all but swallowed the irises around them.

Clinically, its gaze roved over the naked flesh revealed by its open robe. The salted wounds would take longer to heal, especially in its current state. Fluids and blood seeped between its thighs, still fresh and pungent. The pain that burned from the inside out was a familiar companion.

Its visitor would be so disappointed to discover that she was, after all, not that original in her depravities.

Ever so slightly, its lips parted on an icy breath, revealing the glinting tips of its vampire fangs.

Abruptly, its face and form changed to an altogether different visage. And again and again, it transformed until it confused even itself what its true form was.

Finally, as if in exhaustion, its body shed the false skins, unable to maintain the mirage any longer, and the creature regarded its real reflection in the overhead mirror.

A tear of blood welled in its soulless eyes and slid unrepentantly down its cheek.

Stupid tear, it thought as its lips twisted to disguise an infinitesimal quiver.

Just because something ached in the vicinity of its chest did not mean it possessed a heart. Just because the acid in the back of its throat tasted of shame did not mean it possessed any pride.

The smile turned mocking and derisive.

Just because it longed for something it could never have, missed and mourned the absence of that lovely dream, did not mean it would ever know love.

*** *** *** ***

Inanna spent most of the night driving aimlessly in her Lamborghini. Hours of tunnels and bridges, winding roads and lightless streets.

As if led by a beacon she could not see, her final stop before dawn was "Dark Dreams", Mama Bear's bakery, tea and antique shop.

The woman in question opened her shop door before Inanna even raised her fist to knock.

"Come in, come in," she said in her musical accent, ushering Inanna inside with a warm, welcoming smile.

"You look worse for wear, my dear," Mama Bear observed, peering at Inanna with wise eyes over her bifocals. "I know just the thing to set you at ease."

She hustled into the back of the shop beyond a curtain of beads while Inanna settled in her favorite chair. She could not quite determine the time and place from which it originated, but she was sure it was ancient enough to be priceless.

Mama Bear returned with a fresh batch of scones and home-made jam. On the tray she held were also a small pot of chamomile tea and two dainty China teacups dating back to the eighteenth century, probably the "newest" items in her shop.

"Now tell me what troubles you, my dear," Mama Bear encouraged, laying a comforting hand on Inanna's shoulder before seating herself in an adjacent chair.

Always the same words or some version thereof, Inanna reflected briefly. Did she only come here when she had troubles? She couldn't recall another person she'd ever unburdened herself to. Not her father, certainly. But there was...

Inanna squeezed her eyes shut to block the memory from surfacing.

It was imperative that she didn't remember, she knew. For the sake of self-preservation if nothing else.

"I got married," Inanna said, looking at the teacup in her hands rather than the woman she was speaking to.

As such, she missed the sharp glance that swept her face before returning to neutrality once more.

"Congratulations, my girl," Mama Bear said softly, sincerely. "I wish you all the happiness in the world."

Inanna sighed heavily and sipped her tea for a time, silent with her own thoughts. And then—

"I love him you know," she admitted out loud, and the confession loosened something within her.

"That's as it should be," Mama Bear agreed.

"But I think he hates me, or at least he should."

"Hmm," came the circumspect reply.

Inanna replaced her teacup on the tray, leaned back in her chair and closed her eyes. "I've wanted him for what seems like forever."

Mama Bear's silence only prodded her to go on.

"I feel like he's always been a part of me. I've watched him and yearned for him from afar for so long… but he doesn't know me at all."

She let out a burst of breath, a laugh that was half a sob. "I hardly know myself when I'm with him. I wanted him, so I took him."

Mama Bear maintained her silence, though the small slurping noises she made as she sipped her tea were strangely comforting.

"And now we're in this together and there's no turning back."

"Do you regret your choice?" Mama Bear finally bestirred herself to ask.

"Never," Inanna replied immediately, resolutely.

"Then the answer is simple, my dear," Mama Bear declared, as if Inanna had actually asked her a question. "You must only look forward. The past cannot be changed, even should you wish it to. Nurture the love in your heart. Cherish the man with everything you have. If nothing else, for the next time you are sitting in that chair telling me that you have no regrets."

Inanna opened her eyes and looked directly at her friend, her support.

Wise eyes looked steadily and empathetically back at her, ancient yet timeless.

"Every so often, the Balance shifts, the Way is lost, and Devastation ensues. In this time of darkness, the Light-Bringer will rise and deliver us from lies."
—*Excerpt from the Ecliptic Scrolls.*

Chapter Ten

Sophia lay on her stomach on the top bunk of the double she shared with Aella.

Her guard and real-life Amazon sat cross-legged below, communicating online through a secure channel with the Shield, the Pure Ones' home base, currently located in Boston, Massachusetts.

Sophia could hear the furious tapping on Aella's MacPro, and once in a while her friend would huff a held breath, whether in exasperation, alarm, or relief Sophia didn't know.

Cloud had gone out earlier to rendezvous with two of the Chosen on a mission. He was also planning to meet up with their human Chevalier who had gone deep undercover in the fight clubs.

Sophia felt frustrated that she couldn't help much—as usual. She felt certain the vampire Queen of the Greater New York Hive, Jade Cicada, was much more purposeful and effective. Honestly, her legend preceded her.

Jade Cicada was known in both the Pure and Dark worlds as one of the most beautiful women of all time, past and present—and likely future as well. She was sometimes capricious, sometimes deadly serious, and always awe-inspiring. She ruled her realm with a velvet-encased iron fist; those who strayed did so at their own risk, for her punishment was swift, irrefutable and inescapable.

Sometimes, though, she liked to toy with her prey, give them a long leash, before closing in on the kill.

Now Sophia, on the other hand, was none of those things. Half the time she didn't know what was going on around her, and the other half she wasn't of much help when she did clue in. She didn't rule anybody with anything, although through some twist of fate (the Goddess had a strange sense of humor), she was chosen to be the Queen of the Pure Ones. All of them.

And she wasn't even one of them—yet.

Depending on one's perspective, she was fortunately or unfortunately still a human, with all the human vulnerabilities, fragility, foibles, but also with one major advantage. She didn't technically have to obey the one Cardinal Rule.

Not that she'd ever toed the line. You never knew if there was an addendum to the Zodiac Scrolls with fine print that obliterated that technicality.

Sophia had a Pure soul. One day, could be soon, could be in the next life, though she suspected that those around her suspected that it would happen in this life, else why bother putting her on the figurative throne—she would have her Awakening and join the ranks of the Pure Ones.

So she wasn't all that interested in toeing the line, given what she knew of the consequences, in case the fine print on the Cardinal Rule included the likes of her.

The Dozen, her intimate circle of protectors and advisors, tried to enable her to lead the semblance of a normal teenage life. When she wanted to do this exchange program in NYC with Columbia University, they quickly devised a way for her to do so, while keeping her safe and efficiently dealing with situations like the one that was currently brewing in the vampire world.

It was just another brief chapter in their long, often turbulent lives.

Sophia had a lot to learn.

She navigated her iPad to download some new songs while she multi-tasked some research for the Ancient Persian Civ paper that was due on Monday and kept tabs on her progress in *Hearthstone: Heroes of Warcraft*, her earphones plugged into the device.

Suddenly, a song started playing automatically in her ear, and an icon on the screen showed that it was downloading into her synced devices—phone, pad and pod.

The melody and words caught her attention immediately. It also had an additive *accent* from background drums that seemed to inject the song's rhythm directly into her heart.

A webchat popup flashed in a corner of her screen with the words:

"I have missed you, lovely Sophia. Have you missed me?"

Sophia inhaled a startled breath and held it, lest the popup disappear and the words were a hallucination. She quickly looked down at Aella, saw that the Elite guard was preoccupied, and settled back against her pillow, focusing 100% on the webchat.

"Are you back in Boston, Ere?" Sophia typed with two fingers on the iPad keyboard that asserted itself. That she ignored his question was a given. It was almost a ritual for them.

"Actually, no," he replied. "I am in the City."

Sophia could scarcely dare to believe it. A shot of joy bubbled within her like champagne. Just to be safe she asked, "As in New York City?"

"Yes," came the one word answer that all but made her squeal in delight.

"I'm here too," she managed to keep the exclamation mark out of the sentence. "I didn't get the chance to tell you that I'm here on a study exchange program for a month." Although, why she'd take the initiative to tell him and why he'd expect her to were mysteries for another day.

"How is the Ancient Persian Civilization class at Columbia? Do take copious notes so we can see what it takes to add it to the curriculum next year."

Ere had been her teaching assistant for one of her classes in the Fall semester.

"Wait, how did you know I was here at Columbia? How did you even figure out my web ID?"

From the moment she met him, Ere enjoyed surprising her by showing up when least expected, sending her handwritten letters and mp3s. Saying outrageous things to turn her lobster red in mortification.

"I have many skills," was the answer that told her nothing at all. "Do you like the song?"

Sophia had it on repeat so she could quickly memorize it. She'd memorized all of his songs. Or rather the songs he shared with her.

She concentrated on the lyrics now even as he typed them line by line in the webchat:

"Time Machine" —*by Jason Chen*

In my head I'm going back through all the little stupid things I said
And I'm trying to figure out the moment I lost my head
A combination of sentences that put us in the red, in the red.

Something inside me pushed to be right
Until I found myself too far gone.

If I only had a time machine
I would take you back to the moment
That you fell in love with me,
And stay there forever.

Don't you know that I'd do anything
To make you understand,
Understand that you are everything, to me
If I only had a time machine.

Love was the only thing that was ever between us,
Now you're miles away and I'm missing your touch
And the pain inside is just getting to be too much, way too much.

Something inside me had to be right
Until I found myself in the wrong, so wrong…

If I could go back, admit I was wrong
I would take it all back and you'd still be mine.

Sophia never knew why he chose the songs he did to share with her. When she had received the first one back in fall, she thought maybe it had some sort of message in it for her, but try as she might, she couldn't figure out what it was, because the words didn't reflect anything recognizable in their brief "relationship." She decided that he just liked the singers or melodies and wanted to share an enjoyment with her.

And obviously the lyrics. He always wrote out the lyrics for her even though she could have easily Googled them online.

"Jason Chen," she wrote, "I haven't heard of him before."

"He rose to popularity singing on YouTube."

Ah. It was so easy nowadays to put content on the Net, and a few talented and/or lucky individuals changed their whole lives for the better because of it.

"The version of the song I sent you is a remix on a lower key," Ere continued to type.

"I like it a lot," Sophia responded. "In this version the singer's voice almost sounds sort of like yours."

She blushed after she wrote that last bit, hoping he didn't pick up on the feelings that accompanied those thoughts. She liked Ere's voice, as she'd just implied.

A lot.

It was one of the most attractive things about him. And there were sooo many to choose from.

"Alas," he teased, and she could almost hear his affected sigh, "I do not have the talent for singing."

"But you have many other skills," Sophia teased back, recalling his earlier words.

"I do indeed," was the reply. "Perhaps one day I shall show you."

Sophia's fingers paused on the keyboard.

Was he flirting with her again? She could never tell. A, because she didn't have experience in this sort of thing and B, she was never clear-headed and objective where Ere was concerned anyway. Just concentrating on not making an ass of herself took all of her brain power.

"But it is late," he started to write.

Sophia interrupted before he could finish his sentence, "What are you doing right now?"

Online silence greeted her inquiry. Had he already logged off?

"I am thinking of you, lovely Sophia."

Abruptly, Sophia thought of the Pure soul she sensed in him from the moment they had met. "Would you be able to meet me here in the City?" she asked rather daringly.

Their encounters had always been orchestrated by Ere thus far. But why shouldn't she initiate contact, Sophia thought defiantly. It wasn't as if she were chasing after a guy she crushed on—she didn't have the self-confidence and nerves to do that. She was just doing her job helping to recruit more Pure Ones for their cause.

Another long silence made Sophia gnaw on her nails, which her Guardian Ayelet found to be a disgusting habit, unfit for the Queen of the race, though she only sighed in begrudging acceptance whenever she saw Sophia do it. As mentioned, her caretakers tried to let her have a normal teenage human life.

"Do you like to dance?" Ere finally asked.

Sort of, Sophia thought to herself. She liked moving her body to music, especially if it had a Latin beat, but that didn't mean she was any good at it, which the question usually implied.

"A little," she replied to manage expectations, "is there a club nearby you want to go to?"

"There is."

"Is it for twenty-one and under?"

"I shall make sure you get in," he promised.

Cloud and Aella would not let her go alone, Sophia knew, but maybe she could convince them to give her some space when they came along. Maybe she could even get only Aella to escort her. The Amazon knew how to fit in no matter where she was, though she would never be one of the crowd.

Sophia thanked her stars Dalair wasn't the one guarding her in NYC, even as she worried and wondered how and where he was.

"When and where?" she asked Ere.

"I'll message you later," was his final reply. "Good night, Sophia."

Sophia turned off her iPad and switched to her iPod, lying back on her bunk and squirming under the covers.

Before long, she was asleep, Ere's song playing on an endless loop in her ears.

*** *** *** ***

When Inanna returned to the Pure Ones' apartment, after connecting digitally with the rest of the Chosen, Cloud and Aella were sitting at right angles to each other on the sleek modern sectional in the living room, heads together in what was obviously a serious conversation.

Their heads raised as one when Inanna entered and they got to their feet.

"Nothing amiss, I hope?" Inanna inquired. "Or rather more amiss than it's been."

"The fight clubs have gone underground—figuratively this time," Aella responded, a slight furrow in her brow. "All of their usual channels of communication, marketing and recruiting have gone silent."

"Our human Chevalier on the inside is the only lead we have right now," Cloud continued. "But I was not able to make contact with him as planned, which is a grave concern. I was, however, able to ascertain that he's still alive."

Inanna nodded, taking the information in, combining it with what she knew.

"Our Queen has dispatched the Chosen to at least freeze the progress the network has been making if not destroy it. Ryu was tasked with shutting down their virtual network, but his first priority was to infiltrate their system to see what their next moves might be. I don't believe it's his efforts that have led to the inactivity we are witnessing."

Aella shook her head in agreement. "They know we're getting close."

"Closer than perhaps we realize ourselves," Cloud said. "Maximus and Anastasia have made inroads with the mafias and gangs involved. Half of the factions are likely to back out after the visits we have paid them this night. But no one seems to know who the orchestrator may be. We were not able to track down the Russian head—his second-in-command revealed that his leader was traveling internationally, specific whereabouts unknown."

"Tristan and Ayelet are on their way to intercept him," Aella added, referring to two members of the Pure Ones' Royal Dozen. "Anything else you can share on your side?"

Inanna gave them a rundown of Jade's missions for the Chosen.

"Devlin's hunt seems to be key," Aella mused, folding her arms. "The female vampire you encountered could be a central link."

"I believe so," Inanna said. "We also have Gabriel."

The two Elite guards visibly straightened with alertness.

"He's still dealing with the *transition*, so he's likely suffering from blackouts and memory loss, the human remnants and vampire side of him battling for supremacy. But once he's stable, he might remember important clues about the other fighters, the spectators, even the vampire who bled him."

It was almost unnoticeable but Inanna sensed rather than witnessed the undercurrent of exchange between Aella and Cloud.

"What is it? What are you not telling me?"

Aella sighed. "I would rather be certain first rather than add to the confusion," she said with some reluctance, "but suffice it to say that Gabriel might be more than meets the eye."

That would not surprise her, Inanna thought. She had sensed something special in Gabriel when she bumped into him six years ago at the hospital on Christmas Eve. She just didn't know what it was.

All she knew was that his fate was inextricably entwined with hers. She had merely sealed it with the *turning*.

Inanna hesitated before asking, "How is he?"

Aella looked at Cloud and confirmed, "We haven't seen him since our powwow hours ago. You were with him last."

"I heard him go out after two, shortly before I left for the rendezvous," Cloud interjected, making both females regard him sharply. "He has taken my leather jacket and boots."

Before he finished his sentence, Inanna had exited the apartment in a blur of movement.

In his current condition, Gabriel was extremely vulnerable and in a world of pain, both physical and psychological.

She needed to find him before someone else did.

*** *** *** ***

Gabriel didn't bother to close the jacket he was wearing over his naked chest. It was more to make him less conspicuous as he walked aimlessly along the riverside rather than a cover to shield him from the elements.

After all, he did not mind the cold.

The boots he borrowed from Cloud protected his feet from lacerations as he walked over rocks and glass right on the edge of the bank, but he could easily have done without them.

What were a few more wounds compared to the ones he'd sustained already and was still healing from? And besides, his speedy recovery time in his new state of being should take care of any sores on the bottoms of his feet before they rotted off.

Gabriel huffed a dark humorless chuckle.

Maybe he shouldn't test his healing abilities. After all, if his feet did rot off, he'd have to endure eternity on inconvenient little stubs.

Where was this new wellspring of morbid humor coming from, he wondered carelessly. Maybe he was turning over a new leaf. So much for his ascetic training with the Shaolin monks. The peace and tranquility he experienced there seemed like eons ago.

He'd always been a tightly controlled person. Simple. Sober. Temperate. Now he was the direct opposite of those adjectives.

His life was anything but simple right now. The complexity of his new reality was mind-boggling. His mind had never been muddier, as if he was spiraling endlessly into a yawning unknown. Hardcore drugs probably had this effect on addicts. Maybe he should have tried some in his human life so he could better deal with the dizzying effects now.

And never mind temperate. He'd never felt such extremes of emotion all at once, all mixed together, tearing him apart from the inside out. Hate. Desire. Bitterness. Hope. Anguish. Elation. Fury. And that persistent dark humor that made him want to throw his head back and laugh until his stomach cramped and his lungs could no longer draw air.

After all, he'd cheated death. Wasn't that worth celebrating? And all he had to do was…

Actually, he wasn't quite sure what he had to do to remain among the living. Maybe Nana Chastain had been about to cover that part before he attacked her mouth in a frenzy of anger and lust.

Off the balcony went temperance again. He could barely recall what the concept meant.

Did vampires drink blood to sustain themselves? Did they kill their victims in the process? Did they have to hide from the sun in crypts and sleep in coffins? Wasn't that the sort of thing that pervaded popular literature and media about the bloodsuckers?

Would he at some point turn into a bat?

A corner of his lips tipped up as he conjured the image of his furry, be-fanged self, flapping tiny little bat wings furiously in the air.

Gabriel's stomach chose that moment to clench hard, almost doubling him over in pain.

He'd been parched and starving for hours, but still he had no interest in water or food, the very idea making him nauseous. Did that mean he needed blood? But he hadn't felt any temptation to attack the few humans that he passed along his rambling walk, nor had he felt anything when he'd put Benji to bed, thank God.

He *did* feel particularly ravenous when he was near Nana Chastain, but he couldn't tell if it was nourishment he sought or a long, hard fuck. He'd sure as hell been starving for both.

Ah yes, sex.

Yet another experience he'd never had and never been particularly obsessed with. It wasn't so much denial as simply a familiar cloak of self-discipline that he wore. He'd wanted to be physically intimate with Olivia, but the word *fuck* had never crossed his mind. Not in relation to any woman.

Until Nana Chastain.

And now he wanted to lose himself in the pleasures and pains of the flesh. He wanted to release over and over and over until he was wrung bone dry and then he'd start all over again.

But not alone. No, he was done with his left and right handshakes. She said they were Blooded Mates. *Married*, in other words, or the equivalent of.

And they hadn't even had their wedding night.

He owed her at least a lifetime times infinity of fucking to repay her for *saving* him so generously and binding them together for eternity.

Gabriel was not proud of his own violent, derisive thoughts. Rage was a new emotion too that he was just now trying out like a new pair of shoes.

"Nice jacket, man," someone called from a much closer distance than Gabriel realized, lost in inner turmoil as he was.

He looked up to see a lean, mean-looking bastard headed his way, accompanied by a dozen or so of his buddies.

"Bangin' boots, man," one of mean-looking bastard's friends echoed. "Can we borrow those?"

Gabriel's eyes narrowed, a surge of adrenaline and bloodlust blazing through his body. "Don't think they'd fit you," he replied quietly, casually.

The group of misfits had by now surrounded him from all sides, some looking grim, some mocking, all evil.

The assumed leader of the horde stared at him unblinkingly, his eyes glittering like a wan moon reflected in a murky well.

"I think I'll try 'em on for size anyway," he said menacingly, his mouth stretching into a toothy smile. "Right now."

Some rustling and clanking ensued. The gang members were outing their various equipment of torture, Gabriel saw from the corner of his eye. At least no guns. He was feeling a little too bone weary to dodge bullets tonight.

"Hey," a guy in the back piped up, "he's that fighter from the videos." He pointed to Gabriel like he was a freak sideshow at the circus, all goggling eyes and gaping mouth.

Recognition swept the rest of the group, and a few even stepped back a decent amount of steps out of respect for what they'd seen Gabriel do.

The hothead leader didn't seem much impressed, if his snide expression was an indication.

"Well, what do you know," he said in a sing-songy voice, "a celebrity right here on our humble turf. I might have to get your autograph after I take those shoes and that jacket off your hands."

Gabriel stood relaxed and loose-limbed. "Sure," he said casually, "where would you like me to carve it in your fetid flesh?"

The leader let out a half-bark, half-snort, as if he couldn't believe the soon-to-be dead man's audacity. Reigning fight club champion or not, there was one of him and more than twelve of them. And the idiot was unarmed too by the looks of it. It was going to be *fun* teaching him a lesson.

The lanky bastard raised his hand and twitched his fingers. The two biggest members of his squad stepped up to face Gabriel, each of them a few inches taller than Gabriel and twice as bulky, one had a club and the other just cracked his knuckles ominously. Both began to close in on him, one from each side.

Of course he had thugs to do his fighting for him, Gabriel thought. Maybe the leader liked to watch. It's just his luck that Gabriel felt accommodating tonight.

With a feral growl, Gabriel received the first attack, going low as one of the giants charged him. Crouching on one knee, he pumped his left fist into the man's kidney, his right fist into the man's balls. Down the first giant went with a shriek several octaves higher than what Gabriel would have expected to be his normal voice.

Staying low, he swept his leg in a swift circle behind the shins of the second giant, taking him down to his knees. Gabriel leapt up in a flash and dropped kicked the guy on the crown of his head, K-O'ing him instantly.

Damn, he felt good!

Gabriel barely registered how many men came at him next, maybe they came all at once. He didn't give a shit. His stronger, nimbler, harder body was on auto-pilot.

As if apart from himself, he observed the ridiculous ease with which he dispatched his attackers. He didn't make any effort to avoid their knives and clubs and steel bars because the pain only fueled his inner savage.

Besides, what was the point of avoiding injury when it healed right away like it never was? Kind of like, what's the point of living when there was no end to life?

Maybe he shouldn't be taking near-strangers' words for fact. But he was in a mood to take risks tonight. He wanted to break rules. Straight up shatter them.

It might have been five minutes, probably less, by the time Gabriel incapacitated the last man standing, the cocky leader, with a jab to the throat, an elbow to the diaphragm, finished off by a roundhouse kick to the back of the head.

Oops, missed one.

Gabriel watched as one of the gang backed up from the carnage, turned tail and scrambled up the embankment to the main road.

He wasn't worth the chase.

As adrenaline slowly ebbed from his system like receding tides, Gabriel realized he was slick with blood, mostly his own. He fell on his ass in a sprawling heap and decided to take a short breather.

Go ahead and heal, he told his battered body.

But his body ignored him, and his life's blood seeped steadily into the cold, hard ground.

"What is Fate but pearls of choices strung together? What is Destiny but a path we walk on of our own free will? Remember, Dark Ones, that nothing is written in the fabric of time until you decide where, when and what shall be the first verse."

—Excerpt from the Lost Chapters of the Ecliptic Scrolls

Chapter Eleven

It's hard to say what miffed it the most, incompetence or over-confidence. And when the two traits were found together, well, it was almost stirred to annoyance.

On the other hand, setbacks offered interesting surprises, twists and turns in a well-mapped plan. It did love a good surprise, even if the unpredictable rerouting developed into a completely different map with a new destination.

After all, when one had lived untold millennia with untold more to look forward to, surprises were rare indeed and must be cherished for the treasures they were.

Besides, it wasn't as if it cared about the outcome.

As the old adage went: 'twas the process that mattered most, not the end.

"You say the network has stopped spreading," the creature in its oft-used vampire guise hissed softly, spearing its prey with serpent-like eyes.

The female vampire's expression remained placid. "I am looking into it."

"No doubt. And I understand the accounts have been frozen as well," the creature leisurely rose from its bed to approach the vampire, whose eyes cautiously tracked its every move.

"A temporary situation."

"Hmm. I do wonder, my dear," the creature said as it stood within striking distance of the vampire, "whether our partnership will be just as fleeting."

The female made no response, wise woman. She simply stood arrested by the creature's dark, bottomless gaze, like a rodent captivated by a viper.

The creature gently ran one long-fingered hand down the vampire's cheek. "Haven't you enjoyed your rewards from me?" it asked in a purring voice, as raw, undiluted sex oozed from its very pores.

"Yes," came the breathy response, as the female closed her eyes, seemingly in the throes of recent memory.

"If you want to continue being rewarded," the creature coaxed while gliding the hand ever so lightly over the vampire's breasts, fluttering its fingertips over her taut nipples, "then you might want to reconsider your strategy."

Her throaty moan was her only answer.

"At least there is one silver lining in all of this," it continued, "you might want to check the latest video upload on the network."

Abruptly, it receded from her body. Without seeming to have moved, it was lounging back on its massive bed.

The vampire opened her eyes and blinked rapidly as if to clear a sex-crazed haze. "Video?" she had the presence of mind to inquire.

"Looks like the human you so admired is alive and well, and demonstrating once again why he's the most popular fighter in our club."

This was obviously news to the female, whose brows drew together in serious consideration. What had she been occupying her time with, the creature wondered with a tinge of impatience. Verily, good help was so hard to find.

"I shall deal with it," the female said, all business now that the sexual fog induced by the creature's closeness had lifted. Without waiting for its response, she turned heel and stalked out of the windowless chamber.

"See that you do," the creature said to her parting back, not really caring one way or the other.

It had other priorities to see to.

*** *** *** ***

Something delicious was steadily trickling into Gabriel's mouth.

The aroma. The taste. If ambrosia could be found on earth, it must be like this.

Gabriel lifted his head slightly to gain better access to the source of the nectar and was rewarded by the application of something silky against his mouth, such that he could take deep draws rather than simply wait and receive.

Involuntarily, his canines punched through his gums, longer and sharper, and he sank them into the soft fruit, finding unerringly a deeper source of the life-giving juice.

Somewhere in the back of his mind, he was conscious of a hand smoothing the unruly waves of hair from his face, the fingers gently massaging his scalp. There was a voice that might have formed words but all he heard was its rich, womanly timbre, full and voluptuous, almost like a lullaby that eased him into a deep, enchanted slumber...

Third millennium BC. Silver Mountains Colony, hinterlands of the Akkadian Empire.

"*Inanna, to me!" Alad shouted above the din of the clashing armies.*

After decades of cold war and skirmishes, the vampires had finally launched a full-on assault on the Pure Ones' stronghold, their target the General and the Elite warriors he had trained to defend their Queen. The Pure Queen herself was in a different citadel some distance away, but attacking her fort directly would not necessarily squash the Rebellion.

And that was the vampires' ultimate goal: to put things back the way they had been for millennia past.

Queen or not, the Pure Ones followed the General.

He was the reason they believed in freedom, believed that they could actually protect their independence against all odds, against the awesome Akkadian Empire ruled by vampires. Their erstwhile Masters had more power, more soldiers, more food supplies, more weapons—just more. *But the Pure Ones had the General, and he was enough.*

Inanna's father knew the ins and outs of the royal Akkadian fortress, could predict their military and political moves with stunning accuracy, and trained Elite warriors to fight with a skill that made twenty-to-one odds in favor of the vampires seem like a draw.

If the vampires captured the General—again—the Pure Ones' hard-won freedom would die a quick, bloody death and their decades-long Rebellion would be naught but an ink blot on the scrolls of history.

Inanna unleashed her chained whip on two of the enemy soldiers blocking her path to Alad, slashing them across the face with deadly accuracy. She leapt in the air as they crumpled to the ground, used one of their backs on the way down as a springboard and jumped even higher, two feet above the shoulders of the fighters between her and her goal, and kicked a jaw here, whipped a throat there, leaving a tangle of writhing bodies in her wake as she reached her destination.

Once with Alad, she stood back to back against him, rounding on the enemy soldiers that surrounded them. They had fought together for many summers now and knew each other's moves as well as their own. Together, their deadliness increased tenfold, as if they harnessed energy from each other's presence.

The more they fought, as long as they were together, the stronger they became.

Inanna's lips curled in a smile of deadly intent as she engaged the enemy. She was loving this!

She could do this all day.

At one point, Alad reached back and hoisted her over his head by her arms, flipped her so that he had her by the ankles and spun her with dizzying speed in a circle while she cleared a whole circumference of enemy fighters with her short swords.

There were more than fifty soldiers, half of them human, half vampire, that gained the mountain path behind the fortress in a surprise attack, but now the battalion was laid utterly low by two of the General's finest warriors.

Alad and Inanna took in the small victory with a brief, but intense look. A look that communicated their elation, pride in each other, triumph.

And love. Always love.

Though they dared not tempt fate and their races' sacred laws by Mating, they had given all of themselves to each other, save for their bodies. Perhaps one day they would find a way to be together completely, but until that day, they would forsake all others. Their hearts, minds and souls were already one.

Just as Alad grasped Inanna's wrist, intending to pull her into a brief embrace and check for injuries, a burst of color blazed in his peripheral vision from the valley below. She caught it too. And with eyes wide in horror, they began scrambling down the mountainside toward home.

The fort was being bombarded by boulders lit as if from within with unholy fire.

The surrounding villages were also under fire attack, from boulders, from flaming arrows and spears, and even from afar, Alad and Inanna could hear the screaming, shouting, crying, the falling ramparts, crumbling towers, collapsing bridges. On top of all the chaos and din, they heard the deafening whistle of the fire boulders launching through the air, projected from giant catapults pulled by water buffaloes, toward the objects of their destruction.

As they reached bottom and made in a mad sprint for the fortress, they could see that the base was surrounded on all sides by enemy battalions. Foot soldiers advancing from the West, cavalry charging from the North and East and heavy artillery combined with archers assaulting from the South.

Goddess above, this was a massacre! It was as if the entire Akkadian army had descended upon their fort.

Inanna and Alad both knew that the battle was lost, but they continued their suicidal dash toward the nexus of the fighting because they knew that if the enemies captured or killed Inanna's father, the war would also be lost.

The odds were ridiculously against them, but they had to try. They had to find the General and protect him at all cost.

They took the least conspicuous path through the tall wheat fields that remained despite a fire that was rapidly scorching a path from the South, the blaze traveling fast with aid from a strong southerly gale.

The vampires were cunning to wipe out their food source in the event of a prolonged siege. But from the looks of the steady bombardment, it would only be a short time before the fort collapsed.

Alad and Inanna met with minimal resistance along the way, knowing their surroundings as they did the back of their hands.

They entered through a hidden sewage tunnel at the base of the fortress, only slightly visible above ground, mostly blocked by weeds and bushes. This tunnel would take them through the underbelly of the fort where the cellars for food and drink were kept, as well as a storage hall for weapons.

There they stopped to grab a few extra throwing knives, daggers, and anything else they could strap easily to their bodies without impeding movement.

Alad sheathed his sword over his back and took down a double-pointed long spear from the wall and a coil of rope.

Inanna favored the chained whip he had specifically made for her given her combat strengths and preferences, but she loaded up on bow and arrows just in case.

Though muffled by the thick stone walls, they could hear the battle waging violently outside. The enemy was storming the gate now with a battering ram. The whole fortress seemed to shake with the resounding assault.

Wordlessly they made their way out onto the spiraling steps that led to the highest rampart. The General's quarters were immediately below it and could be accessed through a large window facing the mountains.

But even before they gained the top step they could hear fighting close at hand, as well as the whistles of arrows that shot past the parapet.

With an audible indrawn breath, Inanna shot past Alad before he could react. She ignored all else but for the lone figure, taller than most of the fighters surrounding him, battling his way through what must have been dozens of enemy soldiers.

Inanna flew into action, accurately dismantling a number of the fighters closest to her with rapid-fire arrows and throwing knives.

Alad was only half a step behind, protecting her from the continuous onslaught of arrows flying over the wall and fighters who moved from their target to engage them.

Inanna had only one goal, to reach her father and pull him to safety.

From the glimpses she had of him, he looked as if he'd been fighting for a while already. Though his moves remained swift and lethal, his precision unerring, she could tell from the grim line of his mouth that his strength was waning. His face and body were streaked with blood, his or his enemies' she could not discern, but if these were the odds he had been facing for Goddess knew how long, she must assume he had sustained heavy injuries.

The fighters were not only numerous but well-trained. There were no humans in the lot, all vampires. Stronger, more deadly.

In a heart-stopping moment, Inanna saw her father go down on one knee.

No! He had to get up!

In that position he would be at their mercy, his chances of victory slim to none.

But he did not rise. And in her haste to reach him, she did not avoid the sword that slashed through her side, the spear that stabbed into her thigh. Distantly she heard Alad's shout of warning, but it was too late.

A flaming boulder struck the tower not six feet away, shattering the stone bastion and watch spire that anchored the fortress.

Out of the corner of her eye, Inanna saw the lifeless body of her father being dragged away by two vampires and down the opposite spiral of steps that mirrored those she had climbed just a short time ago. She did not register the watch tower crumbling above her, the stone and wood reinforcements shattering, until it was almost too late.

Something heavy and hard knocked her flat onto her stomach, walloping the breath out of her in a loud oomph, *but otherwise, as she lay still on the stone ground, she was unhurt. Whatever covered her entire body from head to toe took the blunt force of the falling rocks and debris from the blast and the disintegrating tower.*

"Be still," Alad's deep voice rasped beside her ear when she tried to move, and Inanna realized that his body was the shield that prevented her from harm.

All around them the destruction continued, arrows zinging into the ground inches by their faces, many carrying flames and torching whatever object they hit, whether wood and straw debris or fallen bodies.

The tower groaned, cracked and snapped as it collapsed in ruins around them. Inanna saw that all the remaining vampires on their stretch of the rampart were silent and motionless where they lay, the dead that caught fire crackling into the air as their bodies turned to ash.

When the storm of falling debris finally abated and the fortress gate was simultaneously breached, Inanna twisted her body and clawed her way out from underneath Alad, unscathed save for the wounds she had sustained earlier.

Once free, she immediately reached for his hands, intending to help him climb out of the rubble, for they had no time to lose.

Any moment now, enemy soldiers would swarm the ramparts, having already entered through the main gate and were now scaling the stone outer walls, the Pure soldiers stationed at the parapets dead or fallen. Inanna and Alad needed to pursue her father's abductors if they could still detect a trail. If not, they needed to escape the ruins, heal, plan and fight another day.

But while Alad took her hand, he did not budge from his position, and that was when Inanna realized that he was crushed under the stone ruins and wood beams, only half of his upper body visible beneath the wreckage.

No! Dear Goddess No!

As if hearing her inner screams of anguish, Alad tilted his head to the side as if resting it idly on his outstretched arm and smiled.

"Go ahead without me," he rasped out, barely able to prevent his facial muscles from contorting in excruciating pain, "I shall catch up in time."

Inanna lay herself flat on the ground and pulled on his arm, hard, and Alad could not help the shout of agony that tore through his throat.

Inanna managed to hold back tears, but her mouth began to quiver with fear and anguish for she had never heard Alad utter such a sound of sheer torture.

When Alad had caught his breath once more, he swallowed hard and said with barely any voice, "'Tis no use. My spine is severed. My legs are crushed…Too much internal bleeding."

Inanna gasped at the words that seared through her heart like the flaming arrows that continued to fall around them. Even with Pure Ones' healing abilities, this was too much. There was no hope of survival and death would be slow and agonizing.

"Stop," he commanded her with what was left of his broken voice. And it was only then that she realized she had been frantically shaking her head, the tears she'd desperately held back flowing freely down her face.

He took another shuddering breath, and she could tell that every inhale hurt terribly, most likely due to punctured or damaged lungs.

"Come here," he murmured, so softly she could barely hear him, only reading his lips.

She inched as close as possible to his body until her face was beside his and his arms could hold her. She wrapped her own arms around his shoulders and conformed her body to what was exposed of his beneath the ruins.

"You must take what is left in my veins," Alad said with surprising strength, still issuing orders even now.

Inanna snorted through her tears and the knot in her throat at the ridiculous command and was about to respond when Alad squeezed her hand to stop her.

"Do not waste time," he rasped out, *"you must take all I have to give to heal quickly and build strength. You will need it to survive this night. Let me do this for you. Let me inside you one last time."*

Inanna was back to shaking her head, but she could not speak to save her life, the gasps and shudders of her silent wails preventing words from forming and leaving her lips.

Alad had closed his eyes and could not see how she flailed like a person drowning, but he could feel the racking breaths tear through her torso.

"Quickly now, Libbu,*"* he quietly urged, *"save me from this unending pain. And allow me to save you in return with my blood. I wish..."*

He paused to draw breath and had to inhale in short bursts with great effort. Inanna knew the end was near, knew he was succumbing to the ravaging torment of the mortal wounds. She held onto his body tighter as if she could physically prevent his soul from leaving.

"...I wish I could have given you everything," he finished on a sigh, almost wistful.

"Do not leave me," she finally whispered, *"please do not leave me. I do not want to live without you. I love—"*

"'Tis but a brief separation," he cut her off, for the pain of hearing her heartbreak was even more unendurable than the pain of his physical wounds.

He sounded so certain she almost believed him. "I shall find you again, I promise."

Using what strength he had left, Alad tilted his head closer to hers so that her lips grazed his throat. "Do it now, Libbu. Take my pain away. Take my strength for your own."

Inanna distantly heard footsteps approaching the spiraling stone steps, shouts of soldiers drawing near.

As if he knew how to push her past the last hesitation, he vowed again, "I shall find you, no matter where or when, I shall ask the Goddess to guide me…. always… find you."

He bit the inside of his mouth and brought his cold, quivering lips to hers in a tender kiss. As he intended, the blood from his mouth trickled into hers, awakening the vampire within.

Unable to resist, her heart shattering, her tears scalding, she struck.

As Inanna drew on the vein at his throat, she could taste both his rich, heady life's force and her salty tears. She let the venom from her fangs flow steadily into his body, replacing pain with a numbing pleasure, cold death with radiant heat.

As his last breath faded away, softly and painlessly, Inanna completed his vow in her heart: I shall wait for you always.

My Mate.

My love.

But Alad had lied.

When the Goddess met him at the gates beyond life, he asked only one thing of her:

To make Inanna forget him.

Forget what he all but forced her to do. For he knew that she would blame herself if she remembered. Even though she had saved him from unimaginable pain, she would only recall that she had been the means that infinitesimally hastened his end.

To the last, Alad wished only to protect her.

If the Fates were kind, if their souls were to meet again... then...

Then he would claim her.

Forevermore.

"Upon her choice, the future rests. To welcome the Darkness or create a New Light, only her heart can show the rest."
 —*Excerpt from the Lost Chapters of the Ecliptic Scrolls*

Chapter Twelve

Sophia and Aella entered the exclusive nightclub in the poshest part of the Upper East Side through a VIP-only door that was barred by lethal-looking bouncers in black leather and dark shades.

Why did people wear sunglasses at night? Sophia wondered. Did the fashion statement really trump being able to see one's hand in front of one's face?

Given that she was certainly no arbiter of fashion, she did not have the answers. It would have to remain one of the greatest mysteries of life, she supposed.

She had wheedled and whined and bargained and entreated, and she was finally able to convince her overprotective guards that only Aella need accompany her this night.

It worked out because someone had to stay with Benji while Inanna and Gabriel remained at her apartment for the duration. Based on Aella's second-hand message, Sophia got the gist that the pair had some unfinished "Blooded Mates" business to attend to.

And if Sophia was not mistaken, the stoic warrior was relieved to stay with the boy rather than accompany the females. Perhaps Cloud did not enjoy loud music and scantily-clad bodies bouncing up and down and bumping and grinding in the dark, Sophia thought with a silent snicker, but she rather thought it was because he didn't particularly relish the experience with Aella as a partner.

Or perhaps he wanted it too much.

Oh well, Sophia would let the adults sort through their complex and convoluted feelings themselves. She had her own drama simmering on the stove, thank you very much.

Ere had texted her the location of the nightclub during the day, as well as the time to meet him: midnight. How he knew her top secret phone number she chalked up to one of those handy skills he spoke of, for she had never shared it with him.

If Sophia paused for a second to think about it, she might begin to have a doubt or two about her resourceful ex-teaching-assistant. He was just a tad creepy if his actions were viewed with a *Criminal Minds* serial-killer sort of lens, though the thought reminded her of the first mp3 he gave her, "Creep" by Radiohead. However, her curiosity about him and the desire to see him overruled what few reservations she had.

And besides, she was almost certain he had a Pure soul.

As Sophia and Aella wound their way slowly through the packed club, Aella subtly but surely discouraging any male or female from getting too close or too friendly, Sophia searched the dark, laser and candle-lit warehouse for the beautiful Ere.

A dance remix of "Sadness" by Enigma was thumping through the blackness of the club, the melody haunting and voluptuous, the words sensual yet full of pain. Countless bodies tangled and collided as they moved to the seductive rhythm, reminding Sophia of reefs swaying in a stormy sea.

With her head turned to the side, looking entranced at the mass of strangers around her, she collided with something hard and immovable.

Wincing to herself, she looked up at the wall she'd run into and stared directly into Dalair's smoky gray eyes.

All thought vanished as Sophia held his gaze. She should have been thinking, *where have you been? What have you done? Why are you here?* But all she thought was, *finally.*

Finally.

It was perhaps just as well that she'd forgotten about Aella behind her, for the Amazon retreated into the crowds when she saw the Paladin with the young Queen. Sophia knew nothing else but Dalair's familiar yet different face before her, perhaps because she viewed him through different eyes.

Ah. How she missed him.

How she hated him.

How she wanted him.

Wordlessly and without touching, a hair's breadth separating their bodies, they began to move to the flow of the music, just as the cult classic "Closer" by Nine Inch Nails began playing, the raw, angry, hungry words clawing into their bodies, electrifying their nerves, heating up their blood.

Sophia was the one to close the distance between them, inexplicably needing physical contact, as if to reassure herself that Dalair was truly here, within reach.

As if in a trance, her mind a blank canvas, Sophia's hands reached for his. Once she found his fingers, warm and calloused, her own wandered upwards along his arms, skimming feather light across the thin cashmere that covered his skin.

They kept roving upwards, those seeking fingers, past his biceps, then inwards to his pecs, which jumped reflexively at her almost-but-not-quite caress. Upwards still to the turtleneck collar that covered his throat, and around, where they laced loosely at his nape, a couple of stray digits exploring the silky hair there.

He, however, did not touch her, his arms staying resolutely by his sides. But his silver eyes bore intensely into her, and he bent his head downwards, ever so slowly as if giving her a chance to retreat.

Scattered inklings of thoughts chased each other like disoriented beads in the pinball machine that was Sophia's brain. Zigzagging nothings like *I've never danced before now. My body feels so heavy and foreign, my blood thick as molasses.*

So this is lust.
So this is desire.
I want I want I want I want...

As if he heard her inner ramblings, Dalair dipped his head the rest of the way until his full lips were a whisper of a breath away from hers, until his thick, long eyelashes fluttered against her sensitive cheeks, and Sophia gasped at the sheer eroticism of the touch.

Eyelashes, for Goddess's sake!

But still he did not touch her, though he clenched his jaw so hard, she saw the vein at his temple throb.

Sophia tightened her arms around his neck and, standing on tiptoe, molded her over-heated body to his, hips to hips, chest to chest.

As their cores fit together, the thick bulge between his hard thighs slotting into the notch at hers, a guttural growl vibrated through their bodies, and Sophia couldn't be sure whether it was he who made the sound or her.

Probably her.

Because she'd never known the primitive drive to possess another being before now. She wanted to mark him for her own, climb his body and crawl under his skin.

She wanted to *own* him.

What she did was bite him on the neck, hard enough to draw blood even through his sweater.

Dalair hissed, and as if the desperate little nip had awakened him from a deep hypnosis, he took a step back, separating their bodies, and another step so that her hands unwound from his neck and they were no longer touching.

After a long, deep inhale, he said, "Choose me. Not him."

Sophia blinked in confusion at his nonsensical words.

Was this a new sort of greeting? For they were the first words he said to her in months. Was this some secret code the Dozen had neglected to teach her?

"Choose me this time," the Paladin repeated, his voice deep and husky, vibrating with raw emotion.

The command tugged at an invisible tether within Sophia, hitched to something in the region of her heart, and she swayed forward involuntarily.

Abruptly, Dalair's eyes shifted above her head to something or someone beyond her.

Sophia turned around to see what had caught his attention and saw that Ere stood on a platform above the dance floor, looking down at them.

She could not see his expression clearly but she felt a wave of negative energy radiating from Ere toward Dalair, just like the first time the two males had met.

Sophia swiveled back to Dalair to ask what that was all about, only to find the Elite warrior gone.

She craned her head left and right to search for him in the crowd, but he had disappeared as if she'd imagined him. Aella must have seen the distress and confusion on her face, for she started making her way back to Sophia's side.

No, can't lose him, can't lose him again.

Sophia turned this way and that looking all around her for the Paladin, a desperation she'd never known choking her lungs.

But there was no sign of him anywhere. And when she turned back to look for Ere, almost as an afterthought, the platform was empty.

*** *** *** ***

The vampire watched the screen before her as if mesmerized.

And perhaps she was. For she'd seldom seen such deadly elegance, such lethal efficiency. The fighter in the streaming video moved so fast that if she didn't know better, she would have thought the clip was doctored by special effects.

But she did know better. She even knew what he was.

Vampire.

Someone had *turned* the delectable human Gabriel into a Dark One, and the vampire had a good idea who.

Oh, this was too good to be true! She would have an opportunity to finish what she started. The creature had just recently sated her needs, but watching Gabriel fight had rekindled the lustful inferno within her.

She had to have him. And she knew just the way to go about it.

Even her mysterious "partner" must appreciate her next move, chess master that it was.

Two birds with one stone was hard to beat.

*** *** *** ***

It was the heat that awakened him.

Unbearable, stifling heat. As if his veins flowed with lava and his skin burned with fire.

Gabriel clawed at his arms and chest only to realize that his upper body was already bare. Someone caught onto his frenzied movements and helped him shuck the rest of his clothes until only his skin and hair blanketed his swollen flesh.

Still it was not enough. Water. He needed water. His throat was parched, and it scalded his lungs to breathe.

As if an angel heard his silent supplication, something infinitely soft, silky and blessedly cool enfolded his body, and a hand gently pressed his face into a faintly fragrant hollow.

His fangs punched through his aching upper gums and into the tender skin against his mouth.

With his first swallow of the thick, honeyed liquid, relief flooded him. But another hunger flamed through his body, making his internal temperature all but steaming.

The silky form that wrapped around him shifted smoothly to lie directly beneath him, until his body draped on top heavily, lethargically, and cool limbs wrapped around his back, his hips.

Gabriel became even more restless, though he maintained the seal of his mouth against the source of thirst-quenching nectar. Helplessly, he undulated his body against the softness, wanting to submerge himself in the cool haven.

The haven responded, moving with him, against him, creating a maddening yet delicious friction that both soothed and stoked his flames higher.

And then the hottest part of him slid against a slick, satiny notch.

Gabriel groaned deeply and gutturally.

Yes. More.

The limbs around his hips tightened so that he pressed slightly into the notch. Wet, heavenly warmth welcomed him, gently yet inexorably drawing him further inside.

Gabriel froze in that moment, holding himself utterly still, every muscle clenched, every bone locked, as if he poised on the edge of Destiny's precipice.

Slowly he opened his eyes.

And stared into pools as deep and as blue as the fathomless sea.

I know you, a part of him whispered in the recesses of his sub consciousness. *I found you.*

My love. My heart.

"Inanna," a voice that was his own yet also apart from him uttered reverently, as if all the hope, desire, pain, and passion were embodied in that one word.

Her eyes widened in response, and a gasp escaped her lips.

The small sound triggered a primal need within him that could be denied no longer.

Gabriel stopped thinking, stopped fighting himself. And surrendered to the voracious compulsion to claim. To penetrate.

To Mate.

His mouth took hers without preamble, his tongue plunging inside the same moment his sex thrust fully into her core.

Yessss. Mooore.

Every sensation became magnified and multiplied. The tight clasp of her vagina. The rhythmic contraction of her strong inner muscles. The wet, hot pressure from the squeeze and pull of her core as he moved within her. The silky soft embrace of her body around his. The sucking, nipping and rubbing of her mouth and tongue against his.

His buttocks clenched in sync with powerful, surging thrusts. He reached beneath her knees and wound them higher up his back as he deepened the slow, steady strokes, hitting the hardened knot inside of her. Again and again. Over and over.

Inanna arched her back and moaned in abandon as her vagina convulsed around him in great shuddering gulps, her nails scoring his shoulders and arms with the violence of her release.

And Gabriel fell from the precipice into a dark unknown. His body clenched painfully from head to toe until the veins raised against his skin, held for an instant and an infinity, and released in a torrent that filled her to the brim.

A pleasure like he'd never known flooded his weary, aching body, banking the fires, washing away the pain.

Finally, he was home.

*** *** *** ***

As far as Silver Lake Preserve, White Plains, Maximus, trailed closely by Simca, and Anastasia followed the lead Cloud had given them.

The warrior had not been able to connect with the Pure Ones' human agent last night. And though he received a sign that at least the agent was alive, he'd also read between the lines and perceived that the human was in a precarious position, hence his message to his vampire allies to do some reconnaissance.

The closer they came to shutting down the fight club operations, the more dangerous it was for the human who remained undercover in the network. Yet, he could not pull out until they discovered and dealt with the true mastermind behind it all.

The two Chosen came upon a small clearing amidst a concentrated circle of pines based on the precise military coordinates the human had left for Cloud.

A fight was currently in progress.

Despite the night's below freezing temperatures, two human fighters faced each other, clad only in loose trousers, their bare feet noiseless in the recent snow.

One had dreadlocks, moved in the style of Brazilian jujitsu and held a long, serrated dagger. The other had a close-shaven haircut, barely moved at all, merely holding a combat stance—knees bent, fists raised, shoulders tensed—and held a similarly deadly looking knife.

A tight ring of silent spectators stood around the fighters. The difference in this crowd versus those that Maximus and Ana had seen on video footage was that the observers here neither made sound nor movement, barely even blinking as they concentrated all of their attention on the fight at hand.

The scene was almost ritualistic in its intensity. This was not a performance. This was not entertainment.

It was a fight to the death.

The grim onlookers were witnesses to a sentencing. Perhaps a punishment being meted out. Based on the way some of them held themselves, the Chosen could tell even from a distance that they were vampires.

Dreadlocks made the first move, aiming a low spinning kick to take out his opponent's legs. Close-shave shifted marginally to avoid the swipe, raising one foot, then the other. His movements were concise and brisk, calculated with a precision that minimized effort and maximized impact. His small incremental moves also allowed him to maintain closeness with his opponent, keeping his target within arms and legs reach.

As Dreadlocks threw one fancy attack after another at Close-shave, the latter merely diffused the impact of the moves with efficient counters and continued to close in. Their knives flashed quicksilver in the pale moonlight, each slash meant to deal a mortal or, at a minimum, debilitating blow.

Close-shave was now within one foot of Dreadlocks, close enough to use knees and elbows. He dialed his movements up a notch, his hands and feet striking on a faster beat, like the tempo of a dance speeding up. One, Long Knee to stomach. Two, elbow strike to back of neck. Three, quarter-turn. Four, dagger across throat.

It was over in less than a minute.

Dreadlocks lay dead in a pool of darkening red snow. Close-Shave stood over the body but didn't bother checking on his opponent, so sure was he of the result. Instead, he stared expressionlessly at the ring of observers around them as if awaiting judgment.

The smallest figure in the crowd took one step forward and addressed the fighter. Maximus and Ana could not make out the appearance of the figure, for the large hooded shroud she wore, except to note that it was a female. Nor could they hear what she was saying to Close-Shave.

Based on Devlin's description of the female vampire Inanna encountered and his evaluation of who she might be, this figure was obviously not one and the same. She was much smaller in stature and did not move with the training of a warrior.

But it was obvious she called the shots, for when she ended her speech, the crowd of spectators began to depart with her in the lead, flanked by two vampire guards.

Four vampires remained with the fighter, however, and shifted menacingly in his direction.

Wordlessly, Maximus signaled to Ana that he and Simca were following the female with the entourage. In all likelihood, the fighter still standing was the human undercover agent. Ana would stay behind to ensure his safety.

Not that he appeared to be needing her help, she saw as she moved stealthily closer to the clearing so that she was within assistance range.

The fighter had upped the tempo of his deadly dance yet another few beats, much to Ana's appreciation.

Though he was human, he held his own remarkably against four well-trained vampire assassins. They were stronger and faster, but the human was more strategic, as if he anticipated their moves based on an internal algorithm of possibilities and outcomes.

And he had obviously been coached on how to fight and win against vampires.

Use their strength and speed against them. Aim to debilitate rather than kill—the eyes, ears, throat, groin. Slash ankles, backs of knees.

Even so, four vampires to one human were impossible odds, and the fighter was sustaining more than a few injuries, the fresh scent of his blood only fueling the vampires' fervor for more.

Ana stepped into the fray when she saw that the human was locked in combat with one vampire, while another was charging him from behind. She suspended the second vampire with her mind and forcefully slammed him against a nearby pine, the impact shaking heavy snow loose from the canopy of needles.

The vampire who currently had the human in a choke hold and was about to take a bite out of his throat was the next to experience the strength of Ana's telekinesis as an invisible force held him immobilized.

Quick to take advantage of the opening this paralysis provided, the human reacted by twisting around and punching his dagger up through the bottom of the vampire's jaw, puncturing his jugular in the process.

With a gurgle, the vampire fell. In seconds, his death would be marked by an ignoble disintegration into dust.

But the human didn't wait for that event. He pivoted and let fly his dagger into the heart of the vampire who was easing himself up against the tree where Ana had flung him.

Meanwhile, Ana efficiently executed the other two vampires who had been crippled by the human.

And then all was silent and still.

Ana faced the human fighter from a few yards away, close enough to see each other clearly.

The human inclined his head slightly in acknowledgement of her aid. Ana gave a nod back, as well as a slow, sweeping, appreciative appraisal from head to toe.

Battle often made vampires sexually aroused. And Ana was a full-blooded female warrior. Blood, sex and war were her specialty. Vampires likely invented the words "bloodlust" and "bloodthirsty."

Ana had a hell of a time controlling her primal needs at the moment. The human was one fine specimen of maleness.

Perhaps he recognized the gleam in her eyes (not that she bothered hiding it), for the corners of his lips curled in a wry smile, drawing her attention to said scrumptious lips and to the faint indentation in his sharp, angular chin.

Keeping his eyes on her, as if he wasn't entirely sure she could hold back her baser impulses, the human picked up the leather trench coat and pair of boots a nearby pile of vampire ashes no longer needed and put them on.

He walked backwards, facing Ana, in the opposite direction that Maximus and Simca had gone, and when he was what he estimated to be a safe distance away, he gave her a mock salute, turned and entered the surrounding forest with long, purposeful strides.

Ana watched him walk away with a contemplative smile on her own lips. *Mmm*. The man could move.

She went to the tree where the human's dagger had punched through the chest cavity of the slain vampire foe, embedded in the thick bark, and retrieved it.

An LHR combat knife. Military issue. Customized specs.

Ana looked it over appreciatively. She did love her weapons, and this one was a beauty. She sheathed it at her hip before breaking into a run in search of Maximus.

She would hold on to it for the human should their paths cross again.

"With his surrender, the sacrifice is made. Death is near and Darkness surrounds, as the race's Adversary raises its blade"
   —Excerpt from the Lost Chapters of the Ecliptic Scrolls

Chapter Thirteen

Gabriel flipped the eggs over easy in the skillet and moved around a few pieces of bacon frying alongside them.

He was learning a number of new things about his "wife" over the course of the last little while.

For starters, he wasn't sure how long she'd been in this world, but she still hadn't learned how to cook in all that time.

If he had to attribute her lapse to skill or will, he would guess will. After all, frying eggs and bacon while toasting some bread was not a difficult activity to learn. When she informed him that she could boil eggs but sometimes forgot the water, or the heat, or the time, he decided to take over cooking their impromptu meal in the wee hours of the morning.

Second, despite the badass, mysterious, cool, calm and collected first impression she gave with her icy beauty, black leather and long trench coats, she was rather cozy and down-to-earth at home, currently watching him prepare their food on a barstool at the kitchen counter outfitted in a long blue cotton sleep shirt with a cartoon of Snoopy on it. When he'd looked at it quizzically, she murmured that Benji had picked it out on a shopping trip.

Gabriel was slowly accepting the fact that Nana Chastain had been, was, and would be an integral part of his son's life.

And his own.

Third, she seemed rather shy despite her no-nonsense directness.

I want you.

A few minutes ago, she'd had him well and good.

But when both their stomachs growled loudly, she'd sprung from the bed like a skittish colt, threw on the cotton T and muttered something about a late supper as she dashed out of the room without a glance his way.

Gabriel wasn't an expert in post-coital protocol—by any means—but he thought maybe a cuddle might be appropriate. Perhaps an affectionate kiss or two which might develop into another round of orgasmic bliss.

He was certainly up for it.

But then, what did he know.

Aside from being "Blooded Mates," they didn't exactly have a relationship based on emotional attachment. Everything was backwards with them. First came "marriage," then sex, and now...

He didn't know what came next. Should they go on a first date? And if he was extra suave, he could sneak to second base?

All he knew was that they'd just had mind-blowing sex— naked, messy, greedy, noisy sex—and they didn't know what to say to each other.

Hell, he wasn't even sure he liked her.

But, good lord, did they have chemistry!

He was wearing a bath towel around his waist in lieu of the torn and bloodstained trousers (he was unreasonably happy to find that she didn't stock up on menswear in her apartment, a good indication of either lack of male company or protection of privacy and discretion), and she was covertly eating him up with her eyes, a rosy blush adorning her cheeks. When he'd asked her mundane questions like what did she have stocked and how she'd like her eggs, she'd provided half-coherent muttered answers without meeting his eyes, her blush getting deeper the longer he held her gaze.

If he didn't know better, he would have thought she was a teenager crushing on her first guy.

But that didn't make sense. She was who knew how old, and looking the way she did, with her charisma and effortless allure, she was certain not to have been lonely for male company in her long existence.

And he assumed that she didn't know him any more than he knew her. It was simply a sexual attraction and now a biological imperative that brought them together.

Gabriel had figured out in the brief orgasmic aftermath that the process had been necessary for his body, perhaps for hers as well. Like air. Like water.

What he didn't yet understand was why she'd chosen *him*.

And why, despite everything, he felt like he'd chosen her. *Inanna.*

The name echoed in his mind, but he did not know the context for it.

It was as if he were submerged in the murky waters of a deep well. Every once in a while he glimpsed a flicker of light, an image, registered a sound, but then the clue would dissolve into shadows and echoes, and whatever that was buried inside of him remained dormant and hidden.

"How old are you?" he asked while he found the plates cupboard and served up the food. He might as well start there since it was on his mind.

She paused for a moment, seeming more surprised by his speaking to her than by the rather blunt question itself. "Over four millennia."

Now it was Gabriel's turn to pause. "Huh," was all he could muster.

She shrugged one shoulder. "I stopped counting the actual years a few centuries in. Time becomes irrelevant after a while. What one does with it is the only thing that matters."

Gabriel put her plate of hearty fare in front of her on the counter with accompanying silverware and said dryly, "And in all those years you never learned to cook."

She peered closely at him for a few seconds, as if trying to decipher whether he was teasing her or whether he was truly deploring her lack of culinary expertise.

Wow, they were awkward, Gabriel thought, as he tipped one corner of his mouth up to indicate that he was just teasing, not judging.

She visibly relaxed and the rosy flush faded by a few degrees. Conversation seemed to help her find her aplomb. "You are twenty-six," she recited, to level the informational field so to speak, "birthday just this Christmas Eve past."

Gabriel nodded as he dug into his own two plates heaped with six eggs, four pieces of toast slathered with butter and jam and at least a pound of bacon.

Finally, he wanted food. It had been days since he'd had a meal.

"When's your birthday?" he asked around a forkful of eggs.

"In the summer," she replied, pausing in her own eating to watch him in fascination, as if she'd never seen a man chew before. "I don't recall the exact date. In the ancient world, the calendaring was different, I'm not sure the date translation would be accurate."

"Where are you from?" he continued to inquire, because that seemed like the next logical question, and he wanted her to keep talking because her voice was a joy to his ears and because he wanted to focus on devouring as much food as he could.

"I belonged to the Akkadian Empire, which spanned much of modern-day Middle East. I grew up in a valley at the base of the Silver Mountains in the Fertile Crescent."

She tilted her head to regard him, again sharing a tidbit about his life that he didn't realize she knew, "You were born in the City to Italian-Spanish missionaries and lived in China for a number of years before returning here."

Gabriel paused in his chewing and said, "You seem to know a lot about me."

"I do."

No explanation as to how or why she knew. Just that she did.

Gabriel put his fork down. He could afford to wait a few minutes before starting on a second course. He needed to get a few things off his chest first.

"Thank you for saving me," he said quietly, solemnly. "Again."

Vaguely he recalled the fight by the river, slipping in and out of consciousness. Inanna finding him sprawled on the rocky shore. Carrying him to her vehicle. Bridge lamps flashing by as she drove them across the City. Infinitely gentle hands washing away the grime, the blood...

She looked into his eyes and became completely still, as if she were holding her breath.

"I've neglected to tell you that," he continued. "I've felt... a number of emotions I haven't felt before meeting you. It's been a surreal few days. But I am grateful to be alive. To be able to take care of Benji, and God willing, to watch him grow into a good man."

She held his gaze unblinkingly, but she did swallow, as if suppressing some intense emotion.

Gabriel looked down at his hands, and for a long while did not speak.

Dislocated images came to mind. Pieces of his childhood, meeting Olivia for the first time, rocking Benji to sleep as a baby. And other fragments that seemed like memories—waiting beneath a copse of tamarisk trees, walking beside a young girl with golden blond hair and rosy cheeks, grueling training with fighters he somehow knew then but didn't know now.

He didn't understand his life any more. Nothing made sense.

It was time to take back control.

Finally, Gabriel raised his head, as if coming to a decision.

"I want to know you," he said, as if making a vow, his deep, husky voice sending shivers down her spine. "If you allow me, I want to know who you are, what... we are, what, if anything, I can do to make things right. The others said we are at war, and it has something to do with the fight clubs. I'm a fighter. I can help."

He reached across the counter and extended his hand, palm up. "I want Benji to have a good future. A safe future. I think—no, I know—you want that too. So tell me. Teach me."

She stared at his outstretched palm as if she'd never seen one before, but her own hand reached out of its own volition.

He grasped it and held on. "We are 'married', you and I. Mated. We're partners, right?"

She blinked rapidly at their joined hands as a bittersweet emotion swelled in her throat, tearing her eyes.

Goddess above how she loved him!

For years she'd watched him from afar, seeing the kind of father he was to Benji, the husband he was to her friend.

The man he was.

A good, strong protector. Always giving, always loving. Perhaps she had loved him from the first and didn't know it. Perhaps she had hidden the truth from herself. She felt now as if she had loved him forever, that she *knew* him in the depth of her soul.

She swallowed back the tears and took a deep, calming breath. This was a new beginning. For the first time since she was a very young girl, Inanna felt truly *alive*, not merely living.

"Yes," she answered his vow. "I will tell you everything you need to know. We will face it all together."

*** *** *** ***

Sophia and Aella entered their apartment in silence.

The Amazon knew better than to interrupt the young Queen's contemplative mood with questions.

Aella had watched Sophia grow up step by step and probably knew her best of all the Dozen. She was sometimes a big sister, sometimes an indulging aunt, but always a close confidant and friend. She had seen all kinds of tantrums, emotional spats, sulking and mood swings.

But this was different.

There was an aura of sadness and longing, confusion and pain that hovered like a cheerless raincloud above Sophia's head.

Aella did not know what was exchanged between the Paladin and the Queen, nor did she know the depth of their emotions—she doubted they knew themselves—but she did perceive that however their relationship had evolved over the years, their feelings were intense and complex and needed resolution.

Unfortunately, no one could help them sort it out; they had to do it themselves.

As such, Aella purposely stayed in the living area and turned on the TV as if she couldn't wait to catch up on a Congressional broadcast on CNBC while Sophia trudged into their shared bedroom like a senseless zombie, climbed onto the top bunk and flopped face down on the coverlets.

What was going on with Dalair?

What was she going to do with Ere?

What did she feel for the two men?

What did it all mean??

The questions and permutations thereof kept circling each other like hungry vultures in Sophia's imaginative teenage mind, while at the same time she felt complex, multi-layered emotions that didn't seem to belong to an eighteen-year-old girl. They seemed to have developed and evolved over decades, centuries.

Even millennia.

Sophia was so torn and frustrated she could scream. She muffled her face in her pillow and did the muted version.

Not nearly as satisfying.

Her phone vibrated against her thigh as a new text came through.

"I am sorry I missed you, lovely Sophia."

Ere.

Sophia immediately lifted up on her elbows and responded, "I saw you on the platform earlier. I was on the dance floor. Why didn't you come down?"

A pause. Then, "You seemed preoccupied."

Sophia did not know what to write back. She had indeed been preoccupied. She had not thought of Ere even once while she had Dalair in her sights, even though she was there at the club to meet another man.

"If I may be so bold as to ask—is he a friend?"

Sophia stared at her phone screen long enough for it to self-lock. "He used to be. I don't know what he is any more," she answered once she punched in the key code.

"He seems very important to you."

Sophia considered the truth of this observation but neither confirmed nor denied it. It felt strange talking about Dalair with Ere. Especially with Ere.

"I'm sorry I was distracted," she finally wrote. "I'd like to meet you some other time if you're up for it."

A long silence.

"Of course, lovely Sophia, we should meet."

Perhaps it was a spurt of inspiration or a dig of conscience, for Sophia wrote next, "I'll bring Aella. You've met her—she's my best friend, remember? She was also at the club with me last night."

Another pregnant silence.

"Yes. You must bring your friend. I shall look forward to it."

Sophia could almost see Ere's rueful smile. If he had been flirting with her and was hoping for some private tête–à–tête, his plans had just been discouraged.

Not that Sophia thought he was flirting with her. Nor did she think she was in a position to discourage him. It's just that she needed time to sort through her own feelings first, the most pressing ones centering on the Paladin.

Call her a two-timer and call her fickle, but it wasn't like she *wanted* to feel these things toward Dalair. She wanted normality. She wanted to experience all the things average human teenagers experienced. Ere would have been the perfect crush. Beautiful, charming, sophisticated.

But as long as Sophia had these gut-wrenching, breath-stealing feelings for her sometime personal guard, Ere would have to wait.

*** *** *** ***

Gabriel sat in silence in the passenger seat of Nana Chastain's luxurious ride, staring unseeingly out the window as she drove them across the City to Morningside Heights.

So much information to process. His head felt too tight for his jumbled thoughts.

He had gained basic knowledge about his race, the Dark Ones, their history, their relationship with humans and the Pure Ones, the Great War thousands of years ago, and the fragile truce they had maintained since that time.

She'd debunked many myths and lore that humans created about vampires. Dark Ones did not burn when exposed to sunlight and turn to ash; they simply felt the biological imperative to sleep and rest. Sometimes the pull was so strong, they could not stay awake even if they wanted to.

And they did not sleep in coffins in dark and dreary crypts, Gabriel was relieved to know, though of course every story had some basis in truth, however tenuous. Being sealed in complete darkness seemed to promote better rest, especially for the less powerful vampires. In ancient times, whence the practice originated, tombs were sacred, secure and luxurious. Many civilizations, across all social hierarchies, believed in living a richer afterlife.

In many ways, Dark Ones were animalistic and primal in their nature, with heightened senses, strength and powerful base urges. Compared to Pure Ones and humans, they were much more instinctual, sexual creatures. They relished the passion and drive to eat, drink, fight and fuck.

She had not put it in those terms, exactly, but Gabriel got the gist.

For all that, Dark Ones had an extremely sophisticated societal structure. At one time they had ruled all sentient beings. But the Great War had changed their place in civilization, perhaps permanently. They now stayed to the shadows and kept mostly to themselves within the confines of the Dark Laws. Those who strayed were mercilessly hunted down.

Garlic, crucifixes and the like had no special power over them. They did not adhere to one religious system since religions changed with the times and their race had existed across untold millennia and civilizations. The ancient ones among the race, however, did believe a Dark Goddess protected them, if not created them.

Not much was known beyond that.

Coming to the present, Gabriel downloaded what they knew about the fight clubs and how the chaos and violence were spreading. The dangers of this happening were manifold: civilian casualties, power concentrating in the wrong hands, destruction and social unrest, and last but not least, potential mass exposure of their two races to the public.

Maybe Armageddon really was upon them. It boggled the mind.

He also learned more about his Blooded Mate—his partner in this new phantasmagoric life. She was a warrior, one of the Chosen, the personal guard to the vampire Queen of New England, Jade Cicada.

Apparently, Gabriel would need to be presented to Her Majesty soon.

Or was it Her Highness? Her Worship? His Mate hadn't used any honorifics when describing the Queen, so he supposed he could just follow her lead.

She told him about the rest of the Chosen warriors, as well as their Pure allies. Gave him a rundown of their backgrounds and abilities. Prepared him for what to expect. She wasn't yet sure what it meant for her position on the Queen's inner circle now that she was Mated.

One could never take anything for granted where Jade was concerned.

She confirmed what he had suspected about their bond as Blooded Mates. Their survival depended on each other: they were one another's source of Nourishment.

Like a limitless supply of energy for an all but limitless rechargeable battery. They only needed to consume each other's blood, no one else's, Gabriel was relieved to know, and not with the same frequency as the daily meals they would still eat. They could survive as long as months without taking blood, but they would suffer dearly for the lapse.

She had not said how she'd lived before choosing him.

As for the sex... it was a case of "the more, the better."

He could feel it very keenly.

Whenever he was near her, his body hummed, his senses buzzed, as if he were a human tuning fork vibrating to her specific pitch. And only to that pitch.

Just sitting next to her in the Lamborghini he was fully aroused. A shared sideways glance told him that she was too.

She cleared her throat, perhaps to distract them both from the palpable sexual heat between them.

"We need to tell Benji," she said softly. "Because he is your... our son. He is now inextricably part of our world."

Our son.

Somehow those two words sounded so right.

"Would we watch him grow up, grow old, and..." Gabriel couldn't finish the thought, "While we stay as we are?"

For a long time she did not reply.

And then she said, "It is heart-wrenching, the loss. To watch loved ones wither away and disappear. I cannot even contemplate that for Benji. Every Dark One, and I suppose Pure One as well, deal with this consequence of longevity differently. Some prefer not to form attachments at all. They become isolated, jaded and devoid of joy. Death seems preferable to such a hopeless, lightless existence. For me, every soul has something to give, something to teach us, and it's our responsibility—no, privilege—to give what we can, love when we can."

Gabriel thought of Olivia. His time with her had not been fulfilling. He had tried his damnedest to make her happy, take care of her, lift her up, but he recognized in hind sight that it was never in his power to do so.

But if he could do it over again, he would still have made the same choices. Because he had made her life more bearable. He had sheltered a lost soul. It had been a worthwhile endeavor.

And because of Olivia, he was a father. He had Benji, who was happiness incarnate.

And through Olivia he met the female sitting next to him.

"You have suffered many losses over the course of your existence," Gabriel stated rather than asked.

"True," she returned, "but I have received many gifts of friendship and new beginnings. Life is so much more precious, is it not, when death hovers on the other side."

"You are very courageous to know loss yet continue to love," he said quietly.

"You give me too much credit," she said, "I do not know how I would be if I ever *fell* in love. I think I am only brave enough to love once, and once and for all."

I do not know if I could ever bear to lose you, Inanna thought to herself.

And then strangely she added in her head—*never again*.

"We have arrived."

*** *** *** ***

"That is so cool! Way better than elves!"

Elves was what Benji called the Pure Ones.

Inanna and Gabriel exchanged a nonplussed look.

This conversation was not going as expected. But then why should they be surprised? Five-year-olds didn't know the meaning of "impossible" yet. Of course there were vampires and elves. Maybe werewolves and witches too.

"You mustn't tell anyone," Inanna reminded him, "it's a secret, okay?"

Benji nodded vigorously, eyes like saucers. "I can keep a secret."

Indeed he could. He was amazingly tight-lipped for one so young and unused to the ways of the world. He had kept Olivia and Inanna's secret from Daddy, after all.

"But where are your fangs?" Benji asked, poking at Inanna and Gabriel's upper lips with both his little hands. "Are you going to suck my blood?"

He didn't seem too worried about that prospect, even seemed to relish the potential experience.

"No blood will be sucked," Gabriel answered. At least not between anyone but himself and his Mate, and Benji didn't need to know those details.

His son looked somewhat disappointed. "Then how can you say you're vampires?"

Inanna smoothed golden curls from his brow, a gesture so affectionate and maternal, Gabriel's heart skipped a beat.

Seeing her next to Benji, both with their golden blonde looks and large blue eyes, anyone would assume they were truly mother and son. And then there was the open adoration in their eyes when they beheld each other, something Gabriel had never seen between Benji and his biological mother, even after Olivia had turned over a new leaf with the onset of her cancer.

There were many different forms of love. Nana Chastain's love for his son was true and abiding.

"One day, you will understand," she said to Benji, and before he could interrupt, for his scrunched brow indicated he wanted to do just that, she continued, "That day will come sooner than you think. You have to be patient and watchful."

She lowered her voice to a whisper and put her head against his. "It's more fun when it's a mystery, is it not?"

Benji seemed to agree with that logic. Sotto voce he asked, "Am I a vampire too?"

"No," Inanna replied, while injecting her voice with new excitement, "you, my love, are a very, very special human."

Benji seemed satisfied with that, grinning widely, because really, how could he feel otherwise when a beautiful golden goddess looked at him as if he were her entire universe.

"Are you married now? Are we a family?" the boy asked, naked hope and expectation in his eyes.

"Olivia wanted you to be my new Mommy," he said to Inanna, then looked at his father, "and Daddy's new wife."

"She told you that?" Gabriel and Inanna all but asked at the same time.

Benji nodded solemnly. "She said the three of us will always have each other and be together. She promised."

In a sudden realization, Gabriel understood that while he had been focused on taking care of Olivia, she had also tried her best, in her own way, to take care of him. Had she known the truth of Nana Chastain? Had she known that things would turn out this way?

For the first time since his world turned upside down, Gabriel felt like the puzzle pieces were starting to fit. What the finished puzzle looked like he did not know, but there was a sense of rightness to where he was and who he was with.

"Are we going to live here from now on?" Benji asked next.

"I thought we could live at my place," Inanna replied, "you like it there, right?"

Though she asked the question of Benji, her eyes were on Gabriel. She knew that she was making a lot of decisions for the three of them. She knew that he'd felt out of control since the moment they had met.

But something had changed since last night. He seemed to have found his center of gravity, his innate calm and patience, once more.

He looked steadily back at her and gave a slight nod, aligning with her suggestion.

Benji nodded his consent more enthusiastically. "Is my room still the same? Are all my toys and books still there?"

At that, Gabriel cocked a brow. *His room?*

Inanna's smile held an apology for keeping so much from him. "Just the way you left it," she said to Benji. "We can go there today."

"Together, all three of us," Benji wanted to confirm.

"Yes," Gabriel was the one who answered. "Always."

"While the Bond between Blooded Mates is sacred and immutable, it can be contested if a Dark One has prior claim, either of the flesh or of the blood. A formal Challenge must be made. A fight to the death shall ensue. For only through death can the Bond be broken."
—*Excerpt from the Dark Laws, verse thirty-five of the Ecliptic Scrolls*

Chapter Fourteen

The vampire ignited two small candles in the pitch black chamber, the better to appreciate her lover by.

If one could call the creature her lover.

Verily, there was no love, not even an iota of affection or care, between them. They simply used each other for gratification.

She used the creature for blood and sex, and it used her to further its plans. What those plans were no one but the creature knew.

It just so happened that the creature's plans aligned nicely with her own. It was high time a new Queen sat on the vampire throne.

Jade Cicada was too weak, ruled too loosely, did not take full advantage of the might of the vampire race. Humans were but cattle yet she attributed them with more worth. Pure Ones should be slaves yet she treated them as equals.

Everyone knew she kept a Pure pet in her private chambers. Ostensibly he was her Blood Slave, though it was never announced as such, but she accorded him many privileges and listened intently whenever he spoke. She took his counsel more often than not.

She was not even a True Blood.

Neither was the vampire, but that only meant she was the Queen's equal, not her inferior. There was only one True Blood the vampire knew of within the New England Hive: Inanna Sharru-kinu, one of the Queen's Chosen.

Why the ancient Akkadian did not challenge the Queen directly for the throne herself, the vampire could not comprehend. Inanna was much older, and by that virtue, also much stronger. There was speculation among the elite of the population who her antecedents were; some even suspected she had royal blood. But no one was entirely sure.

The fight clubs' profits had filled the vampire's and her allies' coffers nicely. The chaos and destruction the network distributed destabilized Jade Cicada's reign and raised questions about her ability to rule. The international expansion helped the vampire build more alliances to strengthen her own bid.

It had been such a clever plan. But the Queen was more resourceful than the vampire gave her credit, even calling the Pure Ones to her aid.

No matter, the vampire was putting into motion a new piece of her plan to get the fight clubs up and running again.

Inanna, however, was another obstacle that had to be removed. The vampire could not have her own right to the throne publicly challenged, and the Akkadian might just do that if Jade's seat was overthrown. For some mysterious reason, she was extremely loyal to the present Queen.

"You are most attractive when the wheels of your Machiavellian mind are churning," the creature murmured, breaking into the vampire's thoughts.

She turned her attention back to her "lover" and slowly assessed its body, bared by the open satin robe, with an avaricious and sadistic gleam.

So much gorgeous, smooth flesh to mark and claim as the vampire chose. So much pain and suffering to inflict. Such strong veins to feed from. Where, oh where, should she begin?

She approached the platform bed still fully dressed and unsheathed a stiletto strapped to her hip. "I want a male today," she demanded.

"Any male in particular?" the creature asked solicitously.

"The fighter," she responded immediately, "you know the one. *My* fighter."

With a faint, shimmering glow, the creature shifted its form and looks until Gabriel D'Angelo lay against the sleek crimson coverlets.

The Gabriel before her opened his hard, muscular thighs and invited in that rich, husky baritone, "Will this do?"

Plans and schemes momentarily forgotten, the vampire stalked on all fours until she knelt directly at the juncture of her lover's groin. Slowly, meticulously, she slid the stiletto from ankle to calf to inner thigh to that beautiful staff lying half aroused against a tightly ridged abdomen, leaving a thin trail of blood along its wake.

She knew just how to arouse it fully and proceeded to savor her delectable meal.

*** *** *** ***

Aella and Sophia pulled Inanna aside while the males played a round of Mortal Combat on the latest Playstation in the living room before Gabriel, Inanna and Benji had to depart.

The same was true the world over: anyone with a Y chromosome would be addicted to video games if they had time to play, even Cloud Drako, who had the demeanor of a wizened, vice-less old monk while he looked like a ridiculously hot and sexy mixed-Asian Armani supermodel.

Aella threw a long, covetous glance in the warrior's direction, heated enough that Cloud's shoulders visibly tensed, though he did not look back.

"Aella," Sophia said impatiently, indicating she'd called her name already, "pay attention please."

Aella focused on the powwow at hand and said, "Right." She gave Sophia and Inanna her full attention. "Do you intend to present your Blooded Mate to your Queen?" she asked the Chosen.

"I do."

The Pure females shared a look. "My understanding of vampire law is superficial at best," Aella admitted, "but I seem to recall that Dark Ones can only Mate within their own."

"Yes," Inanna replied, though her statement had a question mark at the end. What was the Pure One trying to get at?

"Well, you see," Sophia attempted to explain, "I didn't want to say anything until I was certain, and mind you I'm not *100%* sure, but maybe 99.9%..."

"We suspect your Mate has a Pure soul," Aella finished for the young woman lest she lead them too far down a rabbit hole.

Inanna's only outward reaction was a knitting of her brows.

"We do not know how the *turning* affected him, but Sophia is certain he still possesses a Pure soul. Technically, even as a vampire, he could still be Awakened."

Aella referred to the process by which humans with Pure souls experienced a critical event that merged their present with their past lives and triggered their Gift and immortality.

If they survived the process, that was.

Inanna had not foreseen this. If what they said was true, who could predict what the Awakening would do? She knew of no such example from their race's history to rely upon.

"Perhaps he will remain vampire, just with a Pure soul, though we have not seen examples of this before," Aella said, echoing Inanna's own thoughts.

"But there is also the chance he could transform into a Pure One, overruling the vampire side, since the Awakening comes *after* the *turning*, not before."

In which case, their Bond was forbidden by the Dark Laws, Inanna understood.

And no one knew what the union between a Dark and Pure one would do. Would they still be each other's Nourishment? Or would he endure the excruciating process of the Decline because she, as a vampire, could not provide the energy he needed as a Pure One?

"How much do you trust your Queen?" Aella asked when Inanna remained silent. "Would she allow your union to stand?"

Inanna did not know. Jade had been lenient thus far, turning a blind eye to the *turning* and to the subsequent Mating. But to be Bonded to a Pure One... Inanna did not know of any precedence for it.

"If you permit us, our Seer, Eveline, who currently keeps both the Zodiac Scrolls and the Zodiac Prophesies, might be able to find some relevant information in the ancient tomes. Do you have the same for your race's histories?"

Mutely, Inanna nodded. Simone Lafayette, the Keeper, safeguarded the Ecliptic Scrolls for the Dark Ones.

"Yes," Inanna finally uttered. "I would be grateful for any assistance in this matter."

She started when she felt a gentle touch on her arm. The young Pure Queen was regarding her with empathetic eyes.

"Worry not, Dark One," Sophia said in a tone of voice that belied her age, "love will win against all odds. You must keep faith."

But Inanna could not arrest the panic that was building inside. This seemed all too familiar. It felt like déjà vu. She had been down this lonely, perilous path before. Though she did not understand why she felt this way, she knew one thing for certain:

She would not survive losing him again.

*** *** *** ***

"You look exhausted," Gabriel noted when they arrived at Inanna's apartment across town.

In truth, Inanna was dead on her feet, barely able to hold herself upright.

The fact that it was midday did not help. Although she was not as susceptible to the sun's effects as most Dark Ones, she still experienced the drain of energy from her body, the fog that settled in her head. On top of that, she had not slept in days, nor had she fed her thirst since fulfilling the Blood Contract with Olivia.

Making love... or rather, having intercourse, with Gabriel had helped restore her somewhat, but it was not nearly enough. The *turning* had depleted her reserves as she funneled her life force into her Mate. She had not wanted to overtax him with her own demands since then, while he had been adjusting to his new, bewildering situation.

There were so many things they needed to do.

Decide what to do with Benji now that he was under the care of two vampires.

Protocol must be followed, though Inanna did not know of prior examples. The three of them living together at the Cove was out of the question. And Benji needed to continue his education. Taking care of a child from afar when he had both his human parents was but a smidgeon of the type of responsibility she must shoulder now.

She had to figure out what to do with the new information about Gabriel.

Before she shared it with anyone else, she needed to better understand the potential implications herself. Perhaps she could solicit Simone's help without telling her the full details.

They needed to formalize their union before their Queen.

Not many Blooded Mates existed in the Dark world, as vampires were by nature solitary, polygamous creatures. Those that did exist had to be recorded and announced, for vampire progeny can only come from such Bonds, as far as Inanna was aware. And True Bloods were revered as treasures for the entire race.

She still had the vampire assassin to identify and track down.

Though Devlin was given that particular assignment, Inanna knew that she, and likely Gabriel, might be able to provide more clues to aid his effort.

The list seemed endless. And at the moment, all Inanna wanted to do was sleep in her Mate's arms and take Nourishment from his body for the next... oh, decade or so.

As such, Inanna couldn't quite muster up the false reply, "I'm fine." She tried to smile at her Mate in reassurance, but it came across as a grimace.

Gabriel understood her pained expression all too well. He'd seen the same in the mirror for the past few days, and he now knew what it meant.

His Mate needed to feed.

From him.

Without another word, he ushered Benji to the living area and turned on National Geographic. Unlike most other kids his age, Benji had never seemed to enjoy cartoons. He liked all things documentary, be it about history, geology, animals, space—one of his first words had been "Mesopotamia," and his first full sentence, "There are eight planets in the solar system."

Gabriel took no credit for his son's undoubtedly off-the-charts IQ. All he knew was that in times like these, when he was busy with work or needed an extended period of privacy, Benji's ability to keep himself gainfully occupied for hours on end was a priceless boon for any parent.

He made a plate of PBJ, chips and yogurt for Benji, scrounging together what he could find in the kitchen, and set it on the over-sized coffee table with a glass of milk and cutlery.

Benji was already absorbed in the latest series about African tree frogs when Gabriel tucked a paper napkin into the neckline of his son's shirt.

"We're going to take a nap," Gabriel told him, "See you later buddy."

Benji nodded absent-mindedly and waved him off.

Gabriel came back to Inanna, who had not moved since entering the apartment's threshold, save to take off her boots.

"How do you do that?" she managed to whisper in awe. Her times with Benji had always been joyful and easy, but the boy's energy seemed boundless. There had been occasions when Inanna had felt every single one of her four thousand plus years.

Gabriel shrugged, pleased more than he cared to admit that she didn't know Benji as well as he did, after all. She would learn quickly, and he would help her, but it felt nice for now to be the world's foremost expert on his son.

Instead of answering her likely rhetorical question, he took her hand and led her into the bedroom at the end of the hall that they had shared earlier.

Wordlessly, he locked the door, and in one smooth motion, pulled the borrowed sweater over his head. As he doffed his trousers with the same efficiency, he kept his eyes on his Mate's face.

Her gaze, however, was darting like a nervous rabbit all over his naked body as if she couldn't decide where to look first. Inanna swallowed visibly as her mouth went dry. But only for a moment, before it flooded with saliva and her fangs extended from her upper gums.

Gabriel closed the distance between them until he was standing immediately before her. Her lips quivered with anticipation like a predator about to devour a long overdue meal, her canines long and sharp and dripping with saliva.

He took another half step and enfolded her in his arms. Bending his head to give her better access, he gently but inexorably urged her face into the crook of his neck.

"Take as much as you need," he said, his voice deepened with anticipation and desire.

He wanted her to feed from him just as much as she wanted it. His blood roared in his veins, begging for her attention. His body vibrated with tension against hers, yearning to be possessed. In every way, he wanted to be inside of her.

No further encouragement needed, Inanna bit into his throat.

At the first draw of his blood, her body clamored for more. Unconsciously, she wrapped herself, still fully clothed, around him, like a lioness trying to subdue a large prey, lest it tried to escape her clutches before she'd had her fill of it.

But his arms drew tighter around her instead, seeking the danger of her embrace rather than retreating from it, and he widened his stance so that she could have more leverage as she all but climbed his body.

A delicious aroma filled the air as both their scents effervesced in the sexual heat, mingled and bloomed.

Ah, ambrosia, Inanna thought as she nursed at his vein in deep, satisfying gulps. Somehow he tasted so familiar, though she knew this to be the first time she'd drank from him. Tears pricked the back of her eyes as she continued to draw from his throat. Why did she feel as if she'd done this before? Why did so much anguish and torment besiege her whenever she tried to remember?

His large, calloused hands smoothed their way from her thighs to cup her rear and squeeze, pulling her against his hardness, distracting her from painful thoughts.

Yes, she hissed as her hips took over and she rode him through her clothes. The pressure of his naked cock was exquisite against her weeping core, so ready for him the fluids from her body wetted them both even through the sturdy fabric of her jeans.

She disengaged her fangs from his neck only to plunge them into his left subclavian vein, directly beneath his collar bone.

Gabriel shuddered with the force of her strike and made short work of peeling off her jeans. After that, he had to rip her blouse and underthings from her body because she refused to break the airtight seal of her mouth to his chest.

The moment she was as naked as he, she took him with one powerful surge of her hips fully inside her body. They both moaned helplessly at the indescribable pressure and bliss.

With two deep pumps, taking him to the hilt, the thick, satiny head of his penis hitting her G spot with unerring precision, Inanna came on a keening cry, her entire body convulsing with the pleasure and relief of her release.

As her inner muscles contracted around his manhood with a pressure that was almost painful, Gabriel surrendered to his own climax, his seed surging within her, flooding her womb.

It had only been a few minutes, but Gabriel felt like he'd run a marathon. They were both breathing heavily, their nostrils flaring. They hadn't even bothered to sit or lie down, still standing at the foot of the bed, he supporting all of her weight with her strong legs and arms wrapped around him like tentacles.

She licked the wounds at his throat and chest closed and rested her face against his heart. The organ was working double time, pumping more life-giving blood throughout his body, keeping his penis hot and fully erect within her.

Inanna sighed. Now that the edge of hunger was dulled, albeit only slightly, she could focus on the finer details of their mating.

Like how his skin felt like satin stretched over steel and smelled of sunshine and ocean. How his blood blossomed on her tongue with a rich explosion of flavor, tangy, sweet, uniquely Gabriel. How his manhood still throbbed tantalizingly within her, fitting to completion as no male had before him.

His hands had moved from her ass to her back and were now stroking her spine gently, soothingly.

She felt cared for. Protected and loved.

Again, tears threatened at the back of her throat.

How she'd missed this.

In all her long existence she'd never had this soul-deep feeling of belonging and peace.

Except with him.

It didn't make sense. How could she miss something she'd never experienced?

"I love you."

She hadn't meant to say it out loud, and she said it so quietly she wasn't sure he heard her. But the words refused to stay inside. Strangely, she'd wanted to say them the first time she encountered him years ago. And every time she'd seen him since they hovered on the tip of her tongue.

And finally, her heart would no longer be denied. It demanded to speak its truth. Only to him. Always to him.

Gabriel stilled at her confession, even his breath froze. Only his heart increased its frantic pumping, as if it was trying to beat its way out of his chest and into her hands like a faithful hound charging toward its owner.

He could feel it, her absolute possession of him as his Blooded Mate. His body was attuned to her every need. His blood rushed to quench her thirst. His heart... his heart yearned to answer her pledge so badly he hurt physically from the strain of holding back.

Those words were a vow. Once said, he would never unsay them.

He had already grown to care for her deeply within a short period of time. He admired her sense of rightness, her honor and commitment, her courage to find joy even amidst death and destruction. He loved that Benji adored her and the feeling was exceedingly mutual. Children were the most ignorant and yet the wisest of us all. Their innocence allowed them to discern the truth beneath veneers. They saw people not as titles, stations, backgrounds and skills, but for who they were when everything else was stripped away.

And if Benji loved her, it spoke volumes about who Nana Chastain was.

And yet... and yet Gabriel did not fully know her.

Starting with her name, which he never felt comfortable saying. There was so much of her history he didn't understand. And for that matter, so much of his own that he was still unraveling.

He didn't know whether it was an effect of the *turning* or not, but he was frequently flooded with images from another time, images that felt like memories. Memories which held him back. Because he felt as if he'd already given his heart away, though he knew it wasn't in his human life. Were there past lives for every soul? Did past lives hold sway over the present and future?

He needed to answer these questions before he answered her vow.

Eventually, he would.

He knew that without a doubt. They were Mated. He belonged to her. But when he surrendered all of himself, he would do so with full knowledge of who he was and who he had been.

Then, he would give her everything. Forevermore.

Presently, he carried her a couple of steps to the bed, never breaking their intimate connection, the slide of his penis within her making her emit a sound that was half purr, half growl. Music to his ears.

As he laid her down on the soft down comforter, he moved with her, still joined, and covered her thoroughly with his body.

Her arms loosened around his neck so that her hands could go exploring across his shoulders and back, following the deep groove of his spine to his taut buttocks. There they stayed to pay proper homage to the tight, firm muscles, kneaded and squeezed, pushing him deeper within her.

Gabriel gave her bursts of small but potent thrusts to massage her pleasure center inside while his pubic bone pressed deliciously on her clitoris with every rub. Within seconds, she convulsed tightly around him, milking his sex with voracious pulls.

He couldn't hold back his release even if he wanted to. His body knew its duty and gave her the Nourishment of his seed in wave after hot, surging wave.

Still he kept moving, his hips maintaining the rhythm of their heartbeat, the cadence of their breaths, stroking her inside and out endlessly, until one orgasm triggered another, and another, like a fuse lit along a string of fireworks, exploding through their bodies one by one, each more glorious than the last.

Sweat and fluids from their bodies tangled the sheets around them. His sex was sore and well-used, still swollen and hard within her, throbbing with a delicious pain that reached down into his balls, into his bones, though the contractions of her inner muscles were less wrenching than before.

He raised up slightly on his elbows and looked into her eyes as he continued the steady, pulsing thrusts.

She wore the expression of a woman slain by ecstasy, her eyes barely open, her lips parted on languorous, contented sighs. She blinked once slowly, and as if her eyelids were simply too heavy to keep lifted, her lashes swooped down over the deep blue orbs and a satisfied smile curled her lips.

Gabriel dipped his head down to cover her smiling mouth with his own, wanting to taste the sunshine and sweetness of her joy. She opened her lips obligingly and welcomed the entry of his tongue. Leisurely, she sucked at him, while below, her vagina continued to milk his cock.

As she crested over another orgasm, she nipped his lower lip hard enough to draw blood.

"Mine," she growled huskily, and lapped at the small wound with her tongue, savoring every drop of him.

Gabriel groaned as his own release followed closely on the heels of hers, flooding them both with thick, gushing semen.

At last, his hips stilled, though both their bodies quivered and shook with the intensity of their passion.

Everywhere he felt a tingling soreness, from the toes of his feet to the roots of his hair. He had never felt so exhausted and replete in his life. He could probably lie here, on top of this bed, his body inside of hers, for an entire lifetime, so contented and at charity with the world was he.

Yet even so, his wayward shaft jerked insistently, as if wanting to start another round of orgy. Clearly, it did not know its own limitations.

Before Gabriel could either give his penis a lecture or give in to its boasts, a muffled voice came from beyond their bedroom door.

"I heard a loud noise, Daddy. Did you fall and hurt yourself? Can we go outside to play now? Can we go ice-skating too?"

An indelicate snort sounded in Gabriel's ear, and then another.

He looked down and saw that his Mate was trying unsuccessfully to control her chortles, her mirth wetting her eyes, squeezed into crescent moons from her laughter.

An answering grin spread across Gabriel's mouth and his throaty chuckles joined hers.

Ah, parenthood. And all the exquisite timing it wrought.

No matter what changed in his life, he could always count on that.

"Any issue from the union of a Dark One and an inferior Breed must be a monstrous abomination, fitting into neither world, reviled and mistrusted by all. Such a union must be prevented at all cost. If it cannot be averted, then offspring must not be allowed to exist. If it exists, then it must be hunted down and destroyed."
—Excerpt from the Dark Laws, verse forty-seven of the Ecliptic Scrolls

Chapter Fifteen

"You are up late in the day. What keeps you?"

Simone Lafayette looked up from her ancient tome to see Devlin Sinclair leaning casually against the entrance to the library, one floor below the throne room in the Cove, where the most valuable written records of their race were housed.

She shut the volume gently and placed it back in its cage, which locked itself the moment the book was inside.

The library was a giant oval with concentric ovals of stacked gold cages from floor to ceiling, suspended by gold cables overhead, each metal box containing a priceless piece of the Dark Ones' history.

There were thousands of volumes in this chamber, each with hundreds of pages, which contained small, painstakingly written words in countless languages, lost and current, most of which were written in blood, for it was far more permanent than ink.

Even so, if the Dark histories were the sands of the Saharan desert, the records here represented a single grain.

"I am researching our mysterious guest, the Pure Ones' Consul," Simone replied, coming to stand before another gilded cage. At her touch, the box unlocked and opened to reveal the treasure inside.

"And what have you found?" the Hunter inquired. "Or is it classified information for our Queen's ears only?"

Even though the library was dedicated to the Dark Ones' history, inevitably many of the volumes contained details of notable Pure Ones, and humans too, for that matter. The Great War was written about at length, but mostly by historians thousands of years after the fact, based on legends that were passed from generation to generation, likely by word of mouth.

Simone did not know the exact age of Seth Tremaine, hence she had to start as far back as she could. It was a painstaking process requiring a deep understanding of the history of the Races as well as a proficiency in dozens of different languages, especially ones that no longer existed.

"Nothing much to report at present time," she answered, "except that he is probably between three and four thousand years old, likely Egyptian in origin. I will look through those volumes next."

Devlin nodded, his gaze piercing despite his nonchalant posture. "He makes an exceptional Blood Slave for our Queen then, being one so ancient and strong. The benefits she reaps from his Nourishment is readily apparent. She now only dozes at night and stays awake throughout the day."

Simone carefully turned a page in the volume she was holding, her eyes scanning the words. "One wonders how long she intends to keep him to sustain her burgeoning powers. Surely the Pure Ones will not countenance his indefinite absence from their circle."

"Hmm," Devlin said noncommittally. Then, "You are looking very well yourself, Keeper. Have you done something different with your diet?"

Simone flicked a glance at the other Chosen and looked back at her pages. "Nothing in particular, why do you ask?"

His voice was slightly fainter as he moved away, circling behind her. "Lately, you are often out all night while staying busy throughout the day. One would think the lack of rest would take a toll, but you are glowing with health and beauty—as always."

He smiled flirtatiously at her, but she was not deceived.

"You seem awfully interested in my comings and goings, Hunter," she said with a hint of steel in her voice.

"I am curious about everything and everyone," Devlin said dispassionately on a slight sigh. "Apologies if I offend."

For several moments there was blessed silence, albeit an uncomfortable one. At least for Simone.

When she looked up from her book, Simone realized with a start that he was suddenly not two feet away from her, his hand idly passing across a row of cages.

His stealth must come in handy during the hunt.

"Is there a particular volume you are looking for?" Simone asked solicitously, trying to hide her wariness of the Hunter's mood.

The library was implicitly her domain, as the Keeper of the Race's history. And although she did not know Devlin's exact age, the resonance of his blood was much lighter than her own, indicating that he was hundreds, if not a thousand years younger than herself. It was unlikely he could read and understand even a tenth of the volumes present.

He gave a slight shrug as he kept perusing the caged books; only one ring of the hanging "shelves" separated them.

"Just idling." He glanced at her beneath the thick sweep of his long, golden lashes through the mesh-wire chains that held the gold cages suspended in position. "Are all of our histories written in these tomes?"

"Only the most important of us, of course," Simone replied. "Only the royals, nobles, scholars and artists of great repute."

"And the most dastardly of villains and traitors, I imagine."

Simone paused and held his gaze. Alarmingly, she felt like a mouse hypnotized by a deadly viper about to strike. Her discomfort was increasing exponentially by the minute. What was he after?

The Chosen had been together for many years; some of them had known each other for several lifetimes. But the Hunter was a relatively new addition to Jade Cicada's inner circle, and though he was usually friendly and charming, he was also extremely private and unknowable. Simone and his working relationship had been mostly limited up to now, as they operated in vastly different spheres. They could certainly not be called friends.

"Yes," she admitted, "both the famous and the infamous have been documented to the extent they could be. But what we have here, and frankly, what we have in the entire world of our Race's history, is woefully incomplete. And likely biased, as all histories are."

Devlin seemed to consider this. "Every story has many perspectives, doesn't it? One person's truth is another person's lie. One person's love is another person's hate."

Simone replaced the volume she was holding back in its cage and walked briskly to the library's solid gold and oak double-doors. She breathed a small sigh of relief when he did not pursue her.

"I must attend other duties," she said by way of farewell, "Do let me know if I can assist you another time."

He inclined his head and smiled ironically, his laser blue eyes spearing into her departing back.

Once the doors were shut, Devlin moved to the place where the Keeper was first found standing and took the book she'd been holding from its compartment. He flipped to the page she had been reading and stared for a few seconds at the incomprehensible text. He flipped to a couple of pages before it and a couple of pages after it and did the same. Then he shut the book, put it back and left the library in long, leisurely strides.

It should only take him a few hours to decipher the meaning of the writing on those half a dozen pages he'd memorized with perfect photographic clarity.

*** *** *** ***

Inanna did not know whether it was the love and blood fest they just shared or whether it was because of the Pure soul he supposedly possessed, but thankfully, Gabriel seemed immune to the effects of the sun.

They had carefully ventured out mid-afternoon, two hours before the sun was to set, so that Benji could have the run of the park and enjoy the relative winter warmth before freezing temperatures set in after dark.

Inanna could not remember a happier time. She was with the two males she loved most in the world. She hadn't laughed or smiled so much in the whole of her existence.

They held hands walking through the park, Benji skipping exuberantly between them. They had chocolate fondue at the tourist hotspot and local favorite "Serendipity," made popular by a movie of the same name. They skated together at Wollan Rink, falling several times, first because Inanna wasn't the steadiest on her skating feet, then because Benji thought it was hilarious to drag her and Daddy down in a heap of squeals and laughter.

They picked up a week's worth of clothes, shoes and essentials for the boys at Macy's, to be delivered to the apartment the next morning. Inanna would have the rest of their things picked up from their old studio when it was safe to do so.

Benji was missing his Lamby blanket especially.

They ate beef short ribs, seafood pancake, bibimbap and bulgogi in a hole-in-the-wall Korean restaurant in Brooklyn, and were presently making their way to the subway station that would take them home, strolling off a few calories from their scrumptious meal.

"Let's stop at a tea shop I know," Inanna said on a spurt of inspiration. "You'll love the croissants and shortbread there."

Gabriel smiled in agreement and Benji nodded enthusiastically.

This was the bestest day for him too, Benji thought. All was right in the world when Mommy and Daddy were together with him. He wondered how soon he could ask for a pet chinchilla, like the ones he saw on National Geographic. And better yet, whether he could have a baby brother or sister by next Christmas.

Before long, they arrived at "Dark Dreams." It was already half past nine, but the shop was lit from within by flickering light from antique lamps that bathed every corner with a soft, cheery glow.

Inanna opened the door with a jingle and called, "Hello? Are you open to visitors? I have a couple of introductions I'd like to make."

A few moments later, Mama Bear appeared from behind the curtain of beads, took one look at Inanna and added more wrinkles to her round, merry face with a beaming smile.

"Well, come on in, my dear," she welcomed as she ushered the three of them inside and seated them at the same table she always sat with Inanna at. "I just received a new tea from India I'm dying to try out, and I've baked a fresh batch of scones. You're just in time to share them with me."

Inanna grinned so brightly Mama Bear seemed momentarily stunned, having never seen such joy on the young woman's face before.

"These are my guys," Inanna said, gesturing to Gabriel and Benji, who nodded a greeting and waved in turn. "My... husband and son."

Mama Bear dropped the oven mitts she was holding and stared at the three guests incomprehensibly.

For a worrisome second, Inanna thought she was unwell, the way the old lady seemed to have stopped breathing.

Gabriel retrieved the oven mitts form the floor and handed them to their host, their fingers brushing briefly in the process.

With a gasp, Mama Bear whirled into motion again, clucking at her own clumsiness.

"Goodness me, I must be having a senior moment," she exclaimed, fluttering her hands at her face, "it's not every day a girl receives such handsome gentleman callers. You sit tight while I get a tray."

The smile on the old woman's face did not quite match her lighthearted words, for the smile was more of a line stretched across her lips, which were forcibly turned up at the corners.

Something was wrong.

"I'll lend a hand," Inanna volunteered and got up to do just that.

That Mama Bear seemed too preoccupied to fuss at her to sit back down was very telling. Inanna followed the shop owner into the back room beyond the beaded curtains.

"I do apologize that I brought guests so late," she said when they were out of hearing range. "If you are busy, we—"

"No, no, I'm so happy you came to visit with me, dear," Mama Bear interrupted, shaking her head. "I'm just so happy..." she paused to take a breath and swallow, "just so happy you brought your menfolk too."

Inanna relaxed a little. Even though she didn't know how to describe her relationship with the old lady, Inanna cared for her deeply.

Some of the Chosen and even the Queen herself could be counted as friends, comrades, but Inanna had no family. She'd never met her mother, had not a shred of memory to keep alive in her heart and mind.

And she'd lost her father a very long time ago. She didn't even know whether he was dead or alive. Surely if he lived he would have found a way to let her know? Surely he would not have left her alone unless he had no other choice?

Inanna had been alone for too many lifetimes. Mama Bear was a near stranger, whose name she did not even know and had never bothered to ask, so wary was she of forming attachments. But for all that, she seemed like family.

"It only happened recently," Inanna felt the inexplicable need to explain. "Else I would have brought them here sooner."

Mama Bear busied herself with making the tea and arranging the scones on an antique silver serving tray.

With her back turned towards Inanna, she said, "I am glad to meet them. You have extremely good taste in the masculine variety."

Inanna wasn't very helpful at the moment despite her offer. She simply stood and took in her surroundings, a veritable treasure trove of wares and trinkets from ancient worlds.

Every shelf, cupboard, nook and cranny in the storage room was stuffed with fascinating objects and artwork. Because it was filled to the brim, the room seemed small at first glance, but she saw that it was actually large enough for a fully functional kitchen with a decent amount of counter space, double wall-mounted ovens, an induction stovetop and a small breakfast nook with bench seating in a corner.

A door was slightly ajar in the rear of the room, and the light within exposed a full-size bed piled with hand-made pillows and throws.

Inanna realized belatedly that she had all but invaded her host's private sanctuary, but Mama Bear did not seem to mind.

"Tell me, child, is it a love match? You could barely take your eyes off your swain," Mama Bear teased while she gingerly filled a pretty dish with lumps of fine sugar.

Inanna borrowed a stool from the kitchen counter and gave in to the overwhelming need to *talk* with someone.

So much had happened, and so fast. She felt so many beautiful, frightening, momentous emotions she could burst. The words just seemed to pour out of their own volition.

"I love them both very much," she confirmed readily. "Benji has always been my little angel, and Gabriel… Gabriel is my heart, which I never realized I had lost until I found him."

Mama Bear looked at her for a long moment, assessing her face as she spoke. Apparently satisfied with what she saw there, the old lady smiled with genuine warmth this time.

"He looks like a very good man, your Gabriel. If you've lived as long as I have, you have an instinct for these things, so trust me in this, my dear. You have a keeper."

"I know," Inanna agreed. "I intend to keep him for the rest of eternity."

"And so gorgeous to boot!" Mama Bear hooted, then covered her mouth to stifle a titter. "Goodness, but that man is fine. I almost asked him to stand up again so I could get a better look at him."

Inanna grinned wide like the Cheshire cat who got the cream. "Amen. And believe me the back of him is just as magnificent as the front of him. What's more, he's not just pretty looks, he's got all the right moves."

Mama Bear put a hand on her ample bosom as if all the talk had given her girlish palpitations. "Those are the best, aren't they? Oh, when I was a young girl in the first bloom of youth..." her expression took on a wistful sheen and made her appear decades younger, at least at heart.

But then her face suddenly became shuttered, as if a particular painful memory assailed her. It was but a brief flicker on her otherwise serene, cheerful countenance, and Inanna would have missed it had she not been watching the woman closely.

Mama Bear caught herself and handed Inanna the serving tray.

"You must bring your menfolk around more often," she invited with a smile. "An old woman like me doesn't get the opportunity to admire two fine specimens of masculine splendor such as those very often. It does the spirit good to be exposed to youth and beauty at my age."

Inanna promised to do just that and helped her host carry out the tea tray.

An hour later, the threesome were on their way back to Inanna's apartment. Conversation had been lighthearted and free flowing. It had been the perfect way to end a perfect day.

"Did you like Mama Bear?" Inanna asked Benji, who walked beside her, carefully toting a paper bag with the remaining three scones from the entire batch the shop owner had made.

"She's the bestest," Benji proclaimed immediately, which was the highest honorific he bestowed on anyone.

"But why do you call her Mama Bear? She doesn't look like one at all."

Inanna was amused by this bit of decisive commentary. "Really? You don't think she's the perfect epitome of an elderly, motherly, huggable looking teddy bear?"

"What's epit-me?" Benji asked, brow scrunched slightly in concentration.

"Epitome means example," Gabriel said from the boy's other side.

Benji nodded sagely, then promptly shook his head. "No, I don't think so. She looks more like Arwen from *Lord of the Rings*, except a lot prettier."

Both adults stopped in their tracks, both looking down at Benji as if he'd suddenly grown two heads. Maybe some horns too.

"Benji," Gabriel said with a particular patience, the sort that started all his lectures about Benji's imagination getting away with him, "the nice lady has blonde-gray hair, round, rosy cheeks and a short, portly figure. Exactly what part of that description fits Arwen the princess elf from *Lord of the Rings*?"

It was now Benji's turn to look with sheer astonishment at the two adults. What were they talking about?

"But Daddy, she has long black hair, is as tall as Mommy and has the same..." he fished about for the right word and landed upon, "figure too," emulating what Gabriel had said earlier.

Gabriel and Inanna exchanged a long glance and shook their heads, changing the topic to something less contentious. The lively imagination of a five-year-old never ceased to amaze them.

*** *** *** ***

Anastasia smoothed index and middle fingers together down the long, reflective blade of the combat knife in her grasp and went over last night's events and what they learned in her head.

The fight clubs might have a Pure sponsor in addition to vampires and humans.

She'd caught up with Maximus as they reentered the City from upstate New York. The vampire entourage around the small robed figure who had presided over the death match they'd witnessed dispersed into dark alleys and streets upon crossing city lines. Maximus tracked what appeared to be the vampire right-hand of the robed figure, Simca another henchman, and Ana took the female orchestrator herself.

Ana finally ceased pursuit when the female entered a warehouse-cum-club of some sort, one that was obviously expecting her, since the armed guards at the door she entered parted immediately to let her pass.

The sun was already throbbing in the morning skies, making Ana feel like she'd overdosed on morphine. She kept herself upright and awake by sheer force of will. Enough to memorize the exact location of the unmarked building.

The female, however, did not seem to feel any effects, her pace brisk and purposeful. So it was unlikely she was a Dark One, though not impossible.

The way she moved was worthy of note. It was as if she floated, so graceful and effortless she seemed to bridge distances. Only Dark and Pure ones had that gait: it was the way they moved when they purposely limited themselves to appear more human.

That was a clue, as well as her bright white aura, far more intense than any human.

Maximus had learned nothing worthy of note from his surveillance, nor had Simca when he downloaded the feline's memory banks. (They shared a special connection whereby the man could see and feel in his mind's eye everything the animal saw and felt.)

Nothing new except that the two vampire henchmen were warrior-class from ancient noble families, the involvement of which was something they had suspected since the beginning.

The combination of half a dozen warrior-class vampires with a small Pure female, if that was indeed the case, was an uncommon pairing.

Vampire males were notoriously difficult to control in large groups. Their instinct was to hunt and kill and satisfy their baser urges with all expediency. Throw in a Pure female who was half their size, whose blood was ten times more appealing than the average human female, and the mix could turn ugly in an instant.

True, warrior-class vampires were more disciplined by training, but it took an extremely strong leader to keep them in line. The female must have some awesome powers to restrain her escorts so easily. Else, someone else was doing the restraining for her.

They could have been mindless slaves for all the notice she gave them.

Ana took up a rag and began polishing the borrowed blade until it shone with a blinding luster.

A Pure One thrown into the mix of vampires and humans organizing the fight clubs was both alarming as well as expected.

As soon as they'd reported back to Jade, Seth Tremaine proposed alerting the Shield and having the Dozen find out what they could. Their Queen did not immediately agree, which surprised Ana, for she usually took the Consul's suggestions as given. In fact, the Queen made it clear, though said implicitly, that she wanted this information to be kept amongst the four of them, at most to be shared with the rest of the Chosen. Their Pure allies, however, were not to be notified at this time.

The Consul had said nothing after that, his expression neutral and blank.

Ana lightly ran her thumb along the knife's edge, barely touching at all, but the sharp blade produced a thin red line where it sliced through her skin. Almost instantly, the small cut healed, and Ana barely noticed it as she admired the beautiful weapon.

Deadly. Unyielding.

Rather like a certain fighter she knew.

Perhaps she would do some digging on her own. Jade had not disallowed it. And she knew just the human to tap for information.

*** *** *** ***

After tucking Benji in bed way past his bedtime, Inanna reluctantly left her menfolk to check in at the Cove.

Though the Chosen kept their own abodes apart from their base, it was more home to them than anywhere else.

That had changed for Inanna. Her home now was wherever Benji and Gabriel were.

When she entered the main atrium, one of the Sentries, Maximus' well-trained battalion who protected the Cove, informed her that the Queen was resting, not to be disturbed.

Strange, that.

Inanna wondered when Jade had started to sleep at night rather than during the day. It must have something to do with the Queen's Blood Slave, who was a powerfully ancient Pure One.

Inanna's own biological clock was changing as well, and she wondered whether it was because she'd recently fed her fill of her Blooded Mate, who was a vampire with a Pure soul potentially on the cusp of an Awakening.

Did that mean he was more Pure than Dark?

A shiver of alarm traveled down her spine at the possibility that threatened her Bond with Gabriel.

She inquired another Sentry for the whereabouts of Simone Lafayette and caught the Keeper emerging from her chambers looking fatigued, though she should have been sleeping all day.

"Simone, a word," Inanna said quietly, without preamble.

The Chosen picked up immediately on the urgency in her tone and nodded in reply.

"Shall we convene in the library?" Inanna asked, and Simone gestured for her to lead the way.

Once they were enclosed in privacy behind the thick double-doors, Inanna got straight to the point.

"I need your help in a personal matter," she began, then paused briefly to reconsider.

Simone was one of the handful of suspects in Devlin's hunt for the female vampire who had almost killed Gabriel. She was an unlikely candidate given her station as a Royal Scholar, not a warrior, but there was still a possibility.

After all, Simone had held her own in the battle against the Creature's horde when the Chosen had aided their Pure allies a few months ago.

On the other hand, there was no one else Inanna knew who could help her search through thousands of years of Dark Ones' histories and lore to find what she was looking for, if it existed at all. And time was of the essence.

She decided to take a risk.

"Do you know of any examples in our history where a Dark One Mated with a Pure One?"

At the Keeper's sharp inhalation, Inanna knew that even the question itself was shocking, bordering on blasphemous. Nevertheless, she pressed on. She had too much to lose not to go all in.

"What were the consequences? Why are our Laws so unyielding in this matter? Is it to protect the couple from disaster or is it—"

"It is to protect everyone else from death and destruction," the Keeper interrupted, effectively silencing Inanna from further query.

"Let me show you something," Simone said as she brought Inanna to the center of the rings of concentric ovals where a book encased in gold with gold tipped pages lay open at three feet wide, two feet in length and more than a foot in thickness.

The Ecliptic Scrolls. The Dark Ones' bible, encyclopedia and sacred laws all rolled into one.

Simone deftly turned the delicate pages, so thin they were almost transparent, to a particular chapter and verse toward the middle.

It was a time period shortly before Inanna's birth, during the most dominant era of the Akkadian empire. Although the writing was Sumerian, it was similar enough that Inanna could read the words.

"The only example that I know of was before the Great War," Simone said in a hushed tone, as if speaking too loudly would awaken ghosts long buried. "Some historians attribute the Great War and the Purge of the aftermath to this aberration."

Inanna inwardly flinched at the word "aberration," but she steeled herself and said, "Go on."

"All that was ever written about it is here on this page," Simone pointed to three paragraphs of calligraphy and added, "though the myths and legends around it traveled across generations by word of mouth. Our old often tell this story to young girls and boys as a cautionary tale. A nightmare to be avoided at all cost."

Inanna read silently as Simone stood by and read aloud in the old language:

"In the Third Cycle of our Queen's glorious reign, the Chosen Princess and future Queen, came into her maturity on her twentieth name day. A celebration was held for all to rejoice her beauty, strength and wisdom. As tradition dictates, the Princess must choose a Consort and Protector from among the worthy Dark males, who will eventually earn his place by her side as her Blooded Mate.

During his Training, he will acquire the skills necessary to deserve her trust. He will learn her interests and become expert in them. He will hone his skills as a warrior on fields of valor, both real and procedural. He will become all that she needs in a sexual partner and devote himself, body, mind and soul to her every pleasure.

But when the critical moment arrived, the Princess made a disastrous choice. Instead of her Dark Consort, she chose a Pure Blood Slave, and more shameful, a prisoner of war. Over the years she'd kept him, like an ever-present shadow by her side, polluting her thoughts, confusing her desires. Until one day, she gave into his willful seduction and consummated their union, pledging all of herself in the process. And from this union, death and destruction, chaos and mayhem ensued.

Thus began the Great War."

"Every story has more than one side, like a crystal that captures and reflects different colors of light. Do not take for granted what you think you know, Dark One, for until you hold the entire jewel in your palm, the temptation is to fall prey to illusion and deception."
—*Excerpt from the Lost Chapters of the Ecliptic Scrolls.*

Chapter Sixteen

Inanna took the long way home, driving aimlessly through the City.

What she learned tonight raised more questions than provided answers.

Why was the pairing between a Dark and Pure One disastrous?

What happened to the Princess and her Blooded Mate afterwards?

Could it be inferred that they had actually Mated, for the text did not specifically say so?

What exactly led to the Great War?

Simone had given her more information from what she recalled from oral histories. The union between the Princess and her Pure Mate resulted in offspring.

A boy and a girl. Twins.

The boy had died, causes unknown, and the girl had been lost, never to be found.

The Princess had gone mad with grief and anger, for her lover had betrayed her in the most hideous way. Her mother the Queen waged war against the Pure Ones in retaliation, but ultimately lost.

That was all the Keeper knew. No further answers to all the whys that Inanna wanted to ask but held back, for Simone had seemed distracted and drained, pushed to her limits. But Inanna did learn one shattering truth:

The Princess's Pure Mate had been the leader of the Great Rebellion.

Oh, Papa. Why did you never tell me?

Fragmented pieces of long-forgotten memories began to weave themselves into clear images in Inanna's mind.

Her father's grim mask of heartbreak and anguish whenever she asked about her mother. His pain had been so great it radiated from his body like a physical force, pushing her innocent questions back until they were bottled, buried and consigned to oblivion.

The first onset of her Change.

The horrifying and terrifying realization that she was a stranger and a *monster* to the very people she grew up with and loved. Even worse, that she was a half-breed, an abomination that neither Dark nor Pure Ones would ever accept.

The unconditional love of her father's embrace when she'd run to him, angry, hurt and ashamed.

And there was something else.

An awareness, the shadow of a thought, a tingling that spread like electricity through her consciousness.

There was *someone* else. Someone who made her truth bearable, someone who kept her secret and protected her. Who...

A sharp, stabbing pain almost blinded Inanna's eyes and she swerved to the side of the bridge she had been driving across and slammed on the brakes.

Oxygen seemed to be in short supply as she gulped shuddering breaths, choking on a flood of tears. Gut-wrenching sobs racked her body as she relived the emotions of her long-distant past, though her mind remained ignorant of the actual memories.

Her heart remembered. Her soul remembered.

Alone in her soundproofed vehicle, she released all her pent-up emotions, fears, hopes and desires. Until a voice whispered in the air around her:

Come home, Libbu. *You are always loved. You are never alone.*

Inanna followed the voice, perhaps only in her imagination, but even so it comforted her, calmed her, gave her strength.

Made her feel safe.

When she entered the apartment, out of breath and out of tears, Gabriel met her at the door.

For a moment that was only a heartbeat, yet one that stretched infinitely across time, they regarded each other, frozen with a soul-deep recognition.

They each took a step toward the other, and then she was in his arms, holding on tightly like a castaway to a life raft in a stormy sea.

Gabriel did not speak, did not think. He simply felt with all his heart and being.

He felt her sorrow, pain and fear. Most of all, he felt her deep abiding love for him. It radiated like an inner sun from her every pore. It warmed them both with its uplifting heat. And raised their temperatures with a yearning desire.

How he longed for her.

He lifted her in his arms and took them to their room. Deftly, he undressed them both until she lay vulnerable and exposed beneath him, the windows to her soul wide open as her deep blue eyes penetrated his.

Instinctively, he knew what she wanted from him, what she needed with every fiber of her being.

It was not blood and sex, though his body was hers to command.

She wanted his surrender.

Complete and eternal.

The past no longer mattered. There was only the future. Together.

Gabriel could not pinpoint when he knew he loved her. Perhaps it was the first time he heard her laughter as she fell in a tangled heap with Benji on the ice rink, bubbling and carefree. Perhaps it was the moment she told him, boldly forthright and unapologetically honest, that she wanted him. Or maybe it was the welcome of her body the instant he entered her, as if he was finally home.

Perhaps he had loved her all along.

He gave into love's demands now, gently kissing her tear-stained cheeks, her swollen lips, her quivering chin, as if she was desperately trying to hold things together when her world had just been shattered.

He didn't ask questions, didn't demand answers. He only gave of himself, showed her through painstaking tenderness that she would never be alone. She would always be loved.

Slowly, as if every inch of her that he touched required equal attention, respect and care, he kissed a warm, soothing, arousing trail down the long column of her neck, her collar bone, to her desire-swollen breasts, the small, pink nipples distended into hard little beads. The plump mounds fit perfectly in his calloused palms, and he massaged them gently while his tongue bathed and suckled at the aureoles.

Inanna moaned and arched her spine as passion blazed deliciously throughout her body, chasing away demons from the past. Her mind and heart could hold neither regret, fear nor sorrow when they were full of love for her Blooded Mate.

Gabriel continued his meticulous journey down her torso, kissing each rib, delving his tongue into her shallow navel, his hands holding her hips steady as his mouth closed upon her clitoris.

At the first pressure of his full lips sucking upon the tiny pearl, she began to saw her arms and legs with mindless lust, her hands fisting in the bed sheets, her heels trying vainly to gain purchase. She settled with wrapping her legs around his shoulders, holding his head prisoner against the juncture of her thighs.

Gabriel had no plans to escape, however. He continued to hold her hips down while he bathed her swollen nubbin with saliva, interspersing the deep sucks and draws with licks and flicks.

Inanna's orgasm hit her hard and painfully, the pleasure muted by the emptiness of her core, her contracting muscles drawing on nothing, her womb parched for his seed. She now thrashed in earnest, desperate for his completion of her, clawing to feel the strength of him inside her.

Gabriel answered her silent plea by covering her still shaking body with his much heavier one, trapping her beneath him, stilling her quakes with his soothing heat.

Slowly, inexorably, he pushed his hardness inch by voluptuous inch inside of her.

All sensation focused on their joining. All the blood, energy and nerve endings in their bodies coalesced in the place where his steel plundered her silk, the friction and pressure so exquisite, so consuming, they were enslaved to feeling. The world could have imploded around them and they would not have noticed.

They knew only of the force and depth of his possession. The pressure and pull of her claiming.

When the penetration was full and complete, the most intimate part of him coming flush against the most intimate part of her deep inside, an organism the likes of which Inanna had never experienced started a chain reaction from her swollen core to her clitoris, through her vaginal canal, her limbs, her torso, to explode in blinding bursts throughout her body until even the tips of her eyelashes felt singed.

Gabriel groaned deeply as her inner muscles tightly fisted and pumped and squeezed his tortured cock, drawing upon him with enough pressure to make stars flash behind his eyelids. The rush of his seed from his scrotum to his staff, to gush through the mouth at the tumescent crown, brought delayed but satisfying relief to them both.

When the last shivers ebbed out, and their hearts returned to a more normal cadence, Gabriel rolled them to their sides, keeping himself inside her as if he intuitively knew that she needed the connection and was bereft without it.

She rested her head on one of her arms, the other curled around his waist, her hand absently kneading the muscles of his backside. Her leg hitched over his thigh, her foot hooked around his calf.

As if she couldn't stop touching him, making up for lost time, her hand wandered around to his hip, one finger tracing the jut of his hipbone, the tight band of muscle directly above it, and inwards across his lower abdomen toward the base of his penis.

There her hand stayed, her thumb brushing back and forth, back and forth along the root of his sex, plumping absent-mindedly the vein that throbbed against his hyper-sensitive skin.

I have not had enough of you, those wayward fingers seemed to say. *I will never have enough of you.*

Tenderly, he smoothed a few tangled golden strands from her cheeks so that he could gaze unobstructed into her dark blue eyes.

"Better?" he asked, a small knowing smile on his lips.

Shyly, she smiled in return and nodded.

"Will you tell me what's wrong?" he inquired softly. It was not a demand, not even a request. Simply a suggestion, to do with as she chose.

She opened the floodgates and shared all of herself. Her origin, her birth, her history. She entrusted everything to him.

Hours later, as the first rays of dawn peeked through their bedroom curtains, Inanna's words finally slowed their procession through her lips, having unburdened all of her truths, save one.

She was warming up to that last piece, but she would not hide from him. There would be no secrets between them.

"A vampire's venom is different from person to person," she explained, now lying bonelessly on his chest, still holding him captive inside her.

Their conversation, or rather her monologue, had been interspersed with lovemaking, sometimes slow and languorous, other times needy and ravenous. Always intense, always consuming.

"It depends on the vampire's chemistry, the subject's chemistry and how they combine. In most situations, the venom is like a tranquilizer, numbing the subject from fear, pain and preventing mobility. Other times, it could be an aphrodisiac, or the opposite, an injection of debilitating agony."

Gabriel nodded. He could attest to both extremes.

"When a subject Consents or forms a Blood Contract," Inanna continued, her fingers idly taking a stroll down the smooth, satiny skin of her Mate's side, "the feeding is painless, usually enjoyable for the subject. Otherwise, it can be a form of punishment or torture."

"You collected Blood Contracts before me," Gabriel stated rather than asked, having deduced that much.

"Yes," she answered, her fingers stilling.

Despite the instinct to avoid, she made herself raise her eyes and look directly into his. "I am known as the Angel of Death among my Kind. My chosen role is to help lost souls find their peace, either to be reborn with a second chance or to be taken out of the cycle of life."

Gabriel's gaze probed hers for long, solemn moments, moments in which Inanna did not blink nor breathe.

"Olivia was one of your Contracts, wasn't she." Another statement, not a question.

"Yes."

Inanna said nothing to explain herself.

If he blamed her for hastening his wife's death, even if it was a few minutes or at most hours, she would accept the blame without rationalization.

She owed it to him, whatever retribution he demanded of her for cheating him of those precious moments. If it had been Gabriel on death's door and someone had opened it to usher him through, she would have hunted the person down after she jumped through the door herself to bring him back.

Finally, he sighed and raised a hand to cup her cheek, his thumb smoothing over her skin.

"It must have been hard for you," he said softly, "to witness so much suffering and hopelessness."

Inanna gasped at his innate understanding and compassion. She had not dared to hope for this much.

"For Olivia, in particular, you invested so much of yourself, trying to resuscitate a woman who was already dead inside," he continued in that low, husky baritone, deepened with emotion. "At times the despair must have threatened to strangle your hope, snuff out your joy. It is a slow death to watch someone you care for wither away. It hurts to know that she would rather embrace nothingness rather than life with you."

She knew that he now spoke for both of them. It was all true, every word. And she knew that he'd suffered far more than she in this instance.

His thumb continued to stroke her cheek, his eyes full of love and a bittersweet grief. "You helped her find peace in the end," he said, "eased her from a world of pain. She must have been grateful to have you beside her in the last moments, grateful to have known you and been loved by you."

Tears welled unbidden in Inanna's eyes.

She knew that he wasn't only speaking of Olivia any more.

There was something else, frustrating her to no end with its elusiveness, like trying to capture tendrils of smoke in her hands.

But if not specific memories, *feelings* overwhelmed her, splintered her apart.

Desperate and lost, she moved upon him, taking his mouth with hers, plunging her tongue deep inside as her hips began to undulate against his, her inner muscles squeezing his sex tightly, possessively, almost savagely.

He met her thrust for thrust as she rode him hard and deep, as if she wanted to absorb him into herself, consume him whole within her inferno.

All the while she plundered his mouth, staking ownership, surrendering herself.

And then, as her body seized upon her climax, she pulled away enough to sink her fangs into his throat, his blood filling her mouth at the same moment his semen flooded her womb.

Exhausted and deeply content, Inanna lay still on top of his chest, her face turned into the crook of his neck. She licked the bite wound closed and murmured before slumber overtook her in a muffled litany, more fervent than a prayer, "I love you… I love you… I love you…"

She did not hear his answering vow, "And I, you, *Libbu* mine."

*** *** *** ***

The vampire turned round and round in her head, like Boading balls rotating methodically in a zen master's palm, the interesting new things she had learned, as well as the fascinating secrets she suspected.

What to do with all this tantalizing information?

The Pure One had delivered a message that the human fighter, ex-military, likely Navy Seal, she had bet on to replace Gabriel D'Angelo as the spectators' favorite could no longer be used.

They had no concrete evidence, but there were hints of his duplicity.

Too many coincidences not to proceed with caution. So they set up a death match between him and the other potential infiltrator, a Brazilian jujitsu mixed-martial artist, to take each other out and save them the trouble.

The Seal must have nine lives, for he not only won the death match but survived a bloody execution by four of the creature's finest vampire assassins. He was the rat within their network then, in all likelihood.

As with the Salem witch trials toward the end of the seventeenth century, if the accused died, he was probably innocent. If he lived, however, well... he was most certainly guilty to the depth of his eternal soul.

Pity he got away. She could have used the entertainment value of torturing, bleeding, and killing him by slow, excruciating degrees. The consolation was that either way, they'd rid themselves of the mole they suspected within their ranks.

"You have the look of one who is thinking much too hard," a languorous voice floated her way through the darkness. "Let the game play out of its own accord. We have already set the pieces in motion."

The vampire narrowed her red-centered eyes, seeing into the blackness that surrounded her.

The creature sat idly at a small round table for two, sipping wine and fingering the chess pieces that were laid out on a marble board before it, positioned as if a match was already in progress.

Today, it was in its usual form, looking both female and male, and neither at the same time. But even in this ambivalent state, the vampire knew that it was ten times more beautiful than herself.

It was more than just exquisite features arranged together on a flawless form. There was an aura of irresistible attraction all around the creature. Beauty was in the eye of the beholder, and everyone had their own opinion, yet the vampire knew that it was beautiful to all who beheld it.

Momentarily distracted from her plotting, she regarded the creature thoughtfully, perhaps for the first time with a clear mind.

"Who are you?" she asked.

"Whoever you want me to be," was its usual answer, the same one it gave the first time they had met and aligned their paths.

"Who are you really?" she insisted this time, not satisfied with the brushoff.

There were times in their "partnership" that she felt a powerful mistrust of it, for she never knew what it wanted, what its motives were. But then the pleasures it gave her trumped her misgivings. And besides, she told herself she didn't really care as long as it furthered her own goals.

But she was suddenly curious. Soon she would be betting everything on the line. There would be no turning back.

Failure meant death.

Her death.

What about the creature? What was its skin in the game? What did it have to lose when all was said and done?

The creature sighed deep and long, as if trying to find patience with a slow-witted child.

"An abomination," it finally answered. "Neither one nor the other. Neither here nor there. A freak of nature that wouldn't even be accepted in the Circus. A mutation in the gene pool that hails the end of civilization."

The vampire frowned slightly. It spoke in riddles that made no sense.

"Are you vampire?"

"Yes."

Just as she inhaled a breath at finally getting somewhere, it said after a pause, "And no."

Frustration was building in an ugly black tide within her. "Are you a Pure One then?"

"No."

Another pause. "And yes."

Arrghhh! She wanted to scream, even more so that the creature seemed to treat everything like a game, replying in that sing-songy voice that was neither feminine nor masculine, and yet both at the same time.

"You can't be human," she said through gritted teeth.

The creature seemed to consider this, then replied, "I suppose not. If I ever had any humanity, which I don't know that I ever did, I lost it a long, long time ago."

"Show me your true face," she demanded, advancing upon the creature until she stood between its open thighs, bearing down upon it with hands fisted at her sides.

Unconcerned with her irate mood, shrouded in violence, it tilted its head elegantly to one side and said, "I am not sure I have one. Isn't it better to be someone else? Anyone else?"

The vampire forcefully gripped its beautiful face, her nails digging into its cheeks. "Then show me Jade Cicada, my abomination. I want to fuck her until she bleeds. This is your payment to me for services rendered. Within the week you will get the result you desire."

The creature smiled ruefully as its visage changed into that of the Dark Queen.

"Will I?" it whispered as the vampire descended upon it.

*** *** *** ***

"When will I go back to school?" Benji inquired, squeezed in between Inanna and Gabriel in the Aventador. "I miss my friends."

Inanna made a mental note to invest in a larger vehicle, at least a mid-size sedan.

Clearly, her lifestyle needed to change with a five-year-old in tow. At least the ride had almost opaque black-tinted windows, so that law enforcement wouldn't see enough to pull them over for child endangerment.

Not that most cops would expect to see a child riding shotgun in the Lamborghini in the first place.

"You're taking a long winter break," Gabriel said from the passenger side. "You've just discovered that your parents are vampires and made new friends with elves. Isn't that awesome? We're on our way to see them now."

Benji considered this and came to the same conclusion, but then, "I miss Lamby and Mrs. Sergeyev."

"We should receive your things soon," Inanna said, "and we'll be sure to pay a visit to your friend."

For the time being mollified, Benji requested the radio to be turned to NPR and sat back to enjoy the ride, once in a while asking Inanna what the various buttons on the control panel did.

After all, what male could resist such a fabulous machine?

Inanna had received a text early in the morning from Aella that said she had some new information to share about the private conversation they had.

When they arrived at the Pure Ones' temporary abode in Morningside Heights, the women would video conference with Eveline Marceau, the Pure Ones' Seer and makeshift Scribe.

They had yet to find a replacement for the comrade they had lost in the recent struggle with an anonymous villain.

Cloud Drako was planning to take the boys to the enormous gym in the basement of the building, which also contained an activity room that was perfect for combat training.

Inanna and Gabriel had talked about it earlier, and it made sense for Gabriel to hone his skills as a warrior as soon as possible, given the environment they lived in. He already had the foundation, a formidable fighter even in his human life, but he would need to relearn the moves using an upgraded body, so to speak, as well as acquire new ones to win against much stronger foes, some of whom had trained for centuries, even millennia.

Few warriors were as proficient a trainer as the Valiant, with the exception of Maximus and Valerius.

Sophia met Inanna and company at the door and immediately took Inanna by the arm, leading her to one of the bedrooms the Pure Ones were using as an office.

"Eveline is already on video," Sophia said after brief greetings, "you'll want to speak to her directly."

Introductions were made while Inanna settled into a leather swivel chair around a large round table that seated up to eight.

Sophia sat in another one, and Aella stood behind her with arms crossed. The only other furnishing in the room was a built-in desk that ran across three out of four walls, one of which was sheer glass, overlooking the courtyard below. On top of the desk were various equipment and gadgets, weapons and electronics.

In the middle of the round table was a tripod of monitors placed at sixty degree angles to each other.

One showed live surveillance footage of the building they resided in, as well as the surrounding area within a half kilometer radius. A second displayed various codes of information Inanna could not decipher. And in the third screen a petite, auburn-haired, green-eyed woman stared through the camera as if looking directly at them.

"Have you had the opportunity to check with your own historian?" Eveline asked after the preliminaries were complete.

"I have," Inanna confirmed. "Simone Lafayette, our Keeper, said that the only example in our records was from the height of the Akkadian empire. The Dark Princess chose to Mate with her Blood Slave, who was a Pure One."

Eveline nodded. "That is the same example I found in the Zodiac Scrolls. The only example as well."

The Seer frowned before continuing. "But our records do not mention a Mating. There was no official account of the event in the Scrolls, in fact. I had to piece together what I read about significant figures in the Great War and unofficial, often not completely reliable histories that are more myths than truths."

"But I am relatively confident that such a union took place, at least in terms of the exchange between a Blood Slave and his mistress."

Here the Seer spoke with circumspection. Pure Ones did not take the exchange of bodily fluids, be it blood or sex, lightly. Their Cardinal Rule forbade intercourse with anyone but their destined mate. To be a Blood Slave was the ultimate shame and humiliation, for it went against everything the race valued, in addition to being stripped of freedom.

"Go on," Inanna urged quietly, knowing full well that they were speaking of her father and mother.

"The official history only describes how a Champion who used to be a Blood Slave rose to prominence as leader of the Rebellion. He was an example for all other Pure Ones, slave, servant and free. Stories from unofficial sources diverge from there. Some tell of how the Dark Princess fell in love with him and wanted him for her own, that they were not simply Mistress and Slave. Others tell of how he purposely seduced the Princess so that he could learn the Dark Ones' secrets and better prepare for the ensuing rebellion."

Eveline paused and seemed to stare directly into Inanna's eyes, piercing her with knowledge and insight. "And some stories say that the union resulted in issue. Twins."

Inanna looked away, her heart beginning to pound.

"A girl and a boy," Eveline went on. "I could find no mention of the boy anywhere, so I assume he had died or perhaps your histories talk of him?"

"No," Inanna whispered, "it seems he had perished, perhaps at birth."

"The daughter of the Leader of the Rebellion is mentioned at length, though not by name, only that she was well loved among the Pure Ones and adored by her father. It did not read as if anyone suspected she might have a vampire mother, that, in fact, she was the offspring from that union."

Inanna could barely breathe. She looked anywhere but at the screen, trying to hide the tears that threatened behind her eyelids.

"I admit I had to make some assumptions and leaps in judgment. Nothing was spelled out clearly," the Seer continued. "The stories were extremely vague about the Leader's time as a Blood Slave, for good reason. That his union with the Princess had issue was almost blasphemy to consider much less write down. Those stories were mainly gathered from personal diaries and private speculation. But many notable Pure scribes recorded the fact that he had a daughter, though the girl's mother is never mentioned, which in of itself is an anomaly given our laws. There is no record of his Mating with a Pure female. No record of her death, for that would be the only way he could have a daughter and no Mate."

"But perhaps because of people's respect and reverence for him, no one questioned the specifics, and he never volunteered the information. Then, rather abruptly, all records ended about the Leader and his daughter at the time of the Great Siege. No record of whether they lived or died."

Eveline paused long enough for Inanna to get a hold of herself and look back at the screen, eyes dry, face an expressionless mask.

"I'm sorry I couldn't find more," the Seer said, "this example does not point to anything conclusive about the Mating between a Pure One and a Dark One. I wouldn't have found even this much had it not been for our previous Scribe..." Eveline trailed off as if a particular painful memory assailed her.

She took a deep breath and went on, "Orion was Mesopotamian. He was born hundreds of years after the Great War but his accounts were the most timely, and likely the most accurate. Even so, his records say nothing about a Mating, only a union that possibly produced offspring. We can't be sure the Leader lived because he did not love his Mistress and therefore did not suffer the Decline, or because the union between a Pure and Dark one is valid and sustaining."

Inanna knew that Eveline referred to the "curse of the Pure Ones," as her Kind called it, whereby if one gave oneself completely and in love to another during intercourse, and the other did not reciprocate, the Pure One would die a slow, excruciating death in thirty days.

Inanna nodded numbly, trying to maintain attention despite the deafening white noise in her ears.

"Ms. Chastain."

Inanna started at her name, focusing once more on the screen.

"Legend has it that the child of the Leader is the Light-Bringer. Someone who will appear when the world is in turmoil. This person will help us distinguish right and wrong and find the way to the truth. It is written thusly in the Zodiac Prophesies."

The Eveline in the screen stared straight into Inanna's eyes, unblinking, as if willing the significance of her message to sink in.

"In one of the private journals I found, a noblewoman in the Roman era was recording oral fairytales for her children. The name Inanna came up, just in this one instance, as the daughter of the Leader."

At this point, Inanna had forgotten how to breathe. She had a feeling the Pure Ones already knew her ancient name. Just as the Chosen knew theirs.

Abruptly, Eveline addressed Aella and Sophia, who had not said a word, "I need a moment with Ms. Chastain privately."

Without question, though Sophia cast Inanna a lingering glance, the two females exited the room, closing the door with a soft click.

Inanna's heart was on its way to pounding out of her chest. She did not ask the Seer to continue. She had no voice to do so.

"You should know that when I cross-referenced the name Inanna in all of our surviving archives, not just the ones held at the Shield, it only appeared one more time," the Seer said, and moved her eyes from the camera to navigate the toolbar on her video device.

A yellowed newsprint came up on the screen. The title indicated an archeological find during an expedition to Japan in 1853. In the sidebar of the article, there were faded pictures of some of the oriental treasures, including a sleek porcelain vase that had no ornamentation save two lines of calligraphy.

Inanna did not need the Seer to zoom in the image to see clearly what was written. Her own acute vision magnified and focused the words.

It was not Kanji, the traditional Japanese characters that were Chinese in origin. Instead, it was a stream of block-like symbols that she knew only too well.

In ancient Akkadian the words read:

"Inanna, my child. Wait for me. I shall find you, I promise. You are ever in my thoughts and prayers. —Papa."

"Seek the light, Dark One, when chaos and confusion obscure the truth. Keep faith, Dark One, against the tribulations that will raise your doubt. Be true, Dark One, to the one you love most in your heart. Even if the world falls apart around you, you will still stand tall."
—Excerpt from the Lost Chapters of the Ecliptic Scrolls.

Chapter Seventeen

He's alive, he's alive, he's alive!

That was the only thought racing in a never-ending circle in Inanna's mind. She had not dared to hope, but she had always *known* that her father was still in this world.

True, the newspaper dated back to the eighteen hundreds, and the archeological finds must have dated even further in time. But at her cursory glance, the artifacts in the pictures were probably from the fifteenth to seventeenth centuries, during the Sengoku period. That meant that her father had not only survived the Great War, but was alive at least until five hundred years ago.

He must still be alive somewhere in the world.

She refused to believe otherwise. And besides, he had promised to find her. Her papa never reneged on promises.

"Inanna," the Seer said, "the Sumerian Goddess of sexual love, fertility and warfare. Not a common name."

Inanna broke free of her inner turmoil and refocused on the Pure One. Meanwhile, the door opened again to admit Aella and Sophia.

"You are the daughter described in our histories, are you not?" it was Aella who asked the question.

"Are you really the Light-Bringer?" Sophia whispered, awe in her voice. "I always knew you had a Pure soul." The young Queen glanced triumphantly at her personal guard as if to say "I told you so."

"You and Gabriel are proof that Dark Ones can also have Pure souls," Sophia said more excitedly. "The two are not mutually exclusive as we always thought. Maybe your love will win in the end after all, like the Leader and his Princess. I like that version of the story best."

Inanna looked around her at the Pure females.

She was reminded when she was with them what it was like so very long ago when she lived with her father in the Pure Ones' Fort.

She had been well known by all the villagers, good friends with many. She was reminded that she never felt like she belonged even after she turned to the vampire side because of her biology. Among the Chosen of the Dark Queen's court, she was... professional. Each one of them seemed to hold their own counsel, but she had thought that it was vampires' nature to be aloof and secretive. Now she knew that, in her own case, it was because she was never truly one of them.

"There is much to discuss," Aella cut in. "We cannot do it here. I propose that you come with us back to the Shield where we can talk through the implications at length. We would all benefit from the input of the rest of the Dozen."

"And of course you must bring your Mate and son," Sophia invited. "Since we're unveiling all these lovely discoveries, I should let you know that I sense a Pure soul in Benji as well."

Inanna blinked at that.

Perhaps she had become immune to surprises over the past few days. Hell, it could have been the past few minutes. She no longer even felt winded when someone punched her in the metaphorical gut like that.

But it did take her a while to find her voice.

Finally, she said, "I need to discuss this with Gabriel and Benji. Gabriel, especially, has had so much to absorb in such a short period of time. But I will do it soon. I also need to gain a private audience with my Queen."

She paused. Perhaps Jade Cicada was no longer her Queen. Did all this mean that Sophia was her rightful Queen? Did one get to choose the side she wanted to be on? Why did one have to choose a side at all?

"I have not yet decided what to tell her, a subset of the truth or the whole of it. Give me some time," Inanna requested. "I promise you my answer by the end of the week."

*** *** *** ***

The creature decided, for a change, to bask in the sun this fine winter day.

It had filled itself on Pure blood and was feeling almost perky as it strode down an alley in the Eastern European hoods of Brooklyn.

It wore one of its favorite human disguises today, that of a young man in his prime.

A nonprescription pair of Rayban glasses perched on his high-bridged nose, giving him an intellectual air. Completing his effortless high class look were a Calvin-Klein French cuff shirt with rhinestone cufflinks, overlaid with a Chanel mohair sweater, Armani slim-fitted pants and socks, Ferragamo alligator shoes and a long Armani overcoat that was tailored to emphasize his wide shoulders and lean figure.

An ironic smile tipped the corner of the young man's face.

What a ruse.

What a perfect deception he was having on everyone around him who could not walk by without gawking at his elegance and beauty, as if he were a foreign prince or a world-renowned supermodel stepping out of the pages of a fashion magazine.

If only they knew just how low he was. How dirty, rotten, and savage. Even cockroaches had a leg up on him.

The young man stopped in front of a quaint little shop squeezed in between two seemingly towering townhouses. The name "Dark Dreams" was interesting enough to make him pause, and the tantalizing aroma within of freshly brewed spicy tea and sweet breads baking in the oven invited him to stay.

With a jingle, he opened the shop door and entered, though he did not otherwise announce his arrival. Instead he took time to look around the shop, which had much more space inside than the exterior portended.

He was fascinated by all the little treasures displayed on the shelves that lined every wall in the square room. He did not touch any, only perusing leisurely with his eyes.

Half an hour might have gone by and he would not have noticed, so entranced was he by the dazzling and eclectic collection.

"May I help you, young man?" a warm, feminine voice with a nondescript accent came from behind him.

The young man turned to face a short, plump, elderly woman with gray-blonde hair twisted in a bun behind her head, reading spectacles hanging loosely around her neck, held by a chain. She was smiling benignly yet curiously at him while wiping her ruddy hands on an apron tied at her waist.

"I don't suppose you serve the tea and sweet breads I smelt while passing by the shop?" the young man inquired in a melodious yet deeply masculine voice. "Or sell the lovely trinkets displayed on these shelves?"

She considered him for a long moment, so long that he wondered whether he'd somehow forgotten his disguise and was standing before her in her true form, a naked and ugly abomination.

Finally she answered, "I do not sell the wares you see here, but I would be happy to serve the tea and biscuits. And don't worry about paying," she waved a hand, "It's my treat."

The creature was stunned.

It was to receive something for free?

There was no such thing in the world. A unicorn, dragon and Big Foot might have been standing together before it and it would not have believed in the myth of getting something for nothing.

The young man hesitated indecisively four feet from the entrance of the shop, as if he couldn't convince himself to commit to staying for a short while, just long enough to consume some light refreshments. The old woman came forward and took the sleeve of his expensive overcoat between her fingers.

"Come, come," she coaxed, "I don't bite. You'll be doing me a favor by staying a while and sharing my afternoon tea. It's not every day I get to practice flirting with such a handsome young thing such as yourself. But I must say, my luck's been getting better these past few days."

She chuckled to herself as she ushered him to an antique chair seated at an oval tea table and all but pushed him into it.

"If only I were forty years younger," she said on a sigh, "why, I'd give you a run for your money then, deary." She shot him a wink and a grin. "But as it is, you're quite safe with me."

The creature was charmed, despite itself, by the old woman's chatter. If it ever had a mother—did one have to have a mother or could one be birthed fully-grown like Athena from Zeus' head?—it would have imagined someone like this lady.

"Now you sit tight, my dear," the old woman said as she hustled toward the back of the shop, "I'll bring the tea and biscuits lickity split."

The young man made himself comfortable in his chair and looked around him once more. For some odd reason, his eyes alighted on an intricate wooden comb carved in one piece, the handle in the shape of a crouched leopard, the feline's eyes made of dark purple amethysts.

When the lady came back with a tray laden with victuals, she caught the young man staring unblinkingly at the comb, a glint of something undefinable in his eyes.

"That is one of my favorite treasures," the old woman said as she laid the tray on the table and went to the shelf to retrieve the comb.

The young man's eyes tracked the object as if mesmerized. She gave him the comb to hold, and he took it with unsteady hands.

"It's supposed to be very old," she said as he continued to stare, simmering in silence. "But it's quite strong, so I don't worry that it might break. It is made from African sandalwood and I keep it polished regularly."

As the young man continued to appreciate the comb, now stroking the tines with his graceful, long fingers, the old lady chattered on, "I keep it for its sentimental value. If you're the fanciful sort, the story is that it used to belong to a beautiful Princess, given to her on her birthday by her beloved. He carved it himself, the tale goes, though the amethysts were added later."

The young man's countenance started to quiver, as if he could barely control his facial muscles from contorting. There was a bleakness and despair in his expression that the old woman could not bear to witness. She didn't ask what bothered him. It was none of her business and she didn't want to pry. She just knew that she wanted to make him a little bit better if she could.

She needed it, in fact.

"Keep it, if you like it so much." The words were out of her mouth before she could recall them.

And when the young man raised startled eyes at her unexpected offer, she knew she had made the right decision.

"This must be priceless," the young man finally spoke again. "You don't realize its value."

The old lady smiled, a bit sadly, a bit wistfully. "What's the value of an old comb compared to the joy of its owner for having it? I've had it in my possession for a good bit of time now, and I've appreciated it fully. The older I get, the more I realize that sometimes you have to let things go rather than keep things all to yourself and stay a stingy miser. You feel freer that way."

"And as you can see," she gestured to the veritable treasure trove that surrounded them. "I have too many things holding me back, weighing me down. It's time I let this one go. I'd be pleased as a pickle if you'd take it off my hands."

Wordlessly, the young man accepted her gift and put the comb inside the inner pocket of his wool coat.

"Now let's quench our thirst and make our stomachs a little happier too," the old lady said, pouring her guest and herself two cups of fragrant, steaming tea.

"After all," she said and smiled such a girlish smile at him, he thought she was truly forty years younger in that moment, "I have to tempt you to come visit me some more if I want to see your pretty face again. But honey, you have got to work on your conversation. Maybe the refreshments will loosen your tongue."

The creature in the young man's guise smiled in return, as genuine a smile as it had ever attempted, in any case.

Yes, it would come back. It wouldn't be able to stay away even if it wanted to.

*** *** *** ***

After a light dinner, some movie time with Benji (there was a marathon of Hollywood classics on TNT featuring "There's No Business Like Show Business", one of Benji's favorites), and putting the kiddo to bed after he dozed off in the Second Act, Inanna pulled Gabriel into their room to have a sit-down talk.

Which turned into a lie-down talk. Her favorite kind.

"So you're saying that I can still have an… an Awakening?" he asked, trying to make sense of everything she'd told him. "What happens if I do?"

"You have to survive it first," Inanna answered.

They were snuggled in bed, warm and naked, his pectorals a pillow for her head, one of her arms draped across his taut abdomen, her hand entwined with his at his hip.

"The Awakening is usually triggered by a critical process, where the body and mind that the soul resides in is caught between extremes. Many might call it a 'near-death experience.'"

Gabriel released a long exhale. "Okay. So number one, ensure I survive."

"I have never been through one myself, but now that I know I have a Pure soul too I don't know if I could or would have one."

"What about us?" he asked quietly, "does the dynamic change? Will we still be able to provide Nourishment to each other?"

Inanna shifted and sat up, bracing herself on his chest, covering his lower body with her own, until her sex was flush against his, gliding against it in a hot, wet kiss.

"I don't know the answer to that," she said, staring down into his black-fringed eyes. "All I know is that I will love you whatever the consequences, whatever the future holds. And even if..."

She stuttered on a breath as she swallowed back tears. "And even if we cannot Nourish each other and must survive by other means, I will still love you and only you. This I vow."

Gabriel searched her deep blue eyes and nodded.

It had been seven days since he'd known her. It didn't matter if it was seven hours. He *knew* her. She was his home.

"I want you," she said, her voice turning darker, huskier, her pupils dilating until the blue irises were all but eclipsed.

The reply was past his lips before his mind had even registered it: "Then you shall have me."

He lifted his hips to penetrate her, but she avoided the thrust by moving down his body at the same time.

She trailed scorching kisses everywhere she touched as she meandered her way down his chest, his stomach, to rest at his lower abdomen. She pointed a finger from his navel down the smooth expanse of his abdomen to the coarse thatch from which his manhood swelled, hard and thick and long.

"I want to taste you," she whispered, and her fangs extended from her gums, dripping saliva as lust cranked her hormones into overdrive.

"Here." She took his reddened cock in one hand and suckled the thin stream of pre-cum that seeped out of its fat, satiny crown.

Gabriel gasped and shuddered, unprepared for the sensations she evoked.

This was the first time... every time with her, the first time.

She moved her hand steadily up and down, squeezing rhythmically as she went, suckling slowly but with steady pressure in counter point to her fisting, until his penis was flesh-encased steel and a sweet ache pooled in the sacs below.

As if knowing what he needed, her other hand tended to his scrotum, rolling the balls gently in her palm, in full control of the pleasure she gave, the pace of his climb toward his zenith, the flow of his seed through the most private, intimate parts of him.

"Please," he begged, his breath ragged, one hand tangled in her hair.

But she insisted on having her fill, at her leisure.

She increased the pressure of her sucking, taking more and more of him in her mouth, abrading the hypersensitive skin of his cock with the edges of her fangs.

A shudder racked through him, and she squeezed his scrotum at just the right time with just the right pressure to stall his release, frustrating him, yet prolonging the pleasure and intensity of his orgasm.

If she ever let him achieve it.

Gabriel was beginning to doubt she would.

It seemed like she was settling in at his lap for the duration. Licking, suckling, nipping, squeezing, pulling. While he was on the verge of exploding out of his own flesh for the volcanic heat and pressure she stoked in him.

She took him out of her mouth briefly and he almost wept for the loss of the hot, wet haven.

"Say my name," she commanded. "I want to hear you say my name."

Gabriel parted his lips to fulfill her request.

Yet, the word would not come.

She was not Nana Chastain. That was not her name.

"Say it," she commanded again, skimming her fangs along the large dorsal vein that visibly throbbed against the skin of his penis.

Gabriel gulped on nothing but air. Why wouldn't the word come?

Holding his gaze intensely, she let him watch as she slowly sank her teeth into that throbbing vein, right beneath the glans. Pain and pleasure battled for supremacy in a cocktail of sensations that took Gabriel to the edge.

"Inanna!" he came on a hoarse shout, so violently, his entire body shook as every muscle contracted and released just as his cock shot semen and blood into her mouth, filling her in a tidal wave that could not be contained, the fluids dripping down her chin, her neck.

She sucked him hard and fast, trying to swallow everything, and he came and came, one wave after another, his hand mindlessly pulling her hair as he writhed with such intense pleasure it was almost but not quite pain.

When he was finally wrung out, a glorious soreness settling in his manhood, Inanna released the plump head with an audible pop, licked the puncture wounds closed, then meticulously cleaned the fluids at the glans, and up and down and around the still turgid column of flesh with her nubile tongue.

She finished her ministrations with a kiss against the mouth of his cock and another lingering suck, as if affectionately rewarding a student for a job well done.

But the suck seemed to trigger another obsession, and she moaned as she savored more of him, licking and suckling the most sensitive crown as she would a particularly juicy ripe plum.

He forcefully pulled her up so that her face was next to his, her body draped over him like a human blanket.

"Hurts," he rasped huskily, his eyes barely open. "Give me a few minutes before you do that again."

Inanna smiled a little at his words. "You're willing to give in to me again even if it hurts?"

"Hmm," was his languorous response.

She snuggled close and ran the edges of her fangs against his jugular. "What if I like it to hurt a little?" she whispered darkly. "Would you want me to stop?"

He rolled her onto her back and penetrated her to the hilt with one deep thrust. "Then hurt me some more, *Libbu* mine. I never want you to stop."

Hours later, when both were sated and secure in each other's arms, Gabriel sleeping dreamlessly beside her, inside of her, Inanna's last thought before entering her own slumber was:

How did he know the ancient Akkadian word for heart?

But Hypnos, the god of sleep, had already covered her in his relaxing fog, and the thought receded into the shadows of her mind.

*** *** *** ***

Inanna left Gabriel and Benji with the Pure Ones early in the morning the following day.

Not only must Gabriel continue to train, but he needed to learn more about the other Race's history and laws as well as the Dark Ones'.

He seemed to be taking things in stride, however.

Perhaps just like her, the past few days had inured him of shock. There was an equanimity to his demeanor now that was consistent with the Gabriel she'd always known. A calmness and steadfastness that she'd admired and grown to love.

Benji, by contrast, became a ball of excitement, all but bouncing off the walls, when he learned that not only were Mommy and Daddy vampires, but they were also vampire-elves!

Surely that must be the awesomest of all living beings. He immediately wanted to know how he could become one too, but was then mercifully distracted by the Starcraft game Aella and Sophia were playing in the living area.

Inanna made her way to the Cove with some trepidation. The report in could not be delayed much longer, and she needed to check on progress against the fight clubs as well as seek out Ryu Takamura for a few questions.

As per her new habits, Jade had risen with the sun and was standing before the floor to ceiling windows in the throne room when Inanna entered, having requested a private audience.

The Queen had even dismissed her ever-present "escort," Seth Tremaine, the Pure Ones' Consul.

"I appreciate now why the ancient ones kept Blood Slaves," the Queen said by way of greeting, continuing to stare through the spotless glass with her back turned toward Inanna. "The blood of Pure Ones is dangerously addictive. It allows us, who live for the dark, to also bask in the sun."

Inanna made no response and did not think one was expected.

She could not say for other Pure Ones, but in her own case, if Gabriel could be considered half Pure, she could certainly agree with the sentiment. But it was entirely because of Gabriel, not because of his blood.

"Have you come to ask me for judgment or to quit the sphere of my protection?" Jade asked, still without turning. "I lose count of how many of our laws you have broken of late, but perhaps you are not bound by those laws because of who you are."

Inanna was not entirely surprised that the Queen knew her secrets. Jade Cicada was extremely astute and well-informed.

"I always suspected that you might be the one," she said, turning finally to regard Inanna with large, almond-shaped blue eyes, "the mythical Light-Bringer that walked between our two worlds, Pure and Dark."

"How…"

Jade tilted her head slightly as if preparing to examine Inanna in great detail. "The fact that the sun has less effect on you. The fact that you are extremely selective in your sexual partners and don't exploit that side of vampire nature as almost all of us do. You have had, what, three partners and for only a few nights each in the decades that I have known you."

Inanna cast her eyes downward. Guess her privacy and secrecy had been an illusion, at least where the Dark Queen was concerned.

Jade continued to count off her observations, "The fact that you've chosen a way to sustain yourself for millennia without both the blood and sex. Your Contracts are far more in service of the subjects than yourself. Rather noble for a Dark One, wouldn't you say?"

Inanna looked up at that. "Dark Ones can be noble. Just as Pure Ones can be ignoble."

The Queen did not reply, merely continued to smile. "So what will it be, Light-Bringer? Do you want to take your Mate and leave this circle? Or will you continue as a Chosen and face the consequences of potentially having mated with a Pure One?"

Put like that, Inanna didn't have a choice.

She would never endanger Gabriel or Benji, even if she must leave all that she knew and forge a completely new and uncharted path.

Jade had approached silently and was now immediately before Inanna.

Unexpectedly, she took Inanna's hands in hers and said, "Good choice. You must first and foremost protect your own. But I will miss you, my friend. You were… my Angel too."

Inanna hesitated a moment, but then drew the slighter woman into a heartfelt embrace. She knew about Jade's past, knew how difficult and rare it was for the Queen to trust other females given her experiences. But Inanna was among that closely guarded number. It had been an honor and a privilege.

Jade pulled back and stepped away, already distancing herself as if beginning the process of separation.

"I am afraid I do have to convey one unfortunate message to you before you go," she said, worry and regret in her expression.

Inanna awaited for her to expound.

"A formal Challenge has been issued."

Inanna inhaled audibly. *No! It cannot be!*

"You have been Challenged to the death for the possession of your Mate. You have twenty-four hours to respond or forfeit your right to Gabriel D'Angelo. The Challenger has prior claim of his blood and will fight for possession of him as her Blood Slave."

Every sentence the Queen uttered was a sledge hammer to Inanna's internal organs. Her heart, her lungs, her stomach.

Who?

"Your Adversary is Simone Lafayette, the Keeper," Jade answered her unspoken question. "She has quit the Cove as of yesterday evening. She leaves you these instructions and this address."

Blood roaring in her ears, Inanna took the formal Challenge scroll from the Queen's hands.

"Simone is the traitor we have been hunting," Jade continued in a low voice, "but Devlin cannot pursue her until the Challenge is complete, as it takes precedence by our laws. I am sorry, my friend."

"Pain is transitory despite its depths. Hate eventually eats itself into a hollow void. Sadness can only last as long as life itself. But love, love extends beyond reason and time."
    —*Excerpt from the Lost Chapters of the Ecliptic Scrolls.*

Chapter Eighteen

    Gabriel had used the two hours around lunch time to kill two birds with one stone: one, to escape the grueling, merciless training Cloud Drako enforced upon him, and two, to quickly go by Mrs. Sergeyev's apartment in Brighton Beach to pick up a few of his and Benji's things, the ones with the most sentimental value, like Benji's baby blanket Lamby, as well as give her what's left of his savings for all the help she'd given them in their time of need.

    Benji had been off his sleeping schedule lately because of all the changes in his life and because he'd missed his security blanket desperately. He was a brave little trooper and tried not to dwell on it, but Gabriel had noticed the circles under his eyes due to the lack of a good night's sleep. Those dark bags did not belong on the fresh face of a five year-old.

    He entered the studio apartment with his key and found the place already emptied, cleaned and packed up in boxes. Inanna said that the moving company would bring their things later in the day. Their most valuable possessions were stored across the hallway in Mrs. Sergeyev's apartment for safe keeping, in case the Russian mafia had come looking for them when Gabriel escaped the fight club.

    He did escape, but things did not exactly proceed as planned after that.

In the past seven days he felt like he'd lived an entire lifetime—a kaleidoscope of emotions condensed in an intensely brief period, blazing past the numbness that had characterized most of his human experience, exploding through his consciousness like meteor showers raining upon the night sky.

And now he had come full circle, back to where it had all begun.

Accepting his human past with understanding and clarity. Embracing his present and future with his Blooded Mate and son with hope and conviction.

Gabriel closed his eyes and breathed deeply.

He was at peace.

He was finally *alive*.

"Gabriel."

As he turned toward the strangely familiar yet foreign voice, a sharp stab of pain bloomed in his thigh.

Before he could focus on the hooded figure clearly, his vision grew hazy and his eyelids grew heavy.

It didn't even register when his body collapsed like a house of cards to the cold, hard ground.

*** *** *** ***

Inanna shifted gears and pulled the Aventador into oncoming traffic, navigating the cars coming at her with determined precision, taking the shortest route from the Cove to Morningside Heights, even if it meant driving on the wrong side of the street, ignoring signs and breaking every traffic law in the book.

A deadly calm pervaded her mind and body.

She was in full fight mode, senses heightened, muscles ready.

She had less than twenty-four hours to answer Simone's Challenge, but she needed to make arrangements for Gabriel and Benji first.

Fuck the Dark Laws.

Gabriel was not going to become enslaved even if she lost. She was going to make sure he stayed free even if she had to haunt the Goddess's halls to make it happen.

The Challenge Scroll specified the time and location of their death match.

Midnight.

A ruin in upstate New York, in the woodsy rounded mountains of the Catskills.

It would take her an hour or less if she punched the Aventador past its top speed of 215mph, despite the winding roads and city streets. Good thing she'd outfitted her ride with a turbo charger already. She had plenty of time to plan.

But when she all but blew into the Pure Ones' apartment like a gust of northerly wind, her allies greeted her with grim expressions, Sophia holding Benji in front of her, one hand comfortingly stroking his hair, one arm looped around his chest.

The boy's eyes were wide and frightened.

Shit.

Where was Gabriel?

"He went to his old apartment around noon and hasn't come back," Aella answered Inanna's unspoken question. "We received this note in the meantime."

Inanna took the extended scrap of paper and read: *Come alone and unarmed. I have your Mate. There may not be much left of him if you displease me with your actions. Tread carefully until midnight.*

Inanna fisted the missive in her hand and stood silent and immobile. She had not expected that Simone would Challenge her to a fair fight; she knew it was a trap. But none of it mattered if Gabriel and Benji were safe and well. But now...

"We can help," Aella said, as if reading Inanna's busily churning mind. "We'll make sure Benji is taken to safety ASAP. The Shield would be the best place."

Inanna nodded sharply, still calculating permutations and possibilities.

"Must you answer the Challenge yourself?" Sophia asked, anxiety and worry tinging her voice, "Can't you appoint a Champion or substitute or something?"

"It is for my Blooded Mate," Inanna said, "our Bond will be forfeited if I do not personally answer the Challenge. It is the primal law of Dark Ones, built into our physiology, which is why it trumps all other laws of our Kind. When we Bond, our genetic blueprint transforms to match only with each other. That's why a Bonded vampire can only take Nourishment from her Blooded Mate and no other. A Challenge by someone with a prior flesh or blood claim is the only thing that can break the Bond."

"But you are not entirely vampire," Aella suggested, "perhaps this doesn't apply in your case with Gabriel."

Inanna shook her head. "It doesn't matter. She has him. No one can come in my stead even were it allowed by law. I must prepare for the worst. If..."

She trailed off as she looked upon Benji's small, ashen face. The boy might not understand everything that was happening, but he could sense the adults' emotions.

Inanna knelt before him and drew him into her arms, hugging him tight. "Be brave, darling," she whispered into his ear as he hugged her with all his might in return, "everything will be all right. No matter what happens, know that you are loved. Always."

She wouldn't make him false promises, but she would do everything in her power to return to him with Gabriel safe and whole.

"Come," Sophia gently pulled on Benji's hand and led the boy into one of the bedrooms down the hall, leaving Inanna, Aella and Cloud to discuss next steps more freely.

"If the worst happens, we will make sure Benji is cherished and safe," Aella vowed. "You have my word."

Cloud also nodded in confirmation.

"But that's not going to happen," Aella said firmly. "You will win the Challenge. Tell us what you know about Simone Lafayette. I have done my own research as well. We can compare notes and build a strategy."

Cloud clasped a warm, calming hand on Inanna's shoulder, and as she stared into the warrior's brilliant light-blue eyes, clarity and strength flowed through her like a cooling balm.

"You are not alone, Light-Bringer," he told her quietly, imbuing her with confidence, "we will fight this together."

*** *** *** ***

Gabriel surreptitiously tugged at the chains around his arms, wrists, calves and ankles.

He was bound tightly to an A-shaped solid wood beam with a long bar across the top, his arms wrapped around the horizontal plank at level with his shoulders, his legs braced apart by the lower planks.

Save for the thick musty hood over his head, he was naked and vulnerable against the winter cold.

The good news was that he could feel the flickering warmth from a few torches near his body, close enough to hear the crackle of flames in the freezing air.

The bad news was that he didn't know whether the torches were for the light and the small warmth they provided or because they were there to ignite a conflagration at his feet.

He felt rocks and sticks and some tufts of grass beneath his bare soles. Not enough to start a fire, but they could always pour some oil on his body...

Not a happy train of thought.

Better to focus on the positive.

Which was that he was still alive and unharmed, except for the faint throbbing in his thigh from whatever that had stabbed him into unconsciousness.

Abruptly, the hood was pulled from his head. His eyes adjusted quickly to the dull brightness of the torch lights around him and saw—

A ring of black-robed spectators all hooded so that their faces could not be seen, surrounding a small circular clearing about twenty-five feet in diameter.

There must have been a hundred or more of the shadow-like figures. Gabriel appeared to be positioned toward the middle of this clearing but slightly to the side. Stone and wood ruins stacked behind their circle like additional giant witnesses to whatever was about to go down. Solemn and judging in their eternal silence.

"Welcome to your Challenge match, Gabriel," that eerily familiar voice suddenly purred from behind him. "Though you will merely be an observer in this fight. After all, you are the coveted prize."

Two long-fingered hands, that might have appeared elegant in a different context now looked skeletal in their thinness, slid around his sides, past his ribs and abdomen to grasp his penis and scrotum.

Gabriel gritted his teeth to prevent a shudder of disgust. He wouldn't give the faceless bitch the satisfaction of a sneeze much less a real reaction.

The hands kneaded and squeezed and the purring grew louder, while nausea rose like acid in Gabriel's throat.

Keeping her clutch of his sexual organs, the female slowly came around to face him, the oversized hood concealing her from view.

Freeing one hand to smoothly glide the hood from her head, she raised red-centered eyes to his.

"Remember me?"

The vampire in the tunnels, Gabriel realized, the female who had almost killed him.

She smiled as if pleased. "I see that you do. I have missed you, delectable one." She drew out the *s* in a purring hiss. "We will have so much fun, you and I, once I get rid of your nuisance of a Mate."

Gabriel neither twitched nor flickered. He simply stared back at her with opaque, emotionless eyes, infused with a dose of boredom.

"What bravado," she whispered delightedly, "what a performance. How I will enjoy obliterating that calm exterior piece by piece until only raw, bleeding flesh remains."

"But first a little sip for good luck."

She squeezed his scrotum violently as she held the back of his neck with her other hand. Gabriel managed to swallow a shout of excruciating pain as she raised on tiptoe and struck his jugular with her fangs in the same moment.

A different kind of pain descended like a hail of arrows upon him.

A pain that dragged him into a bottomless pit of despair and hate. The venom from her fangs as she drank in deep gulps at his throat spread like poison throughout his body, decimating everything in its path.

Abruptly, she released him, giving his sex a hard, sadistic tug.

"Just as I thought. A Pure One in vampire guise. I knew there was something special about you from the moment I tasted you."

Breathing hard from the aftermath of her assault, Gabriel gave her no other reaction.

She swiped her tongue meticulously across her fangs, still dripping with his blood, savoring every last drop. She closed her eyes, her expression orgasmic.

"Warrior class. Ancient. Mmmm. There is so much I can do with you. So much to gain."

Over his dead body, Gabriel thought, trying to twist his wrists free of the iron chains. He'd send her to Hell first.

A murmur started among the ring of spectators, all but forgotten until now. The sound buzzed loudly like a swarm of maddened hornets.

Gabriel's heart dropped to his feet at the sight of Inanna striding into the clearing, head held high, shoulders back, hair pulled into a tight braid, dressed in snug black pants, combat boots and a short-sleeved black shirt.

Unarmed.

She did not look at him as she approached the center of the ring, her gaze focused only on the female vampire in front of him.

"Traitor."

Inanna slammed the word down like an anvil, no other opening salvo needed.

"Half breed," Simone returned, smiling evilly.

"Let's get this over with," Inanna said and assumed a fighting stance, knees bent, ready to spring on the balls of her feet.

Simone shook her head, hands ostensibly remaining at her sides, but it was hard to tell with the heavy floor-length cloak that covered her from head to ankle.

"So impatient. You never learned how to savor the violence, sex and bloodletting in all your millennia posing as a vampire, did you?"

Inanna simply stared at her, readying to pounce.

Simone picked up on the coiled energy and *tsked*, "Not so fast. You play by my rules now. See this beautiful piece of meat behind me?"

She made clear to whom she referred by clawing a hand down Gabriel's torso, leaving five long, bloody tracks, "one wrong move and you won't like what I do to him."

Inanna pulled back slightly from her stance, shifting her feet.

A tall vampire male came to stand half behind Gabriel, half beside him, a long serrated dagger in his hand.

"He's going to help me make sure I have your full cooperation," Simone explained. "One can never be too trusting in these situations."

"Are you going to talk all night?" Inanna muttered through a clenched jaw. Goddess above, she wanted to tear the limbs off this filthy bitch. Starting with the hand that left those bloody streaks on her Mate.

Simone tilted her head and seemed genuinely puzzled by Inanna's lack of curiosity. "Aren't you at all interested to know why I've Challenged you and what I plan to do with your magnificent Mate? Why I've left the Cove and renounced my allegiance to Jade Cicada after centuries of service?"

"It won't matter after I murder your ass," Inanna growled, hackles all but bristling. "And then I'm going to kill you again just for the hell of it."

Simone started to shake.

At first Inanna thought she was overcome by some sort of seizure, a stroke of unexpected good fortune, but then she realized that the bitch was laughing.

"Oh I am going to enjoy making you suffer very much," the ex-Keeper said around a chortle. "Your arrogance and over-confidence would be amusing if it weren't so pitiable."

"Back at you," Inanna spat out.

Simone exhaled long and deep, as if she was suddenly tired of the back and forth. It was time to get down to business.

With great theatricality, she slowly unclipped her cloak at her throat, unbuttoned the top and doffed it in a black heap at her feet.

She was similarly dressed, all in black, form-fitting, mobility-enhancing clothes and boots. What was different was that she was armed to the teeth with half a dozen knives secured to a circular holster around her upper thigh, two short swords criss-crossing her back, throwing stars attached to her hip belt, and Inanna could see at least two stilettos in the hidden compartments in each boot.

Simone bared the full set of her teeth in a gruesome grin. "And they're tipped with poison, to which I am immune," she said, as if sharing a special treat.

Inanna had anticipated this. Aella had done a remarkably thorough research on each of the Chosen. She knew more about the Keeper than Inanna, who had lived and worked with her for decades. It made Inanna wonder what else the Amazon knew.

Simone was not to be underestimated.

Despite her station, she was good enough as a fighter to avoid Inanna's chained whip before. They did not know who trained her and for how long, but she obviously had some moves up her sleeves.

Earlier, Inanna and Gabriel had gone over his last fight club in detail to try to round up some clues to help end the network as well as uncover the identity of the female vampire. Their suspicion based on Gabriel's recall was that he had been poisoned by the initial stab wound, which served to paralyze him before she'd attacked in the tunnels. Aella also hypothesized that Simone might use poison if she knew she had to compensate for other weaknesses.

"Better and better," Inanna threw back. "I wouldn't want to humiliate you with a beheading within the first ten seconds."

Hate flared in Simone's blood-red eyes, and she hissed in displeasure before unsheathing the cross swords and launching a blitz attack.

Inanna was ready and countered bare-handed with single-minded precision, using her elbows and knees to block, her long-legged kicks to attack.

It had been a long time since she'd had to engage in such a vicious close-quartered combat, her hunts and battles in modern times mostly done at a distance. But her body recalled rigorous training from the ancient past.

She could almost hear the voice of the warrior who taught her everything she knew in her ear, giving her strength and guidance.

Look for an opening as your opponent attacks.

The more aggressive the assault, the less guarded they will be.

Bring them in closer to your body by side-stepping and turning your torso ninety degrees, making yourself a smaller target while holding your ground.

Use their momentum and strength against them; conserve your energy for the knock-out blow.

Inanna finally got close enough and placed two rapid jabs in sequence to strategic spots on Simone's upper arms so that the locked length of her three middle fingers hit critical nerves like screwdrivers that numbed her opponent's limbs instantly.

With a loud groan, Simone dropped her cross swords to the ground. But before Inanna could follow up with some more debilitating blows, she heard Gabriel's gritted *oomph*.

The male vampire beside her Mate had stabbed him in the stomach with the six-inch dagger, embedding the entire length into his flesh, then pulling it out in a tear that shredded the skin and muscles and potentially internal organs with the serrated edges.

A low, maniacal chuckle bubbled forth from her opponent.

"Are you getting the idea yet?" Simone taunted. "For every hit you deal me, your male gets it much, *much* worse."

Inanna pivoted and stepped back, reassessing her strategy.

A bead of sweat ran from her temple down the side of her cheek. She was barely winded from the fight—it hadn't even been three minutes. But the fear and despair for her Mate that she was holding back was rearing its ugly head.

Out of the corner of her eye, she saw that the ring of spectators were no longer stationary; they were slowly and steadily drawing the circle tighter. Although everything else was covered, their right hands were revealed through the black cloaks.

And each hand was holding a long knife.

Simone had finally recovered the use of her arms and hands, though they shook a little as they each pulled out a stiletto from her boot.

"Be careful you don't step too far back," she warned with false solicitousness. "You wouldn't want to accidentally impale yourself on one of those sharp looking things."

Inanna switched her steps and moved in more of a circle, keeping in mind the steadily decreasing space she had to work with.

Again, her opponent came at her full of rage and viciousness.

Again, Inanna deflected the attack and moved in close, delivering a hammering head butt and dislocating one shoulder as she twisted Simone's arm behind her back while shoving it straight and sharply at an upward angle.

The vampire's scream Inanna barely heard. Instead she was hyper attuned to Gabriel's breathing behind the female who had fallen to her knees.

He did not make a sound this time, but his breaths had become ragged, and her laser vision told her that he had taken a knife between the ribs. One of his lungs must have been punctured.

Inanna calculated with a calmness she had to reach deep inside to harness, even as panic and terror for her Mate boiled close beneath the surface.

He likely suffered from both a punctured kidney and lung, if the darkness of his blood was any indication.

And he was bleeding out fast.

The cold helped to slow the flow, but the wounds were deep. The serrated edges of the knife not only fucked up the organs they stabbed in and out of but also the tissues of his muscles and abdominal wall, making it much harder to heal.

Added to that, his body was also trying to fight against the freezing cold, which weakened its power to heal the wounds.

At this rate, those wounds would be fatal within the hour. And that was assuming the knife wasn't poisoned. Even his new abilities wouldn't be able to save him.

Inanna choked on a breath.

She couldn't do this. She didn't have the strength after all. She couldn't be the instrument of her beloved's death.

Only for a moment did she hesitate, and it was all that her opponent needed to stab a poison-tipped dagger straight into her heart.

"Death is but a phase of life. While it is unwise to court death, there is also no reason to fear it if one's soul is pure and one's heart is true."
　　—Excerpt from the Lost Chapters of the Ecliptic Scrolls.

Chapter Nineteen

Gabriel watched the poisoned stiletto enter Inanna's body as if in slow motion.

In those few moments, his heart lost its rhythm and forgot to beat.

A silent bomb exploded within him, blasting through his body in a blistering heatwave.

A stab in the heart.

Neither a Pure nor Dark one could survive it.

Her death accelerated his own, for his body simply stopped functioning as his receding vision tracked her fall to the frozen ground. He no longer felt the pain from his wounds, no longer heard what went on around him.

No longer cared.

As if his body was on auto-pilot, he vaguely felt himself struggle free of his bonds and stumble the few steps toward his mate.

His soul seemed to be already floating apart from his flesh, so disengaged he felt from his surroundings.

Vaguely, shouting and clashes of steel reached his ears from a distance. He couldn't be sure whether he was remembering the sounds in his mind or if they were happening right now.

He didn't care.

As he reached Inanna's prone body he collapsed beside her.

They lay on their sides facing each other, and he saw that her eyes were open, though unseeing. He clawed with his fingers another two inches to be close enough to touch her face, his lower body no longer obeying him.

If this was their end, then so be it. At least they would enter the afterlife together. They would not go alone.

He would never leave her again.

But as his fingers made contact with her cheek, a blast of energy consumed them both, hot and white and searing.

Was this what it felt like to burn? Was this what it felt like to die?

Gabriel closed his eyes and surrendered himself to the blinding light, keeping the physical connection to his beloved.

And then there was silence.

There was darkness.

A soothing cool breeze teased Gabriel's eyes open. He awkwardly sat up and looked around him.

Nothing but blackness. There was no up or down, no sky and no ground.

Only void.

Inanna lay beside him, as naked as he, seemingly asleep, for her sides moved gently in deep, slow breaths.

He stroked her cheek and saw that it was tinged slightly pink with health and vitality.

How could this be? Where were they?

"You are in the In-between, warrior," a soft feminine voice came to him, carried by an undulating white orb.

Gradually, the orb drew nearer and coalesced into the form of a woman, though she remained faceless, her figure obscured by the dazzling light she seemed to radiate from within.

"Are you... the Goddess?" Gabriel asked, his own voice hoarse from lack of use.

The bright light seemed to smile though he could see no such thing. "Merely a messenger. And here is my message for you, Alad Da-an-nim."

Gabriel frowned at the name she called him. "I'm not—"

A sharp screeching erupted in his ears, abruptly severing his train of thought. Visions and images flooded his mind as long hidden memories were finally released.

When the images that included Inanna began to run like a furiously fast forwarded movie clip through his head, his heart accelerated to keep up. His breathing raced to match. And when he thought he would blackout from the hyperventilation, everything suddenly stopped.

"Do you remember now, warrior?" the voice asked gently.

"Yes," he managed to gasp.

Yes, he remembered *everything*.

"Then you are ready to make your choice."

The bright white figure floated closer until she enveloped him in the warm, soothing glow. "Attend me closely, warrior..."

*** *** *** ***

Gabriel regained consciousness in the middle of a heated battle.

As he rose on his hands and knees in a defensive crouch, he took stock of the situation in a split second with three hundred and sixty degree precision.

Aella and Cloud were engaging half a dozen of the black-cloaked spectators who had drawn long swords in addition to daggers. A couple other warriors he did not recognize clashed with more cloaked foe a few feet away. By the way they coordinated seamlessly with Aella and Cloud, Gabriel deduced they were long-time comrades.

Four vampires fought the remaining black-cloaks back with deadly maneuvers. He could tell they were Dark warriors for the fangs they flashed in the pale moonlight. One of the warriors was paired with a fierce black panther who was like an extension of his body the way they seemed to know exactly where each other was and the way they moved in tandem.

The torchlights had been doused, Gabriel saw. A mound of clothes and boots and leftover ash that the wind had not yet carried away lay beside the beams he had been bound to. His chains had been cut in four strategic places. Someone had released him as he struggled to get to Inanna.

At this reminder, he jerked toward her and saw that she was already standing beside him, one hand stretched to pull him to his feet.

With a smile of triumph and exhilaration, she said, "Let's do this. You remember how."

Gabriel clasped the hand and pulled himself up, using her weight as leverage.

He tugged a little harder as he gained his feet, pulling her close and devouring her mouth in a hard, passionate kiss. One that lasted not even a heartbeat but which communicated a hundred thousand emotions, the foremost of which was:

I love you. I shall never let you go again.

"I remember," he said against her smiling mouth.

They rounded on the black-cloaked vampire assassins who flew at them from every direction, back to back, bare-handed.

He was still naked and sore, but his wounds had stopped bleeding and he knew his body well enough to gage that he was going to heal and live.

And despite the stab to the heart, his Mate appeared to be spritely and energized as well.

They both grinned as if they'd already won.

They were together again. They were whole. They could overcome anything as one.

"Duck," Gabriel grunted as he did the same when a cloaked assassin swung a long sword at his head.

They both kicked out low at their opponents' legs and brought them to the ground where they made quick work of disarming the assassins and using the weapons to deal killing blows, turning them to ash.

Without hesitation, they engaged the next foes to come at them, synchronized in their movements as if performing a deadly dance.

When he stepped forward to attack, she stepped back to lure her enemy closer. When she jumped to avoid a low swipe, he did so as well without being told.

When the odds were more than one-to-one, he used her body as an extension of his own and increased their reach, strength and speed like a lever or a pendulum.

Soon, both of them hardly winded, powered by adrenaline, they faced a circle of empty clothes, footgear, and discarded weapons as their enemies had all been reduced to heaps of ash.

The fighting around them had also come to a halt. Aside from Inanna and Gabriel, eight warriors and one feline remained standing.

In the center of the clearing, Simone was alive and kneeling on the ground, Devlin's sword at her throat.

Gabriel picked up a nearby cloak and put it on. The boots could wait until he finished his business with the female vampire.

"She's mine," he all but growled as he approached his prey, a bloodied long sword in his hand.

"She's ours," Inanna said beside him, a hand on his arm to stay him. "I must complete the Challenge, and even if it doesn't matter anymore, I just want the satisfaction of ending her."

Gabriel nodded, and together they stood before their tormentor, grim and resolute.

Devlin stepped back to allow them the death-dealing blow. As the Hunter, Simone was his prey, but they had a deeper claim.

"Any last words, traitor?" Inanna asked, uncaring of the answer.

Simone merely glared up at her, her lips lifted in a scathing sneer. "You have no idea what you're dealing with," she spat, "you stupid, weak—"

From two different directions two blades swung together to sever the ex-Keeper's head from her shoulders, cutting off her tirade.

As she disintegrated into a pile of black ash as if she never was, her executors turned and walked away without a backward glance.

Devlin's mouth tipped up in a brief, ironic smile. "Good thing I interrogated her before those two got here," he muttered to himself, then caught up with the others who had congregated in a loose group a few feet away.

"Thank you for coming," Inanna said to her former Commander.

Maximus inclined his head and clasped the length of her arm in acknowledgement of her gratitude. "My Queen would not have it otherwise. For old time's sake, she says. Jade sends her regards."

Inanna nodded and with only a slight hesitation, stepped close to embrace her friend and comrade fully. "I shall miss all of you," she said against his chest.

"And I, you, Angel."

One by one, she embraced her former comrades. Ryu, Anastasia, and finally Devlin.

Even Simca allowed a quick smoothing of her sleek fur before she swatted Inanna playfully with her whip-like tail.

"Do you know what you will do now?" the Hunter asked in his nonchalant, casual way.

Inanna shook her head. "I am looking forward to figuring it out."

With that, her old friends departed into the night.

This would not be the last she saw of them, she knew, but still Inanna watched them go with a bittersweet ache. The warmth of Gabriel's arm around her waist comforted her immeasurably.

She then turned to Aella and Cloud and embraced them as well.

In a very short period of time, she had come to rely upon them as trusted friends.

They introduced the two other warriors who had traveled from Boston to their aid, Tristan, newly returned from his international expedition with Ayelet, and Dalair, the Pure Ones' Paladin. Valerius had already escorted Benji and Sophia back to the Shield.

"What now, Light-Bringer?" Aella asked with a knowing smile.

"Now we go home," Inanna answered.

But she was not looking at the Amazon. She was gazing steadily into the eyes of her Eternal Mate.

Her Blooded Mate.

He was both. He was everything.

He was her home.

Gabriel bent down so that their foreheads touched, their eyes closed, and softly he vowed, "Yes, we go home, *Libbu* mine."

*** *** *** ***

The creature watched the Pure Ones, the Angel and her Mate depart the clearing on live streaming.

Simone Lafayette had done her job.

The entire Death Match and the ensuing battle had all been captured on hidden remote cameras in the trees and ruins surrounding the clearing. Real-time edited with slow-motion effect so that human eyes could track the supernatural beings' movements.

And broadcasted on an encrypted channel on the Internet.

Globally.

Already, it could see the number of video views and downloads skyrocketing, reaching over five-hundred thousand in the first ten minutes.

Not surprising, given that it wasn't everyday humans witnessed galactic battles among vampires and elves.

For that was what it looked like on the screen.

Even if most believed the footage was a spoof, wasn't real, was some sort of movie trailer for a new fantasy epic, it didn't matter.

Humans were curious creatures.

There would be those of above-average intelligence who sought the truth behind the videos.

And if they discovered it? The creature could only imagine the chaos that would ensue, gleeful in its anticipation.

If they didn't? The gory violence would beget more, inspire those of average and below intelligence to unleash their base urges, incite destruction and disorder.

Because, after all, it all looked so *freaking cool*.

The fight clubs were not ended, not by a long shot.

This was just the beginning.

*** *** *** ***

Back in her apartment, Inanna and Gabriel washed each other and made love leisurely in her rainforest shower.

Tomorrow, they would leave for Boston with the Pure Ones, where Benji awaited their arrival, and start a brand new chapter in their lives together.

Tonight, at least for the few hours left until sunrise, they would love and feed and revel in the fact that they were *alive*.

"Inanna," Gabriel groaned as he braced his arms against the shower wall in front of him, his long legs spread apart to accommodate his Mate as she devoured his sex with her ravenous mouth.

Inanna clutched his tight, muscled buttocks closer, pushing him deeper into her throat, sucking his hard, satiny length with increasing pressure and a building desperation.

Goddess above, she would never have enough of him.

The water of the shower had turned cold a long time ago, but they did not notice, for the heat from their bodies turned the entire luxuriously large stall into a sauna.

She fisted both hands around his cock and pulled and squeezed as she suckled, nipped and lapped at the engorged head, running her teeth along the fat dorsal vein.

She'd already fed from him here several times. Despite the water rinsing over her constantly, his intoxicating musk filled her nostrils, the tantalizing taste of his seed and his blood danced on her tongue, the feel of his hot, smooth skin and the steely muscles beneath a sensorial feast for her hands, her face, everywhere she touched him.

She couldn't get enough.

She knew he was terribly sore in spite of the continuous and pervasive pleasure of their orgasms. But she couldn't help herself. She had to have *more*.

Gabriel caught his breath and bit his lower lip hard enough to draw blood when she sank her fangs into his tortured cock once more, sucking deeply from the well-used vein there. One hand moved from the shower wall to tangle in her wet hair, his fingers massaging her scalp rhythmically while she continued to suckle him.

He knew that, as much as they took Nourishment from each other, they were also marking each other as their own.

There was a ferocity and desperation in Inanna's claiming of him, in the way that she pushed him to, and possibly beyond, his limits, the way she needed him inside of her one way or another—his blood, his seed, his body, inside her mouth, her womb. It was as if she was trying to consume him, absorb him wholly into herself so that she would never lose him again.

She wouldn't. She might not believe it yet, but she wouldn't lose him again. He would make sure of it.

A shudder racked through him as his balls tightened on the verge of climax. Gabriel increased the pressure on Inanna's scalp to signal that he needed her to release him. He wanted to be inside of her in a different way.

Gently but reluctantly, her mouth let go of his cock and her tongue licked the wounds closed. Her hands squeezed and smoothed their way up his sides, his torso, to wind behind his neck as he grasped her thighs and lifted her, entering her in a long, slow thrust, filling her to the brim.

She locked her legs around his hips and rode him in counterpoint to the deep, mind-numbing rhythm he set. She stared into his dark chocolate eyes, his pupils dilated with passion, his full lips parted with ecstasy.

"Mine," she staked as she held his gaze.

"Yes," he answered, increasing the tempo of his undulating hips and contracting buttocks.

"Forever," she demanded.

"Yes," he groaned, his breath coming faster, a flush traveling from his chest to his throat and flooding his cheeks.

Her mouth claimed his the same moment his orgasm blazed through him, the jerking of his hard cock inside of her triggering her own euphoric release.

Long after the waves of passion had subsided, they continued to make love with their lips, tongues, hands.

The water had not only gone cold but had also reduced to a weak splatter of raindrops rather than the powerful deluge when they'd first turned the shower on.

Without breaking the seal of their mouths, Gabriel turned off the water, carried her out of the stall, wrapped an extra-large bath towel around her and laid her on the bed, finally covering her body with his own.

Inanna kept all of her limbs wrapped securely around her Mate and buried her face in the crook of his neck, nuzzling his throat with her nose like an affectionate kitten.

Gabriel turned them both slightly to the side so that he supported half of his weight and wasn't too heavy for her. By the way Inanna was pulling at him with those long, lean legs deeper into herself, she seemed to want his full weight upon her.

He'd soon give in, as he always would with her, but first he had some questions.

"Happy?"

"Mmm," came her drowsy purr.

He brushed golden locks, already starting to wave as they dried, back from her face and hooked the tendrils behind her ear. His hand then trailed reverently down her collar bone to her breast, behind which her heart beat strongly, steadily.

As his calloused thumb abraded her nipple with gentle strokes, he asked, "What did the Goddess ask you?" for he knew that she had had her Awakening just as he had. She would not be here with him, whole and vibrant, otherwise.

He felt her smile against his neck. "She wanted me to choose between the vampire side and the Pure side."

"And what was your answer?"

Inanna sighed and nibbled along his jaw. "I am both Dark and Pure, so I chose both. My mother and father created me. I don't know what happened, my father never said. But I feel... I believe they loved each other deeply. I do not think I could be here if not. They must have sacrificed much for their love, and if I am the result, I want to honor them both. I do not want to forsake either side."

Gabriel nodded. He could empathize. Until you embraced who you really were, you would never truly feel whole and reach your full potential.

"And you? What did the Goddess ask of you?" she queried in return.

Gabriel closed his eyes and smiled. Her nibbles had progressed to his cheeks and nose. She was now sprinkling kisses against his eyelids and brows like fairy dust.

"The same question she asked of you," he replied.

She had traveled back down to his mouth and was plucking gently at his lips with her own. "And?"

He pulled back enough to look into her eyes, those deep blue pools of bottomless love, passion and hope.

"I chose to be your Mate, whatever it took to make me so," he said quietly. "I'll never let you go again."

Tears welled in her eyes as she stared back at him. "You made me forget you," she whispered, her words filled more with anguish than accusation.

"Yes," he said regretfully.

"Why?" the question came on a broken gasp as twin trails of tears ran down her cheeks.

Gabriel's heart broke at the sight. He'd rather die a thousand deaths than see her in such pain.

He swallowed back his own sorrow and tried to explain. "I didn't know whether we had a future. I...I loved you more than anything, more than everything."

He swallowed again as he remembered the last moments of his life as Alad Da-an-nim, the pain of letting her go far greater than the physical pain of his body crushed under the fallen tower.

"I couldn't risk hurting you if we fully consummated our feelings, and keeping you by my side while not giving you everything you deserved was selfish and unfair. I thought if I made you forget, you wouldn't have regrets because of me. You would be free to love again... someone who could give you everything, who would never be of risk to you."

Her tears flowed in continuous streams down her face, as if a millennia-old dam was finally obliterated by her accumulated, tumultuous feelings.

"But none of that mattered to me," she choked out over a sob. "All I've ever wanted or needed was you. I didn't care if we never consummated our union as long as you could be with me forever. One moment with you is far more precious than a lifetime with anyone else. I died when you did. Inside. I died..."

He crushed her to him to stop her words. They were tearing him apart.

"I'm sorry," he murmured over and over as he held her through the convulsive sobs, hiccups and wails that racked her body from the inside out. As if she were transported back to the moment of his death. As if she were losing him all over again.

When the tears finally dried and the shudders subsided, Inanna felt like she'd put the past to rest at last. She'd finally had the chance to grieve for the love that she had lost. And now she could focus solely on the present and future.

Her true love at her side.

"You owe me millennia of loving," she dictated, looking into his eyes again. She tried her best to put a challenging glint in her gaze but she didn't know how effective that was with the red puffiness of her lids almost sealing her eyes shut.

"Yes," he said simply, caressing her swollen lips with his thumb.

She pushed him onto his back, braced herself on her elbows and undulated her hips against his, pulling him deeper, rubbing the head of his penis against her innermost pleasure center.

"Tell me," she demanded, riding him faster, harder. "You have never given me the words."

He gasped as a fiery climax quickened within him, shooting through his nerve endings like lightning bolts.

"*Ze ki angu*," he vowed huskily, staring into her eyes, spearing into her soul, "I love you."

And she loved him back.

Thoroughly.

Taking everything he had to offer like a sacrifice at her alter and giving everything she had back to him, enslaved by her love of him.

Yet, she was also set free. Nothing was impossible now. There were no doubts, no regrets, no shadows.

There was only light.

Epilogue

My daughter is truly Mated.

She is in love. The kind that never dies, no matter the odds.

I know.

I have seen it in her eyes.

Her happiness is so radiant and bright, it warms the cold, dark places in my heart.

The sorrow of never having held her as a babe, never watching her blossom into a lovely girl and mature into a full-blooded woman. Powerful and primal.

The fury against those who took her away, who made it impossible to be with her, nurture her.

The vengefulness that has spread like poison throughout my soul, making me want to destroy everything and everyone around me.

The numbness that counteracts that hate, that makes me feel entombed in flesh and blood and bones, like someone carrying on in the world yet distinctly apart from it.

Her light is thawing the walls of ice around my heart.

Whether I want it to or not.

Her love for her Mate causes me pain to witness, for it reminds me of the way I used to look upon *him*. As if he were the sun and moon and stars. The past and present and future. Nothing else mattered but him.

But he betrayed me.

Empires have fallen because of my stupidity.

Yet, I cannot help but feel the warmth of her effervescent hope. I cannot help but want to believe in love again. For I feel it for my daughter. And the Dark Goddess willing, I shall feel it for her children.

I have felt it for my son.

From the moment he came into the world and I cradled him in my arms.

It is madness, I know, to dare to dream the impossible.

They told me he died.

It was my fault for sending him away. My heart bleeds when I think of him alone in the world, never knowing he had a mother who loves him, never knowing why she let him go. What if he believes I'd forsaken him? Who was there to comfort and hold him?

It is madness, yet I believe... I *feel* that my son is still alive.

And I shall find him.

Glossary

Awakening: test of courage and strength of spirit which leads to the subject coming into his/her Gift, a supernatural power, if he/she passes the test.

Blood-Contract: Contract by which a human Consents to surrender his/her blood (and sometimes soul) to a vampire for a promise in return that the vampire must fulfill. The vampire has the choice to accept or reject the Contract. Upon acceptance, he/she must fulfill the bargain or risk retribution from the unfulfilled human soul in the form of a curse. See also Consent.

Blooded Mate: the chosen partner for each Dark One. Once the Bond is formed between two Dark Ones, it cannot be broken unless a third party has prior claim of blood or flesh. The third party can elicit a Challenge to one of the Bonded Dark Ones to obtain rights to the other. The Challenge is fought to the death. Save in the case of a successful Challenge, the Bond cannot be broken except through death. Blooded Mates do not need to take the blood and souls of others to survive. However, they must take blood and sex from each other on a regular basis, else they will weaken and eventually go mad and/or die.

Blood-Slave: a human or Pure One, often the latter because of their power and immortality, whose primary role is to provide blood as sustenance to a vampire master. Usually, a Blood-Slave also surrenders his/her body for carnal pleasures to the vampire master. This obligation continues until the master grants release.

Cardinal Rule: Sacred Law number three for the Pure Ones, thou shalt not engage in sexual intercourse with someone who is not thy Eternal Mate. See Sacred Laws.

Challenge: see Blooded Mate.

Chevalier: a combination of Pure and human warriors who stand as the first line of defense against rising vampire Hordes and human menace.

The Chosen: six royal guards of the New York-based Vampire Queen, Jade Cicada.

The Circlet: five royal inner council members of the Pure Queen.

Consent: a human's willing agreement to surrender his/her blood (and sometimes soul) to a vampire.

Cove: base of the New York-based vampire hive, with dominion over the New England territories in the U.S.

Dark Goddess: supernatural being who is credited with the creation of the Dark Ones. She is a deity to which Dark Ones pray. It is unclear how or whether she is related to the Pure Ones' Goddess. See also The Goddess.

Dark Laws: One, thou shalt protect the Universal Balance to which all souls contribute. Two, thou shalt maintain the secrecy of the Race. Three, thou shalt not take an innocent's blood, life, or soul without Consent.

Dark One: supernatural being who prefers to live in the night and who gathers energy and prolongs his/her life by feeding off the blood, and sometimes souls, of others. Dark Ones are born, not made. Sometimes confused with the term *vampire*.

Decline: condition in which or process of a Pure-Ones' life force depleting after he/she Falls in love but does not receive equal love in return. The Pure One weakens and his/her body slowly, painfully breaks down over the course of thirty days, leading ultimately to death unless his/her love is returned in equal measure.

The Dozen: see Royal Zodiac.

Ecliptic Scrolls: events past, recorded by the Keeper of the Dark Ones.

The Elite: six royal personal guards of the Pure Queen.

Eternal Mate: the destined partner to a given Pure soul. Each soul only has one mate across time, across various incarnations of life. Quotation from the Zodiac Scrolls describing the bond: "His body is the Nourishment of life. Her energy is the Sustenance of soul."

Gift: supernatural power bestowed upon Pure Ones by the Goddess. Usually an enhanced physical or mental ability such as telekinesis, superhuman strength and telepathy.

The Goddess: supernatural being who is credited with the creation of the Pure Ones. She is a deity to which Pure Ones devote themselves. She protects the Universal Balance.

The Great War: circa 2190 B.C., the Pure Ones who had been enslaved by the Dark Ones rebelled against their oppressors en masse. At the end of countless years of bloodshed, the Pure Ones ultimately regained their freedom, and the Dark Ones' empire lay in ruins with the members of the Royal Hive scattered to the ends of the earth.

Hive: society of vampires with a matriarch, the Queen, at the head.

Horde: small groups of vampires with no Queen, typically composed of Rogues who band together for ease of hunting.

Lost Soul: describing a soul placed in the wrong body, time or space. Lost Souls seek death and destruction at worst, battle with dark emotions and debilitating depression at best. Their existence detracts from the Universal Balance. Releasing them from their current corporeal capsules to rejoin the world at the right time restores the Balance.

Nourishment: the strength that Mated Dark Ones take from each other's blood and body through sexual intercourse. Once Mated, they will no longer need others' blood to survive, only that from each other. Sexual intercourse is required to make the Nourishment sustaining.

Pure One: supernatural being who is eternally youthful, typically endowed with heightened senses or powers called the Gift. In possession of a pure soul and blessed with more than one chance at life by the Goddess, chosen as one of Her immortal race that defends the Universal Balance.

Rogue: lone vampire who does not belong to an organized vampire society or Hive.

The Royal Zodiac: twelve-member collective of the Elite, the Circlet and the Queen of the Pure Ones.

Sacred Laws (Pure Ones): One, thou shalt protect the purity, innocence and goodness of humankind and the Universal Balance to which all souls contribute. Two, thou shalt maintain the secrecy of the Race. And three, thou shalt not engage in sexual intercourse with someone who is not thy Eternal Mate. Also known as the Cardinal Rule.

Shield: referred to as the base of the Royal Zodiac, wherever it may be. Not necessarily a physical location.

True Blood: a vampire born of Dark parents. See also Dark One.

Universal Balance: underlying order that is essential for the continuation of time. The idea that everything exists in cycles or pairs—good and evil, darkness and light, past and future, right and wrong, male and female, life and death, etc. Disruption to this balance leads to destruction, chaos, and eventually, the implosion of time and space.

Vampire: supernatural being who prefers to live in the night and who gathers energy and prolongs his/her life by feeding off the blood, and sometimes souls, of others. Contrary to prevalent beliefs (see *Pure Healing*), vampires are both made and born. Some vampires are Pure Ones who have chosen Darkness rather than death after they break the Cardinal Rule. Some are humans turned by other vampires. Some are True Bloods that are born of two vampires, more accurately called Dark Ones.

Zodiac Prophesies: events yet to come, foretold by the Seer of the Pure Ones through the Orb of Prophesies.

Zodiac Scrolls: events past, recorded by the Scribe of the Pure Ones.

Excerpt from Book #3 *Dark Desires*

Present day, en route from New York City to Tokyo.

The guy next to her had cheekbones that could cut glass.

That was the first thing Ava noticed when she finally got her above-average-sized assets settled in the luxurious first class seat on Japan Airlines.

Well, okay, the second thing.

The first thing was his smell.

Although the word "smell" connoted foul odors, which was not the case at all. Perhaps *scent* would work better the way Ava was thinking about it.

Or heck, maybe *aroma* would be the most appropriate description for the way the volatized chemical compounds he produced from scent glands all over his body, more commonly known as pheromones, made saliva pool in her mouth as if she had just been presented a decadent, dark chocolate fudge wrapped in a crisp white chocolate casing with a graceful swirl of raspberry sauce and an elegant sprinkle of hazelnut on top.

Presented in the haute-couture artistic fashion of three star Michelin restaurant plates of course.

It was Ava's favorite dessert, guaranteed to make her mouth water.

The raspberry and hazelnut details were her mental attempt to match the impeccable, almost inhuman grace and style of the man sitting in the seat next to her, to the dessert in question.

She'd only had this specific dessert once in an exclusive posh French restaurant when she was attending a conference at the Sorbonne.

And wow. Just wow.

The first bite had been better than sex. The second bite more euphoric than the multiple orgasms she achieved with her best friend the Rabbit Habit. And the third and last bite—she could only make the tiny piece of fudge last so long—had her begging for more.

That was what the man's *smell* reminded her of.

Her internal temperature had already risen a couple of degrees by the time she'd noticed his cheekbones.

Ava tried to regroup by keeping her eyeballs strictly focused on the screen in front of her as a flight attendant in person and in video went through the safety instructions.

She was not the most natural when it came to interactions with powerfully attractive men. *Irresistibly* attractive, rather, if just his smell could make her break out in a heat rash.

With an IQ of over 200 (genius was above 140 and Einstein's IQ was between 160 and 190, but who was counting), a PhD and MD in molecular genetics, another PhD in regenerative stem cell science and being one of the world's foremost experts on these topics at the age of thirty, she should be able to handle a simple human interaction with aplomb.

But no, sadly not.

Not when her EQ was well below average and her social quotient was probably not even on the chart—as in, negative.

Thus, Ava tried to avoid embarrassing herself abominably by focusing her attention away from the glorious male sitting beside her before she caught wind of something even more threatening to her libido than his fragrance and his cheekbones.

And it *was* just his personal scent, she could tell, no artificial cologne on top to distort the perfect combination of molecules that wafted from his skin to her olfactory bulbs. Perhaps just a hint of soap, very light and wintry fresh.

Odor prints were influenced by diet, environment, health and genetics, she knew, and it was as if his smell was made specifically to elicit a force-of-nature response from her.

It would all be extremely fascinating had she not been preoccupied with hiding her now flaming hot cheeks from view.

"What would you like for first meal?"

"What?" Ava blurted, reeling from discovery number three:

His voice might be the most dangerous attraction of all.

The man gestured with a slim, long-fingered hand to the attendant who was bending over Ava with a menu of items.

Ava swiveled around to regard her.

How long had the model-esque stewardess been there? Probably a good while, since her smile seemed frozen in a grimace on her face.

Ava quickly chose the least healthy of all her options for lunch, snack and supper, because her motto was that healthy equaled tasteless, and why go through life eating tasteless food? Thus decided, she refocused on the TV screen.

It was blank.

Blank was good. Perhaps she could channel blankness into her mind.

Fourteen hours! She had to tame her libido for eight hundred and forty minutes! That was a lot of time to be simmering fruitlessly in unrequited lust.

Not for the first time Ava wished she wasn't so hot-blooded. Maybe it was the Latin heritage. Though genetically speaking, she was one-fourth German, one-fourth Japanese, owing to her Brazilian mother, and one-fourth Scottish, one-fourth Welsh on her father's side. One hundred percent American, born and raised in the Bronx of New York.

Maybe it was more nurture than nature.

Ever since she was a child she always felt like she didn't quite fit in. She had the looks on the outside, but on the inside, her brain worked in unusual ways. She viewed the world in mathematical equations, chemical cocktails, symbols rather than words.

But that's not to say she didn't *feel* things. She felt rather too much. She avoided feeling whenever she could because emotions weren't logical, and she very much preferred logic.

She could be downright volcanic when her emotions and *feelings* ran high. It wasn't as if her hormones operated in overdrive 24/7 or even a small fraction of the time. In fact, she rarely had time to notice, let alone indulge, in physical attraction. But when she did feel those powerful bodily urges... well, she indulged.

But she'd never felt *this* magnitude of attraction.

Keeping her gaze unfocused and her eyeballs pointed forward, Ava dug into the giant hobo bag beneath the seat in front of her, pulled out her iPhone, stuck the buds into her ears and turned up the volume on her favorite playlist.

But no matter how hard she listened, all she heard was that voice.

It was what the ocean would sound like if it were male and awakening from a satisfying slumber after a night of mind-blowing sex.

*** *** *** ***

She was not what he expected.

Not that he knew what Professors or Doctors (or whatever one called someone with both PhD and MD as a suffix to their name) in molecular genetics looked like on average, if there was such a stereotype to begin with.

But he thought they might be...*older*.

Gray-haired with glasses and a wizened, wrinkled visage reflecting self-sacrifice (for how else would they have had the time to concentrate on their studies?) and solemnity (for what humor was there in such an analytical, methodological subject?).

For Ryu Takamura, who had been raised for the first ten years of his life in a whorehouse and abandoned thereafter at a Shinto shrine, formal education—hell—*any* education seemed foreign and antithetical to his own upbringing.

Perhaps this was why he always dressed and spoke with meticulous care.

To any observer, he appeared to be the immensely wealthy heir to a Japanese or Korean conglomerate, living a life of privilege and idleness with armies of servants to tend to his every need. His clothes were of the finest quality and tailored to fit his long, lean body to perfection. His wavy black hair was tousled just so, fuller on top and in the back and shaved closely on the sides to emphasize his aristocratic bone structure, all angles and points liked a laser-cut diamond.

He was so blindingly elegant, in fact, he could never have been mistaken for a real Asian heir. He represented what their alter egos might aspire to if they could ever look as resplendent as he. Rather like how K-dramas represented the ridiculously good-looking and wealthy on TV with actors who had undergone countless surgeries to mimic perfection.

If only they knew the truth. Ryu's lips tipped at one corner in dark amusement.

He cast a surreptitious glance at the woman beside him.

She seemed determined to keep to herself and take up as little space as possible though she had plenty of it. She was—Ryu struggled to describe her—a study in contrasts.

Short. At just over five feet.

Round. At least where females were supposed to be round. She was extremely well-endowed in those areas, but relatively slim in others.

Dark velvety eyes like Bambi, full of innocence and ignorance.

Full, luscious lips like pillows, made for sin.

Ryu didn't know whether her instant, palpable attraction to him was a good thing or a bad thing. Her body was still radiating an enormous amount of sexual tension and heat even as she tried to pretend normality and hide in her seat.

Ryu mentally shrugged. He'd deal with it later if he had to. Usually, such attraction came in handy.

And he hadn't fed in weeks.

But for some reason, he didn't feel like using her weakness against her. It didn't seem fair.

He scoffed mentally. Then again, what did he care for fairness. It wasn't as if the term had ever been liberally applied to himself.

Or applied at all, for that matter.

He closed his eyes and reclined his headrest to a more comfortable position, putting the luscious human morsel from his mind for the moment.

He had a mission to accomplish. Several actually.

First, he was following a trail the Russian mob boss left when he hightailed out of NYC after the expansion of the insidious fight club network had started stalling. The Chosen had eliminated one of the heads of the hydra recently, one of their own, in fact, but there were at least two others that they knew of still at large. Their sometime allies, the Pure Ones, had returned from their pursuit of Sergei Antonov with very few clues. But one of them pointed to the fact that Japan was Sergei's next destination.

Second, he was to rendezvous with his ex-comrade Inanna and her Mate Gabriel within the fortnight. Being native to the land and familiar with the language, culture and history, having lived it himself over hundreds of years, he might be able to help them in their search for Inanna's father, whose last and only proof of life was found in Japan, dating to a time Ryu was intimately familiar with.

Third, the New England vampire queen, Jade Cicada, whom he served as one of her most fearsome warriors, had gotten wind of some nasty development in which humans were experimenting with vampires, even gaining traction with some genetic engineering and splicing of human and Dark DNA together. The next step was cloning.

If they were not stopped, vampires, or some concoction of virtually immortal creatures, might soon be mass produced in test tubes.

Why anyone would want such an event was one question. What the world would look like overrun by bloodsuckers was another.

As a vampire himself who often saw the ugliest, darkest, filthiest parts of his Kind, Ryu would rather not contemplate such a possibility.

And if he had any downtime in the middle of saving the world and doing a favor for friends, why, he might just pursue his one personal vendetta that was long overdue.

He did relish multi-tasking.

The white noise of the airplane engine receded into the background as his ears adjusted to the sound, enough that he noticed the restless squirming in the seat beside him.

Ryu raised his right eyelid a fraction and saw that his erstwhile companion was struggling to get the lower portion of her seat lifted to elevate her legs. It was stuck.

"May I?" Ryu murmured, offering his aid.

But she had ear buds in and did not hear him, continuing to alternately push the seat buttons in the electronic panel by her arm and bend down to pull at the leg rest.

He reached across the narrow divider that separated their seats to get her attention just as she suddenly whipped upright and turned in his direction.

Rather than touching her shoulder as he'd intended, his fingers brushed her cheek and mouth. His palm cradled the left side of her face for a heartbeat.

But it was long enough to tilt the world on its axis.

*** *** *** ***

Pre-order or buy Book 3, *Dark Desires* **now.**
Check out Book 1, *Pure Healing***.**

Dear reader:

Thank you for reading Dark Longing. I hope you enjoyed reading it as much as I enjoyed writing it!

Please be sure to leave a review on Amazon, Goodreads and any other social book sharing site of your choice (a short one sentence of what you enjoyed about it will do, but feel free to expound!) I read every single one of my reader's reviews, and I endeavor to take your feedback to heart as I continue developing the series.

Would you like to join my trusted reader list? Read my next book before it publishes for Free! All you have to do is Mail to Aja James (megami771@yahoo.com), and I'll add you to the list of readers who are notified about upcoming books, excerpts, giveaways and promotions! And if you have burning questions about the Pure/ Dark Ones series, well, I just might answer them :)

Give me a shout! And happy reading!

Aja James

Manufactured by Amazon.ca
Bolton, ON